SHOW ME
THE MONEY

Connie Shelton

SHOW ME THE MONEY

Heist Ladies Mysteries, Book 5

Connie Shelton

Secret Staircase Books

Show Me the Money
Published by Secret Staircase Books, an imprint of
Columbine Publishing Group, LLC
PO Box 416, Angel Fire, NM 87710

Book layout and design by Secret Staircase Books
Cover images © Balasoiu Claudia, Jara3000

First trade paperback edition: June 2021

First e-book edition: June 2021
* * *

Publisher's Cataloging-in-Publication Data

Shelton, Connie
Show Me the Money / by Connie Shelton.
p. cm.
ISBN 978-1945422966 (paperback)
ISBN 978-1945422973 (e-book)

1. Heist Ladies (Fictitious characters)—Fiction. 2. Arizona—Fiction.
3. Financial scams—Fiction. 4. Women sleuths—Fiction. 6. Con men—
Fiction. 7. Mystery caper—Fiction. I. Title

Heist Ladies Mystery Series : Book 5.
Shelton, Connie, Heist Ladies mysteries.

BISAC : FICTION / Mystery & Detective.

813/.54

In memory of Shirley Shaw, my longtime editor. In addition to the professional connection, ours became a good friendship with numerous chats about our dogs and families. I loved sharing recipe ideas and hearing about the accomplishments of your grandsons. Such good times. I miss you greatly, my dear.

As always, I am indebted to so many who help each of my books come together. Dan Shelton for keeping our personal lives in perfect working order; Stephanie Dewey, ditto, with the business side of publishing, promotion, and editing; and my team of beta readers who dropped everything and gave their invaluable assistance on this one—Sandra Anderson, Susan Gross, Marcia Koopman, Judi Shaw, and Paula Webb. I couldn't manage it all without you—thank you!

Chapter 1

Nine p.m. Eighty-seven degrees. The 747 emptied slowly. Those in business class were allowed through while the jumbo jet's coach passengers were still fumbling bags from the overhead bins, gathering personal items from seat pockets, and attempting to stretch legs that were horribly cramped from the seventeen hour flight. Paris, London, Phoenix.

Amber allowed the good-looking flight attendant to pull her new Louis Vuitton bag from the bin and flashed him a smile of thanks as he set it on the floor for her. Looping the strap of her messenger bag across her body, she followed a business-suited man with gray hair as he descended the stairs toward the jetway. Traversing a couple of long corridors, she felt her muscles stretch pleasantly by the time a final escalator deposited her in the International Arrivals Hall at Sky Harbor. Home.

She approached a kiosk and tapped the screen to answer the prompts, scanned her passport, and received her immigration slip. Customs would review her declaration form, she knew. Considering the trip had started as business, she'd certainly made the most of the last few days in Paris. After all, what was the point of spending fifty hours a week at a desk in a downtown high-rise if a girl couldn't splurge a little of her six-figure salary on gifts for her friends back home? She waited behind the red mark on the floor for the next officer to wave her over.

The gray-haired businessman was ahead of her and he breezed through with no more than a half-minute's conversation at the desk.

Amber waited for the immigration officer's signal, then wheeled her bag along as she stepped up and handed him her passport and declaration form.

"Amber Zeckis?" he said, eyeing her papers and flashing a glance at her face, comparing. "How long were you in Paris?"

"Five days. Before that, London and Amsterdam."

"Business or pleasure?"

"Business in London and Amsterdam. I work for Blackwell-Gorse Tech, based here in Phoenix. The Paris portion of the trip was vacation."

"Anything to declare?" He repeated the usual items— alcohol, cigarettes, cash over ten thousand dollars ...

She indicated the list she'd written out on the plane. "It's all there. I'm sure I owe some duties."

"Collect your luggage then step over to Window 3." He gave a vague wave to his left.

She knew the drill. Her large blue suitcase had seen

a lot of travel and was a little worse for wear, unlike the new carry-on bag Cody had bought for her. She felt her mouth curve in a smile as she tugged both pieces toward Window 3. Cody. Wow. Fun days. Would she hear from him soon? He'd tried to get on the same return flight but that hadn't worked out. He would be along within a day, he'd promised.

Her mind was still on her new boyfriend—his neatly styled chestnut hair, green eyes behind dark framed glasses, his trim body—as she approached the customs official, hoping this would go quickly. The time difference was beginning to tell; her limbs felt draggy, her brain fuzzy. She hefted both bags to the inspection table and reached into her purse for her wallet. She'd already calculated that she would need several hundred more than she had in cash.

The officer, a weary-looking woman in her forties whose name badge simply said Abbott, glanced over the list. "Looks like you hit the high-end stores. Mind if I take a look?"

Whether Amber minded or not, Abbott began unzipping the larger of the bags. After she flipped through shopping bags from Hermes, Chanel, and Tiffany, she unzipped the new purple Louis Vuitton with the distinctive logo in orange.

"The bag is new, too."

"Yes, ma'am. It was a gift, and I understand I'll need to pay duty."

Abbott was mauling the packets of specialty foods from Harrods. A puzzled expression crossed her face, and she began tapping the bottom of the case with a fingernail. She found the edge of the cloth liner and pulled it up.

"What's this …?"

Amber looked up from her wallet where she'd been

fumbling for the credit card. Before she knew what was happening, Abbott had signaled another official, a guy who looked about eight feet tall and wasn't wearing a smile.

"We'll need you to come with us, ma'am," he said, closing and picking up both of Amber's bags effortlessly, and turning toward a door that seemed to blend into the wall behind him. Abbott was right with him, carrying Amber's passport and declaration form.

"What's the matter? What's this about?" Amber asked, hurrying to match her steps to his gigantic stride.

"Just step inside," Abbott said, standing aside to let Amber follow the tall guy. The moment they were inside the room, the door clicked shut with a dreadfully final sound.

Chapter 2

Gracie Nelson pulled into her suburban Phoenix driveway, happy to see lights on in both of her teens' bedrooms as well as the usual glow from the kitchen and family room. She couldn't wait to get out of the navy blue business suit and heels she'd worn for her presentation at the Rotary Club meeting and to let her shoulder-length hair out of the tight bun. A pair of cotton shorts and a tank top would feel so good right about now, especially if Scott would hand her a beer and massage her shoulders as they settled on their big sectional sofa.

She'd no sooner stepped inside the front door when her phone rang. She pulled it from her jacket pocket and peered at the screen. Amber? Wow, it had been months since she'd heard from her younger friend.

"Hey girl, what's up?" Gracie said, setting her briefcase

on the console table near the door.

"Gracie—I need help." Stress, fear, borderline tears.

"Amber, what's wrong, sweetie?"

There followed some babble about the airport and a giant of a customs agent and some money that Amber didn't know about.

"Calm down a second, Amber. You need to tell me exactly where you are."

Gracie jotted a few words on the back of an envelope on the table. Her husband walked up beside her, a questioning look on his face.

"I'll be there as soon as I can, Amber. Just hold tight."

"Problems?" Scott never asked for details when it included Gracie's group of women friends.

"You gathered that was Amber. I have no idea what's going on but she's really scared. Airport officials have detained her. I'd better get down there and see if I can help. Hopefully, it's some kind of simple mix-up."

He gave her a kiss and turned her toward the front door. "At least you're dressed like you mean business."

She sent him a weak smile and didn't mention how much she'd wanted to get into comfy clothing and snuggle for an hour or so before bedtime.

Back in the car she debated calling the others—Pen, Sandy, and Mary. But it was already after ten p.m. and Amber's little emergency could turn out to be something minor. If she was in the Customs area at the airport, she must have come in from an international flight. No doubt she was exhausted, and most likely what seemed like a disaster now would be nothing tomorrow in the light of day. Their youngest member had probably called Gracie because she lived closest to the airport, and maybe because Amber had been the Nelson's family babysitter back in her college days. The girl felt a closeness to Gracie that the others didn't share. It was as simple as that.

She hoped.

She found parking in the East Economy lot, rode the Sky Train to Terminal 4, the largest at the vast airport, and went to an information desk. There was no point in going to the greeters' area for incoming international flights—she would never get past security to the inner sanctum where only ticketed passengers could be. She would need an escort.

It took some talking, including dropping the name of the customs officer Amber had mentioned in her string of nearly incoherent words—an Abbott—but she finally had a uniformed TSA agent at her side. They took an elevator to another level, went through a keypad-guarded door, and traversed a corridor behind the scenes, the kind with exposed ductwork and pipes.

When she walked into the room where Amber waited (and yes, there actually was a gigantic uniformed agent), Gracie's young friend burst into tears. Her curly hair was wilder than ever, dark smudges showed under her eyes, and her cotton slacks were rumpled.

"What's going on here?" Gracie addressed the agent with the name badge Abbott.

"Are you representing Ms. Zeckis?" Abbott asked.

Sort of ... The woman hadn't actually asked if she was an attorney.

"Your client is being detained for giving a false customs declaration."

"False, in what way?" Gracie stood a little taller in her heels and hoped her business suit still looked somewhat fresh.

"Failure to declare more than $10,000 in cash among

her personal effects."

Amber sputtered but Gracie put out a hand to quiet her.

"How much more?"

Abbott stepped over to a new-looking carry-on bag and raised a flap to reveal neatly banded packets of hundred dollar bills. Gracie did a quick count of the packets—it was a hundred thousand dollars. She felt her eyes widen and her breath whoosh out, but she quickly caught herself.

"It's not illegal to carry large amounts of cash."

"No, but it is illegal not to declare it."

Gracie fumbled for a second. "Sorry, this isn't my specialty. So, what happens next?"

"We confiscate the money and start an investigation. If it's determined that your client is transporting cash obtained through illegal activities, there can be fines and imprisonment."

"What!?" Amber sprang to life once again. "I didn't even know it was in there."

Abbott gave her a withering look, meaning *that's what they all say.*

"I'm *serious*. I had *no* idea. I was getting out my credit card to pay duty on some scarves and perfume. Would I have done that if I could have just pulled out a couple of those?" Amber said with a glance toward the stacks of bills.

Gracie turned to her and whispered, "It's better if you don't say anything right now. We'll get this figured out."

Turning back to the customs agents, she said, "Has the money been fingerprinted? Unless you can do that right now, there is nothing to tie Ms. Zeckis to this cash."

"Not exactly true, ma'am. It's in her possession. Until this is straightened out, she'll remain in custody."

As if to prove the agent's point, the door to the small room opened. A middle-aged man in a rumpled suit entered, followed by a uniformed Phoenix PD officer. Abbott indicated Amber with a nod of her head, and the officer stepped over with handcuffs. The suited man presented his badge and informed them he was a detective with the major crimes division. From an inner pocket he pulled several plastic bags with red Evidence tape across the tops.

"All of this goes into evidence, at least until we figure out what's related to the crime and what's not." With a look toward Amber he added, "You'll get your personal items back."

"Where are you taking her?" Gracie demanded, hating the desperate sound in her voice. A real lawyer would be so much cooler under pressure.

"She'll be questioned downtown. Probably booked and held at the station on First Avenue. You can go there for your allowed attorney/client meetings. Wait until morning, though. Nothing much will happen tonight."

And with that, Amber was taken away in handcuffs. Gracie stood there, numb, clearly dismissed, as the detective and the customs officers counted out the stacks of money and put them in a bag. The designer suitcase was shoved into another large plastic bag. She was about to turn and leave when it occurred to her to get the detective's business card. Mark Howard.

She stumbled from the tiny room into the bustle of the Arrivals hall and walked numbly toward the exit.

Chapter 3

"Why didn't you call us last night?" Penelope Fitzpatrick, the Heist Ladies senior member and the reason the women had banded together in the first place, seemed a little put out with Gracie. It didn't mean her chin-length gray hair was ruffled or her trim black slacks had a wrinkle.

"It was late, I was taken completely by surprise when the cops came in with handcuffs." Gracie had called the Heist Ladies together in her living room as soon as her kids had left for school.

"It's all right," Sandy Warner hastened to assure her. "We know now, and we need to decide what to do."

Gracie had lain awake all night, pondering that very question. What to do? This was the first time one of their team had been arrested. Usually, it was the five of them against a real criminal.

Mary Holbrook piped up. "Amber has been there for each of us, no matter how silly our needs might have seemed. My ex, really? All of you jumped right in to help me that time."

"First, we must secure proper legal counsel," Pen said. "Not to undermine your efforts last evening, Gracie. I'm sure you were brilliant."

"I was terrified. I walked in there as a friend, offering to give a friend a ride home. How was I to know they would assume I was her attorney?"

Mary Holbrook laughed out loud, her spiky white-blonde hair catching the light. "I can just picture it."

"I propose that I contact Benton and get a referral." Benton Case was a retired district attorney, a close friend of Pen's who still had a lot of connections in Arizona courts and politics.

"That's excellent," Sandy said. "We also need to let her parents know what's going on."

Gracie grimaced. "I should do that since I know them fairly well. Edward will want to jump in and take charge. Rich people are like that. No offense, Pen. It's just his way, from working with everyone from movie makers, to investment sharks, to gurus in that ashram where they lived for a while." She noted puzzled looks around the room.

"That's another thing that puzzles me about what's going on with Amber," Gracie continued. "She has traveled internationally since she was a little kid. They lived in Paris when she was a child. She knows the drill, and she surely knew it would be stupid to try to smuggle in that kind of cash."

"And Amber is anything but stupid," Sandy agreed. "The girl is brilliant."

"It's what got her that plum job at Blackwell-Gorse."

Mary looked a little wistful. "I've missed her since she took that job."

Nods all around. Amber had been with the mega corporation headquartered in downtown Phoenix since the first of the year, and in these ten months the group had been all together only a handful of times. All they really knew of her new career was that she was doing what she loved best, something to do with computer technology that was difficult enough to challenge her; it paid enough that she'd moved from her tiny digs near the university into an upscale condo in Scottsdale; she traveled fairly often with the job.

Pen had her phone out already, and her call to Benton went right through. Once she'd quickly recapped the nature of the legal emergency, her end of the conversation consisted of nods, the occasional "all right" and a quick note scribbled on a page from Gracie's kitchen scratchpad.

"He will make the call," she reported. "Mariah Kowzlowski is a *tiger*, in his words, with a reputation for taking the sorts of cases where she shines at protecting her cubs. She's got experience in criminal court and with the US Customs Service, *and* she owes him a favor."

"She sounds perfect."

"He will ask her to meet with Amber this morning, and he feels fairly certain Ms. Kowzlowski can get her released."

Gracie let out a pent-up breath. "I hope so. I couldn't think of anything else all night but our little Amber, cold and lonely in a cell somewhere."

"It's ninety-four degrees already," Mary pointed out. "Doubtful she's cold."

"And knowing Amber, she's bewitched a guard into bringing her extra breakfast and, while he had his back turned, she's figured out the keypad code to the cell door."

Sandy said it with a grin that showed off her dimples.

A nervous chuckle went through the group.

Gracie cleared her throat. "Okay, well, then. I guess I'm up. I don't look forward to telling her parents about this, but—"

"Then don't," Mary said. "Yes, they'll need to know sometime, but it's really up to Amber to inform them, don't you think?"

"I don't want Amber to think I didn't do everything I could to help."

"The best help will be this tiger of an attorney," Pen said.

As if by telepathy, Pen's phone rang. Recognizing the number Benton had just given her, she grabbed it.

"Ms. Kozlowski, thank you for calling." She put the phone on speaker so the others could hear.

"Ms. Fitzpatrick. Benton Case says you're my contact regarding this new client, Amber Zeckis." The voice hinted at a lifetime of cigarettes and a New Jersey upbringing.

"That's fine. Amber is a dear friend. I am quite confident in saying any charges against her are completely false."

Gracie wondered if Pen intentionally played up her proper British accent in situations like this.

"Doesn't matter. My job is to get her out of jail and do my best to keep her out. I can go downtown and meet with her at eleven. She'll need a ride home after that. You planning on being there?"

"Absolutely. I can bring several friends as character witnesses."

"Not today. This is just for me to find out what evidence they have and convince them she's not a flight risk."

"That won't be a problem," Pen assured the lawyer.

The call went dead and Pen looked up at the others.

"Well, I'm going along anyway," Gracie said. "Amber called me last night and I don't want her to think I'm skipping out."

"I'd go, but I really need to take over for Billy at the gym," Mary said. "My women's self-defense class is this morning." Her equally athletic business partner was super accommodating of Mary's outside interests—up to a point.

Sandy shook her head. "If I don't get to the bank this morning, they'll wonder if I'm still their manager. There are only so many dental appointments I can legitimately claim." She stood and smoothed the pale blue blouse that brought out the color of her eyes and complimented her light skin and blonde hair.

"It's fine," Gracie said. "You heard the lawyer. I have a feeling we'd catch some flak if we all showed up anyway."

Pen added, "Besides, until we know more, it might be smart for some of us to remain behind the scenes."

They all knew what she meant. In previous cases, the Heist Ladies had used alternate identities and disguises to track down their quarry. And one thing was certain. Amber had somehow been set up, which meant someone was out there. Someone who'd better watch out because the Ladies were on the trail.

Chapter 4

The downtown main police station bustled with activity, the lobby filled with civilians—about half of whom looked as if they knew what they were doing and where they were expected to go. Gracie spotted Pen and joined her at the edge of the crowd.

"Two minutes to eleven," Pen said. "Seems a popular time of day here."

Gracie chuckled and glanced around the large room, wondering if there actually was any less-popular time in a place like this. She recognized Mariah Kowzlowski— she'd looked up her law firm and the lawyer's profile online before they left home. The heavyset woman with her severe charcoal gray suit and dyed-too-dark hair would never win any fashion awards, but she had a no-nonsense build and a stern bulldog expression that probably made young prosecutors cringe. Pen and Gracie approached.

"I spoke to you on the phone about our friend, Amber Zeckis," Pen said.

"Oh, right." Kowzlowski glanced at her wristwatch. It was now precisely eleven o'clock. "I'll have time for a quick consult alone with my new client and then we'll see what the authorities have to say. I assume you'll be around for a half hour or so?"

She didn't wait for an answer, merely turned toward the duty desk and signed in. Gracie watched as the lawyer was buzzed through a doorway and disappeared. An officer appeared and made an announcement about jailhouse visiting hours, and a number of the people followed him through a separate door and down a corridor. With most of the crowd gone, Pen and Gracie found seats on benches along one wall.

"I'm itching to know what's going on in there," Gracie said.

"For research on one of my novels, Benton once allowed me to sit in the observation room adjacent to an interrogation," Pen offered. "They turn off the microphones when the client and attorney are in there alone, then most likely an officer or two will come in and begin the questioning. If they feel an arrest is imminent, someone from the prosecutor's office may come along."

Gracie closed her eyes, trying not to imagine poor little Amber being grilled about the money. At least she had Kowzlowski on her side. The lawyer didn't seem like she would take any guff from anyone. Thirty minutes ticked by in what felt like two hours.

Finally, Mariah Kowzlowski emerged. The three moved to a relatively quiet corner. "They're letting her out, partially on my recognizance, partly because one of the detectives has a wife who's a big fan of a certain movie made by an Edward Zeckis. Amber's dad, I gather."

"Really? I mean ... that's great," Gracie said.

"They confiscated her passport and she's under orders not to leave Maricopa County."

Gracie made a face. The terms might not sit well with Amber or her parents.

"Hey, she's lucky not to be stuck inside while they dig around for evidence," Kowzlowski said. "Anyway, there's some paperwork and then they'll send her out here. I've gotta get back to my office."

"Gracie will give her a ride home," Pen said.

Gracie nodded and watched the attorney leave the building. She'd spotted Mark Howard, the detective who'd been at the airport last night, heading toward the elevators.

"I'll meet you in a minute," she told Pen as she dashed to catch the cop.

"Detective Howard," Gracie called out, just as he was about to press the elevator button.

He turned. It took no more than a split second before recognition dawned. "You must be pleased. Your client got what she wanted."

Gracie wasn't sure how to read the look on his face. "First of all, she's a friend, not a client. The customs officials were mistaken."

"I know. I just wondered whether you were going to admit it to me."

She forced herself not to grit her teeth. He would notice.

"Tell me this," she said, stalling Howard from leaving. "Why would she be coming back into the US with the cash on her? If she took the money and got away, *why* wouldn't she just stay away? It doesn't make sense."

His cocky smile took a dip. "We're still working the case. There are reasons for everything, and it's my job to uncover them."

"But—"

"Everything will come out later, when there's a trial. I'm afraid I can't discuss it with you. Good day."

Chapter 5

ank into the well-worn seat in Gracie's minivan
groan.

ed sleep," Gracie said, starting the vehicle and
vay out of the downtown parking garage.

leep." The past two days had become a blur—
rnational flight, the ordeal at Customs, the
and the surreal quality of the police station

an attorney, someone she'd never seen before
ared her a little. She'd had no problem being
the detective—the same one who'd showed
at the airport. He seemed all business, not
out not giving an inch either. At least the
ashed forward to getting Amber released.
on of questions she would need to ask later.

"Don't nod off on me just yet," Gracie said. "I know basically where your condo is, but I'm going to need directions once we get close."

"Um hm, that's good." Amber's eyes closed as they entered the ramp for the 101 Loop.

Two seconds later, even though the dashboard clock showed twenty minutes had gone by, Gracie tapped her shoulder. "We're at the intersection of Goldwater and Scottsdale Road. Now what?"

Amber rubbed her eyes and forced herself to look around. "Take a left." She gave instructions for a series of turns, including a final one onto a down-sloping driveway that led to an underground parking garage. The automatic arm rose and Gracie made the turns through the gloomy lot, ending up at a space marked Visitors.

"The elevator is over here. Sixth floor." Amber pointed "I guess the bright side is I have no luggage to haul inside

She felt her voice crack a little at the realization that everything she'd brought back from Europe was gone—the gifts she'd chosen for her friends, the cool new suitcase from Cody. She had her messenger bag with the company computer she was sworn to guard with her life, and her phone. At least her photos would be on there. She hoped. Her passport was gone, but the cops had been definite about that. She wasn't to leave the county.

"Want me to come up with you?" Gracie asked.

"Please. I just need some reassurance that the world normal. It means so much to me that you and Pen came this morning." Again, that tight feeling in her throat as she pressed the elevator button marked 6.

"We got together earlier," Gracie said. "All of us. want to help you figure this out."

"That cop—he's not going to do anything to prove

innocence, is he?"

"It's his job to find a crime and a suspect and to arrest them. I get the feeling he thinks he's on that path."

"And my lawyer? Who is she?"

"Pen found her through Benton. Don't worry. She's gruff but she's supposed to be really good."

The elevator stopped and they got out and walked down a long corridor of plain brown doors, like the interior hallway of an expensive but unimpressive hotel.

"Hey, she got me out of there. I can learn to love her." Fumbling through her bag she came up with a key and opened the door of number 6023. "You haven't been here yet? Gosh, I can't believe I never had everyone over for a housewarming or anything. My job consumed every moment, I guess."

"It's okay. We're here for you, all together again."

They walked into a tiny foyer which opened into a spacious living room. Gracie noted a long white sofa that faced a wall of windows, with Camelback Mountain in the distance. There were two side chairs and a wall-mounted TV on the north wall. Ahead, sat the small dining table for two that had served as Amber's desk in the old apartment; it stood adjacent to a spacious kitchen done in all the latest granite and stainless steel. A narrow balcony opened off the dining area, revealing lush outdoor plantings maintained by the condo association, along with the balconies of more than a dozen other condos that faced the cool inner courtyard.

"I've used one stove burner for my tea kettle," Amber said, with a wave to her left, "and the microwave. Kind of lame, huh, that I don't use a fantastic kitchen like this."

"I get it," Gracie said. "Careers like yours can eat up a lot of your time."

"It's not just that," Amber told her. "I could work from home, at least a few days a week, but I've just never taken the time to make this place *home* yet."

"You will. You know, a few touches like pillows and some art. A few little conveniences and comfort pieces—you'll get the place feeling as if you've lived here forever."

Amber yawned. "Someday."

"Hey, I'm going to let you get some sleep. If you crawl in bed right now, you'll feel a lot better by dinner time. How about if I bring food and come back with the rest of the ladies? Seven-ish?"

Amber nodded, leaving Gracie to let herself out. She walked down the short hall from the dining area, bypassing the empty bedroom she'd planned as her home office one day, if she ever got things organized. A guest bathroom opened on the left, an equally sterile space where she'd done no more than hang a couple of towels. Gracie was right—she needed to begin adding the personal touches that would make this a home.

The second, larger bedroom was hers, and here she had splurged on a top-of-the-line bed and chic furniture that had appealed to her the moment she saw it in the showroom. The climate-controlled condo allowed her to heap on a thick comforter and a couple of angora throws, despite the outside heat. It was the one room where those comfort touches Gracie had mentioned were already in evidence.

She dropped her purse on the dresser, pulling out her phone and checking messages. Only one—her mother, wondering if the flight had arrived on time. Nothing from Cody, which sent a little frisson of worry through her. She fired off a quick text to her mother, promising a call later, and one to the new boyfriend: Everything okay? Did you

catch your flight?

Then she walked into her en suite bathroom and peeled off her travel-worn clothing, dropping everything into the hamper and turning up the shower as hot as she could stand it. Fifteen minutes and liberal amounts of body wash and shampoo carried away the physical residue of the past forty-eight hours.

With one final glance at her phone screen (no messages), she crawled between her bamboo sheets and went dead to the world until her eyes fluttered open and she realized the room was in twilight. Six o'clock, according to her phone. If she caught the parents during their nightly cocktail hour, the news she had to impart might go better.

As for reaching Cody, there was no point in trying now. If he was still in Europe it was the wee hours of the morning, and she knew—from body-tingling experience—that he slept so soundly he'd never hear his phone. It would be at least four hours before she could reach him—maybe more, if he was on a plane right now.

"This is ridiculous," she said out loud. "I've never been the girl who sat by the phone, pining away. Let him call me."

She ignored the pang that went through her and ordered Siri to "Call parents."

"Hey, baby!" came her father's booming voice. "How was the trip?"

Before she could think of the best way to respond, her mother's softer voice with its hints of her Black Caribbean heritage came through. "Hi, honey. Did you get some sleep on the plane?"

Amber physically tilted the corners of her mouth upward, hoping a smile would come through in her voice. She couldn't avoid the subject she didn't want to broach;

her father could read her like a book.

"Well, the trip was mostly great. No, I didn't get any sleep on the plane, so I have some catching up to do, and by the way they stopped me at Customs with some shocking news."

"What's that?" Of course, Dad would be the one to pick up the negative. She felt her resolve crumble.

"Oh, Daddy ..." The story spilled out, starting with the moment that officer, Abbott, had discovered the hidden cash in her bag. There was no way to soften it and no way her father wasn't going to lead her through a series of what-happened-next questions. All too soon, they knew of her detainment and the investigation.

"We'll be on the next plane," Edward Zeckis announced with finality.

"There's nothing—"

"Amber, listen to your dad. We'll come. He can check out this attorney they assigned you, and I'll bring my healing crystals to give you an energy cleansing treatment."

Amber felt her eyes roll. There was absolutely no point arguing with the Greek tycoon and the Caribbean shaman.

"At least wait and get a morning flight. I'm going to eat a bite and then fall right back to sleep." The half-truth gave her a twelve-hour reprieve.

Chapter 6

Gracie spent a productive afternoon, first contacting Pen, Sandy, and Mary. All were eager to help Amber in whatever way they could.

"Her place isn't easy to find and that parking garage is a nightmare to navigate, so if you don't mind carpooling in the minivan ..."

They met at six-thirty in the parking lot of Desert Trust Bank, Sandy's place of employment. Mary brought an assortment of Thai food in takeout boxes, which she'd picked up on her way; Sandy and Pen carried several overstuffed shopping bags with mysterious gifts; Gracie had left her family to fend for themselves with the help of two large pepperoni pizzas.

At 6:45 they were rolling into the underground parking garage and Gracie (after only two wrong turns) managed to find the correct section of the building and an available visitor parking slot. Amber buzzed them up to the sixth floor and met them at her door.

"Well, I have to say, you look a hundred percent more perky than you did a few hours ago," Gracie said, pulling their young friend into a hug.

"Thanks. Other than the fact that my parents are coming in the morning, I feel pretty great too."

"Oh, honey," Mary said, "you'll be glad to see them when they get here." She held up the food containers and Amber led the way toward the kitchen.

"I know. At least I told them everything up front. Dad will have tonight to marshal his forces, and Mom can pack a bunch of cleansing herbs and all that woo-woo stuff she believes in."

"Let's eat," suggested Pen, "and then—there are presents!"

"Mostly, we want to figure out how we can help," Sandy told Amber. She draped an arm across the younger woman's shoulders.

Amber squinted and shook off the emotion prickling at her eyes. "Yes, food will be good. I'm definitely at a low energy point, as my mom would say."

Mary and Gracie took charge in the kitchen, warming the food and locating plates.

"We can take everything to the living room," Amber said. "Afraid my two dinky dining chairs won't cut it."

"At least we can put one of the gifts to use right away," Pen said, holding up bags. Out came two bottles of wine and a set of crystal glasses. "Rinse the glassware, Gracie, and we shall be all set."

They settled around the coffee table and toasted to Amber's new home and the fact that the five were together for the first time in months.

"Okay, I'm dying of curiosity," Mary said, pausing between bites of her pad Thai. "Other than the ending, how was the trip? I caught tidbits about Paris, Amsterdam, London ... What the hey?"

Amber pushed rice around on her plate with her chopsticks. "Well, it started out as business. B-G—um, Blackwell-Gorse sent me, along with a couple of their sales reps. We called on customers who are contemplating massive expansion in their tech offerings, so the sales team was there to put the glitz on it all. I was sent along in case there were technical questions and to demonstrate some of our capabilities."

"Sounds fun," Sandy said.

"Challenging, at times, but yeah, it was cool. We landed in London and spent two days with a big client there, then it was on to Amsterdam for a week and meetings with two more potential accounts."

"And Paris? How did that figure in?"

Amber blushed slightly. "Well, there's this guy ..."

Smiles and nods all around.

"He works in Paris. We 'met' at an online symposium a few weeks ago during a class on the introduction of blockchain technology into the current modes of supply ... Well, you don't care about that. Anyway, we kept turning up in the same live chat rooms and group discussions, so he asked if he could privately message me. And he did, and we started getting more personal ..."

"What's his name?" Gracie piped up, smiling.

"Cody Brennan. Anyway, the more we talked about where we worked and what we do in our jobs, it was really obvious we had a lot in common. So when I mentioned the trip for B-G, he suggested I come to Paris, where he lives."

Pen smiled and raised her glass once more.

"Anyway, I took some vacation days and well ... it was fun. In person he's so much better looking than in his photos, and well, you know. He just had a way about him. He's a fun guy and he knows the city, which I barely remembered from when I was a kid there. So we did the touristy things, but we also hit a lot of quiet little spots. Did some shopping, ate some fantastic meals. Each evening he brought me a single pink rose."

"Aww ..." Mary grinned.

Amber blushed. "Yeah, fun, romantic touches."

Gracie spoke up. "You said something last night about him coming here?"

"Right. That's the cool thing. He was due some vacation time, too, so he wanted to come to Phoenix so we could spend some more time together. He's American, raised on the east coast. I think his parents still live there. He didn't mention his mom much, but his dad, for sure. Cody talked about him some. So, he checked into getting on the same flight I was on, but it was full. He said he could get on another one in a couple of days."

"You mean he could be calling almost any time? Arriving here?"

"I hope so. I mean, I don't know. I don't have a flight number for him, and he might have ended up on standby or something ..."

"Do you think you're ready for him to meet your parents?" Mary asked.

"Uh, I'm thinking not yet. I didn't mention him to them, and with this new trouble ... I think I'd better keep those two things in different compartments for now. Dad wants to meet Mariah Kowzlowski. Knowing him, he'll size her up, check out her record on cases won, and hire someone else if he doesn't like what he finds."

"I guess this brings up the difficult subject," Sandy said.

"The elephant in the room." Amber said it with a little laugh. "I know you're all curious about what happened."

"Well, Gracie filled us in on the parts she knew," Sandy said. "But I still don't really understand it. You had a carry-on bag with cash in it?"

"Cash that I'd never seen before. I hope they fingerprint the bundles and prove that."

"That would be a good first step," Pen said, "although a shrewd prosecutor is going to say you wore gloves when you handled it."

"We need more," Sandy said. She paused, chopsticks in mid-air. "Look at me. Here I am, assuming we'll work on this ourselves."

"I believe we most definitely should," Pen told them. "Right now, who is in Amber's corner? The attorney, certainly, but she will be looking at whatever evidence the police collect and then she'll attempt to contradict or disprove it. But I'm not certain she'll put a private investigator on the case. It's a chance I don't think we can take."

"And Amber's own resources could be limited. I mean, the order not to leave Maricopa County basically pins you down to the metro area. If the trail leads elsewhere, you'll need us on your team, especially if the evidence is to be found in another country."

"Are you trying to sell me on the idea of accepting your help?" Amber asked. "Because you know there's no one in the world I trust more than the four of you."

Chapter 7

Amber rolled over in bed, tempted to pull the pillow over her head to drown out the pesky buzz of some irritating insect. Then she recognized the noise for what it was—her intercom, signaling a visitor. Really? At ... 7:36 a.m.? A voice came through, faint in the distance from the front door to the bedroom, but distinct.

"Amber, aren't you there?" Her mother, sounding worried.

My god, they'd said an early flight, but seriously?

She rolled to the edge of her wonderfully comfy mattress, wishing she could pretend she'd slept through the buzzing. Running her fingers through the tangles of her wildly curly hair, she padded through the dining room and pushed the intercom button.

"Mom? You're here already?"

"Our flight left Albuquerque at 5:43," said her father's voice. "Didn't you get our texts?"

She sighed and pressed the button to allow access to the elevator. In the two minutes before they would be at her door, there wasn't much she could do to appear ready to welcome guests. Peering at her reflection in the glossy window on her microwave, she tried to make some order of her hair and rubbed the grains of sleep from her eyes. Her sleep shorts and tank top would have to do—it wasn't as if her parents hadn't seen her scantily dressed on a few occasions.

She'd pulled out a box of assorted K-cup flavors and was reaching for clean mugs from an upper cabinet when the knock came at the door.

I should have been up early, should have planned what I was going to say to them. This is going to be a disaster.

She put on a smile and held the door, stepping aside to let them in. "Sorry, I didn't get your text. I was exhausted last night and left my phone somewhere …"

"My baby," Mom said, dropping her purse on the sofa and pulling Amber into a hug. "I'm so sorry you had to go through this."

I haven't brushed my teeth yet. Oh yuck.

Her father was studying her face. "There's nothing to it—is there?"

"No! No, I still don't know how it happened, but I swear to you I didn't commit a crime." *At least not this month.* She stifled thoughts of other somewhat-iffy things she'd done in the past. Dad could read her like a grade school primer.

Turning her back, she pointed toward the mugs in the kitchen. "Look, how about if you two make yourselves a coffee, and I'll get dressed. I'll take you out to breakfast."

Preferably at a crowded place where we won't have to talk about personal stuff.

"It's really nice outside this morning. Enjoy yourselves out on the balcony," she said, slipping her phone off the dining table while they were preoccupied in the kitchen.

Closing her bedroom door behind her, she first skimmed through the texts that had arrived since last night. Dad had sent their flight information last night, confirmed when they were leaving the Albuquerque airport, reiterated that they'd arrived in Phoenix and were at the rental car desk. Sheesh. No wonder they expected her to be waiting at her door in full welcome mode.

There was one from Cody: No worries about not meeting my flight. Paris to London flight delayed. Missed connection. Trying for direct to PHX. Will keep you posted. Sleep tight.

It had come in at two a.m.

She set the phone aside and pawed through her closet, deciding on stretch jeans and a V-neck t-shirt. Clean cut, all American girl, nothing to warrant a critique. In the shower, she chastised herself—so far, although shocked, her parents had been nothing but supportive. They'd always had a close relationship, aside from the fact that Dad was used to being in charge. His comment last evening about having her lawyer checked out was just his way. He wouldn't find Mariah Kowzlowski lacking, not if Benton and Pen knew her.

She stepped out of the shower and toweled off, putting on her clothes and taming her corkscrew curls into a high ponytail, sticking in enough pins to create a messy bun. When she walked into the bedroom her phone was ringing. It went to voicemail before she could catch it.

"I got a call from Detective Howard," Mariah Kowzlowski's gritty voice said. "The police have released your personal possessions and you can go downtown and pick them up any time. Not the cash. Don't be surprised if there's fingerprint powder on your stuff. It's how they do things."

Great. Amber couldn't force herself to be excited about walking into the police station, but she would like to have her favorite clothes back, along with the gifts she'd bought for her friends. Before she'd quite decided how to handle the situation, the phone rang again and it was Pen's name on the screen.

"Pen, thank goodness."

"How are you doing this morning?"

"Well, my parents rang the bell before I was even out of bed, and now the police want me to come pick up my stuff downtown. So the day is starting out peachy."

"Handling your parents falls to you, I'm afraid, but I would be most happy to go and sign for your things at the station. I know my way around fairly well, from Benton's days in the same complex."

"Oh, Pen, that would be great."

"Consider it done. Phone me when you're free and would like me to bring your things."

"Actually, can we plan on later this morning? I promised my parents breakfast, which should give them time to chew me out plenty. By ten or eleven I should be more than ready for an intervention."

"I'll text you once I've got your bags. You may then let me know what's convenient for me to casually drop them by."

"Sounds like a plan. And, Pen? Thank you. You're the best."

"I never had a granddaughter, so I'm adopting you. If you don't mind."

Amber thanked her again and they ended the call. She walked out to her kitchen to find her father at the dining table with a near-empty coffee mug. Her mother was strolling through the living room, cupping her mug between her palms.

"You've got some new things," Marianne said. "I don't remember those pillows or that art print. Would you like me to help you hang it?"

Amber smiled and actually studied the room. "Maybe later. Some friends came by last night and brought the gifts. I guess my place is pretty plain and I just hadn't noticed. Gracie even got me a plant for the balcony. Now I have to remember to water it."

"It's a beautiful condo," her mother said. "And how interesting that you see right into the neighbors' living rooms, too."

"Yeah, that took a little getting used to. The guy across the courtyard on the fifth floor watches TV in his boxers and never closes his drapes. I've kind of learned to ignore him."

Her mother patted her arm. "Well, you be sure to get in the habit of closing yours when you're in here alone after dark. You never know who's watching."

"Right."

"I want to talk about this lawyer they sent you," her dad chimed in. "We might need to hire someone better."

"Over breakfast. Remember, I said I'd take you out, and there's a great place just across the street in Fashion Square."

She managed to get them out the door and they walked across to the massive mall, which boasted all the name-brand designer clothing and accessories. Settling into a booth at Sadie's Place, Edward went right to the topic again. What a dog with a bone, Amber thought.

They studied the menu and ordered omelets, and while they waited for their food, Amber managed to convince him that Kowzlowski was reputable and an excellent defense lawyer, according to Benton Case, who would know. Muttering a little, her father switched topics.

"So while this hotshot lawyer works on getting the charges dropped, you need to come home to Santa Fe with us. Our return flight is tomorrow, and I can still get you a seat."

"Dad, you know I can't do that."

"And why not?"

Oops. Forgot to mention the conditions of my release.

"I have to stay in Maricopa County. The cops ordered it." She fiddled with the straw that had come with her glass of orange juice. "Plus, I have a job here, and friends who want to help me. I can't just take off anytime I want."

But did she have a job? B-G was one area of her life that had, so far, remained curiously silent. Had anyone there heard about her night in jail?

Chapter 8

Cody Baker stepped off the escalator at the Tri-Borough Mall and scanned the weekend crowd. He gave a sigh and made his way toward the food court, where he spotted his father sitting alone at a small table, cupping a paper coffee container in his hands. It hit him that his dad was thinner and grayer than the last time he'd seen him.

"Hey, Pop," he said, taking a little pleasure in the fact that he'd startled the older man by walking up behind him.

"Hey! Back from your trip. I gotta hear the details." Woody Baker reached into his pocket and pulled out a dollar bill. "Here, let me treat you to a cuppa coffee."

"Sure, sure." Cody walked to the counter at Cup O' Joe and ordered a latte, adding three more dollars to cover it. Pop had no clue about the cost of things, and he'd likely only ordered the most basic, cheapest cup for himself.

As the barista poured and stirred, Cody turned again to scan the crowd. There was Pop, smiling largely at a family of little kids.

"Sir, your latte."

He dropped his change into the tip jar and picked up his cup. Approaching the table, he watched his dad reach into his pocket again and pull out a coin.

"Hey, wanna shiny new quarter?" he said to a four-year-old in a fluffy pink jacket.

The little girl's mother shot him a fierce look before taking her daughter's hand and leading her away, saying something urgently in the girl's ear.

"Sheesh, what's with people?" Woody complained.

"Pop, you can't be doing that. Times are different now. It scares people."

"Well, it's a shitty world when you can't be nice to a kid." He said it a little too loudly and several people stared.

Cody lowered his eyes and took a long sip of his coffee.

"So, Pop, why the mall? Kind of a weird place to meet up." *Especially considering what we're going to talk about.*

"My bank has a branch here. I want to take a long gander at my balance and then I'm gonna take some cash out, for the track."

Cody pulled out his phone. "People don't do it that way anymore. We can just sign in and see your balance. What's your login and password?"

"Aw, I don't got none of that stuff. Hell, I use the ATM—sometimes. That's modern enough. Besides, all this modern crap just leaves a trail. Cash is king. That's how I work. How we always worked in the old days."

They'd had this conversation a dozen times. Paying for big purchases in cash was considered impressive, back in Woody's day, back before there were dollar limits on what you could deposit or travel with. Moving big money now required computer skills.

"So, you get somebody to bring me my cut?"

"Let's walk around, Pop. I don't want anybody listening in." Cody spoke in a low voice, eyeing the movement of foot traffic.

"Good idea. I'll stop at the ATM and get my betting money." He pointed toward the far end of the long walkway. "So? The mark. She bring the goods in?"

They left the table and moved past a Gap and a Benetton before Cody spoke again.

"There was a snag."

"What snag?" Woody stopped and stared at his son. "She got caught?"

Cody gave a half-nod, noncommittal. "So far, I've been stalling about seeing her. She thinks I'm still in Europe, or maybe England."

"How much did you send with her?"

"About a third."

"A *third* of our loot?"

"Pop, you should see this girl. Not at all the type Customs picks on. Cute as a button, mixed race, obviously well off, travels first class. There was just no chance they'd call her out and inspect her bag. I packed the stash myself. It wasn't an easy find."

"But you think they did?" Woody made a disgusted sound and tossed his cup toward a trash barrel, missing. He walked on without a backward glance.

"Son, what do you know about this girl, anyway? And how much does she know about you?"

"I know plenty. I've been watching her for a couple months now, and not just online. As for what I've told her about myself, she *thinks* I work for this Omni Corporation in New York and I've been assigned to their Paris office. No clue that I live just a few miles from her. She doesn't even know my real name. She knows nothing that ties to you or to Jersey."

Woody muttered, "So now whatcha gonna do?"

"This was a test. And don't forget, this is on you, Pop. You're the one who wanted cash. I moved everything out of that corporate account, in increments that made sense for the business. Set up some offshore accounts, switched it up several times. It was all made to look like everyday business. You're the one that wanted to see good old hundred-dollar bills."

"Hey! Don't start that with me. You're still a whippersnapper in my book."

Cody took a deep breath. Pop believed Cody still needed his ideas and connections to pull off this con, and the next. They walked on, making sure nobody was close enough to really listen. Mostly it was young families, rowdy kids, or clusters of giggling teenage girls.

"Okay, Pop. I get it. Either I picked the wrong girl or luck just went against us. You never had a run of bad luck on a con? Never had an inside tip on a horse go wrong? Just let me think about this. I can get the money moved back here and you'll have access. I still got my inside connections, but I gotta get back to my day job by tomorrow. That's gonna tell me a lot."

The bank was just ahead. They waited until a leather-jacketed guy with tattoos running up his neck finished at the ATM and walked away. Woody walked up and fumbled his bank card into the machine. He muttered a little, until Cody stepped up and helped him select the correct buttons. It was reassuring to see that the account still had a high five-figure balance. At least Pop hadn't splurged it all on some conspicuous purchase.

Woody drew out the maximum allowed and turned to his son. "What do you say we hit the Meadowlands this afternoon? I gotta bunch of good tips."

"Maybe for a little while. My flight's out of Newark at five."

"Ah, plenty of time. C'mon, son. We'll have us some fun."

Cody hoped the old man wouldn't have *too* much fun. He had cautioned him that the money needed to rest a while. Especially now that Amber had been caught, there would be a lot of eyes on her and anyone remotely associated with her. He wished he'd made up a better alias to use in Paris.

Chapter 9

Pen wheeled the two suitcases along the corridor to
Amber's condo. Her text had been terse but almost
cute: Any time now! The door swung open before her
second tap.

"Pen! So great to see you!" It was nearly comical how
overjoyed Amber seemed to see her. "Let's just take these
in the bedroom real quick." Underlying meaning: Sneak
them in quietly.

Pen spotted Amber's mother in the kitchen, rinsing
some cups at the sink. Her father wasn't in evidence, but
he stepped out of the guest bathroom and moved down
the short hall, just as Amber closed the bedroom door on
the suitcases.

"... and I had the spinach, mushroom, and Swiss
omelet," Amber said to Pen. "We'll have to go back there

sometime. Oh, Dad, I want you to meet my friend, Pen."

"Penelope Fitzpatrick," she said, extending her hand. They were standing at the counter which divided the kitchen from the dining area, and Marianna stepped closer. Pen saw where Amber got her looks, the perfect combination of her mother's coffee skin and fine features, and her father's stature and Mediterranean curls.

"Penelope Fitzpatrick, the writer? I *love* your books. So exciting, so much adventure!"

Pen acknowledged the compliment quietly, with a nod and smile of thanks. She noticed Edward relaxed, a touch, at the revelation that his wife knew and approved of Amber's friend. "Amber tells me you live in Santa Fe. Such a beautiful and unique city. Have you been there long?"

Turning the conversation away from Amber's current problems worked to loosen up the couple.

"About ten years now," Edward said. "Before that, we were in Hollywood."

"Too big and too crazy, that southern California traffic," Marianna added. "We love New Mexico, and Santa Fe still gives Eddy the contact he likes with the film crowd he used to work with. Before that, we were in Europe for several years. Paris, in fact, when Amber was born."

"We had hoped Amber would stay in New Mexico, get her education locally, and settle near us."

"Dad … you know computers are much more my thing than the artsy scene where you are."

Edward tilted his head toward Pen, as if to say, *Kids, what can you do?*

She gave her enigmatic smile that could mean anything. "I'm so impressed with Amber's new condo. So, are you enjoying your visit here in the Valley?"

"The whole Phoenix area—no. Can't wait to leave. Too

hot, too much traffic. The condo, yes, it's really something."

"Our flight leaves early tomorrow," Marianna added, softening his words. "We weren't sure, when we came, if we would need to stay a while, but it seems there's nothing much we can do to help our daughter."

"That woman lawyer she's got—"

"Was personally recommended by a dear friend who has long ties to the court system here. Ms. Kowzlowski may seem rough around the edges, but she is one of the finest attorneys licensed in the state of Arizona." Pen said it with a tone that refuted any argument, and she kept her smile in place to let them know the offer had been made with love.

"Well, then, that's … that's good," Edward said. Clearly, the wind had been taken out of his sails.

"I shall leave you to your afternoon together, then. Amber, we'll get together in the next few days? I'm sure the girls will be eager to try that breakfast place you were telling me about." Pen draped her purse strap over her shoulder and headed for the front door.

Amber followed, seeing her out, stepping into the hallway as she left. "Thank you. I'm scared, but I can't admit it to them. They're convinced I'm young and stupid and overly gullible. Your words helped a lot."

Chapter 10

They stayed at the Phoenician and insisted on me joining them for dinner there. It's *way* more my dad's scene than mine," Amber told the Ladies the next morning. "I managed, and I wished them well on the trip home, but I have to say this was the most difficult visit we've ever had."

True to her promise, Pen had told the rest of them about Sadie's Place. It was crowded on a Sunday, but they had managed to get in and the five of them were seated around a booth, eager to try the omelets Amber had raved about.

"Well," said Gracie, "it's a whole new experience for all of you."

"No one said 'arrested' or 'illicit cash' during the whole visit, but it was just *there*, you know." Amber swallowed hard. "My parents and I were always close, but they're having a hard time seeing me as a real grownup. Before, I was a student, still a kid. Now they have to realize that I'll have relationships, my own real home, a job that pays well."

"What's happening there? Do you think anyone has heard about the cash, since it was a company trip?" Gracie asked.

Amber shrugged, waiting for the server to deliver their plates and walk away. "Tomorrow will be interesting."

"It's always a little strange, coming back to work and routine after being gone, especially to foreign countries," Pen assured her.

"Yeah but this is a little different, don't you think? I was held by the police. There are specific clauses in my employment contract about this type of thing."

Gracie looked around the table, eyes wide.

"I suppose we should have anticipated that," Sandy said.

"Well, it just means we have to get busy and find out what really happened, find a way to clear your name," Gracie said.

"And it has to be definitively enough that there is no question left on your employment record. We have to find out who was behind this and we have to get that person put away." Mary was already halfway into her ham and cheese omelet, the one person whose appetite seemed unaffected.

Amber hadn't touched her plate. "I'm afraid to say this, but it occurred to me that Cody could have done this. Unless someone at the Louis Vuitton shop is running a smuggling ring, he's the only other person who touched that new bag. How could I have trusted him?"

Sandy reached over and touched her hand. "Honey, don't blame yourself."

"That's right, Amber. Anyone can be taken in." Mary didn't say it, but they all knew she was remembering back to the fact that her ex-husband had, at one point, left her penniless.

"Let's think this through logically," Pen said, spreading jam on a slice of toast. "You say he's the only other person who had access to your bag, but what about someone else? Baggage handlers at the airport or hotel? Tell us about the sequence of events."

Amber's gaze grew faraway. "We'd been together five days. Paris in the autumn is so beautiful. We'd been corresponding online for a few weeks and we had so much in common. He's a computer nerd too and he works for a big company based on the east coast, but he was assigned to their Paris office so he knows the city really well. We met first just for drinks and dinner. Second day, it was a long walk through the gardens and a visit to the Louvre, another pink rose ... By the third day there was a lot of suggestive talk and we went to his apartment near the Seine. I basically stopped in at my hotel for a change of clothes, but we spent all our nights together."

Who among them didn't remember meeting someone special and the magic of new love?

"On my last day in the city I wanted to do some shopping. He took me to the best shops, and I figured what the heck, I could splurge a little on gifts. And it was at the Vuitton shop where he insisted on buying my new carry-on bag. He said I would need more space to bring home my purchases. Well, everyone does, right? I would have just found an inexpensive little tote, but he insisted. We'd had all these conversations about how lucky we were to be doing so well in our careers that we had money to spend."

"Had he already picked out the bag, or did he let you choose?" Sandy asked.

"I picked it out, but he did have a certain one in mind. He said it needed to be one I would carry on the plane, which made sense to me at the time. But I don't know why. So yeah, I guess he did steer me toward that one."

Pen seemed thoughtful. "I wonder if there was some way he could have had the bag modified in advance. There was a hidden compartment in it."

"And it must have been made of something that would hide the cash from the security cameras at the airport," Sandy suggested.

Amber only shrugged.

"Was he ever alone with the suitcase? I mean, when could he have put the cash inside?" Gracie wondered.

"I don't think so ... Well, the last night of the trip. I told him we should stay at the hotel because I still had to pack and my flight was somewhat early. My stuff was kind of all over the room, and I needed to organize everything. After we got back from dinner, I pretty much gathered it all and packed it. Then I headed for the shower. He was checking airline flights online, hoping to get himself on the same plane with me, back to Phoenix."

"He was coming here?"

"Yeah. We were having such a great time together and he had all kinds of questions about Arizona and said he'd love to visit. You know, raised in Jersey and all ... Apparently he had one more week of vacation coming and he wanted to work it out that he could spend it here."

Thoughtful expressions all around the table.

"So, while you were in the shower, he could have had access to your luggage," Pen suggested.

"I suppose. I didn't think about it, but he was alone in

the bedroom for a few minutes. When I stepped out of the shower, he was there ... well, undressed ... and said he was ready to jump in the shower with me. So ...”

“One thing led to another. It’s okay,” said Gracie with a chuckle.

“He did tell me he wasn’t able to get on my flight, but he’d found another one later in the day that would route him through London and then into Phoenix. He would get here roughly half a day behind me.”

“But that never happened? Have you heard from him at all?”

“I have. By text. There were apparently some delays and rescheduling. And then I lost touch early yesterday. I assumed he was in flight. I was tied up with my parents anyway.”

Pen shook her head sadly. “Did you tell him you’d been caught at Customs?”

“Well, yes. That was my first thought. I needed to let him know something had gone wrong and I wouldn’t be meeting his flight.”

“Oh dear. I’m afraid it looks as though that was news enough for him to abandon you.”

“It makes sense,” Sandy added. “If he put the cash in your bag and knew it had been seized, he doesn’t want to be anywhere near you.”

“He’s probably back in his Paris flat, regretting that he trusted me with the money.”

“Sweetie, he didn’t entrust you with the money,” Mary said. “He used you. I hate to be so blunt, but that’s the bottom line.”

Amber pushed her barely touched plate aside. “I know. I think I knew it yesterday.”

Pen put an arm around her shoulders. “Sweetheart, we

will get to the bottom of this. No man is going to break the heart of one of our own."

Amber leaned into the older woman's shoulder. A loud sniffle escaped her before she spoke. "What I want to know is, why? And where did the cash come from?"

"The authorities will try to find the source of the cash, and if they believe it came from an illegal source—say, drug dealing or money laundering—that's when the real trouble will begin," Pen pointed out.

"But that's dumb," said Gracie. "For one thing, if she's guilty of a crime like that, why would she take the money to Paris and then bring it back to this city? No one would do that."

"No one has said she obtained the money here in the US. They will be looking abroad too, won't they? And if there's criminal activity in Paris that they can connect, you may be looking at international extradition," Sandy said.

"So we have two mysteries to solve. The hundred-dollar bills in my bag are one thing, and maybe my so-called boyfriend really is a dirty rat. But the larger question, the one that could potentially land me in bigger trouble than a romance gone wrong, is why do the police believe I had all that cash with me?"

Chapter 11

Sandy convinced Amber to box up her uneaten breakfast and take it home. "You'll be hungry later and you'll be glad to have this."

"Always practical," Amber said with a laugh. She picked up the Styrofoam box and set out for the short walk to her condo, leaving the others to their own Sunday plans.

Home alone, at last, she gathered clothing and started a load of laundry. The large blue suitcase got stashed away in the guest room closet, but she'd been thinking about the discussion over breakfast, about how easy or difficult it might have been for Cody, or someone, to place the money in her new Vuitton bag.

As it turned out, not difficult at all. She laid the empty bag out on her bedroom floor and unzipped it. With the cover folded back, she began to probe the bottom of the section where her clothing and new purchases had been so neatly packed for the trip home. Discreet Velcro tabs let go, allowing her to lift the padded cloth bottom of the suitcase. With three sides peeled back, it was easy to see the spare half-inch of space that had been filled with bundles.

She devised a test, bringing in a ream of computer paper and dividing it into packets of about the same thickness as the banded money. Set carefully into the extra space, with the cloth bottom neatly Velcroed back in place, she could see how nearly invisible the hidden stash could be. And the padding disguised the shape of the edges of the paper.

When she closed the bag and lifted it, it was definitely heavier than empty, but would she have noticed that? The bag was new to her and the unfamiliar heft and weight of it hadn't caught her attention, but it might have been the way the Customs officer knew something was amiss.

Something had prompted them to search her. She would probably never know what had tipped them off.

She pulled out the paper packets and closed the bag once again. For an item that had thrilled her when Cody insisted on buying it for her, the bag now only held revulsion. She couldn't imagine that she would ever use it again, not without resentment over the way she'd been used. Instead of storing the new bag in the closet with her older one, she wheeled it to the front door. Maybe the luggage shop in Fashion Square would take it and sell it on consignment. Or maybe she would leave it in the dumpster for some lucky drifter to find. Determined to have no reminders, she wheeled it to the elevator and down to the garage. It vanished through the lid of the trash receptacle.

Back in her own kitchen, she was finally feeling hungry for the breakfast she'd never eaten. While it warmed in the microwave, she checked her messages.

Cody: Sorry, baby, still stuck in London. Horrid weather here. How are you?

Did he honestly think she couldn't check the current weather in England? She deleted it without responding.

Monday morning dawned with a new crispness to the air. October was often the turning point for the weather here in the Valley. After months of triple-digit temperatures, it looked as if the oppressive heat might be letting up. Amber's mood improved accordingly, as she dressed in her business attire, admittedly somewhat more casual than many of her coworkers who seemed to think pencil skirts and five-inch heels were necessary for everyday wear. She had bought two cute dresses in Paris, but now she could barely look at them. Instead, she put on dark slacks and a vivid blue shell, topped by a black silk jacket. The air conditioning in the corporate high-rise was always set too cold.

Twenty minutes later, she swiped her employee ID badge at the entrance and steered her Prius into the parking garage. On level three she found a spot, gathered her company computer and purse and headed at a brisk pace toward the elevators. Sometimes she climbed the twenty-three flights of stairs, just for the exercise, but arriving in a lather on her first day back would not necessarily be impressive.

She found her thoughts drifting to the rest of the Ladies. She'd spoken with Pen, who had phoned right before bedtime, and told her about Cody's latest blatant lie about being stranded in London. Once she'd told him about being stopped at Customs, it must have pretty well sealed the fate of the relationship. She could see that now. He wouldn't be coming to see her.

But why had he texted? She couldn't figure it out, and Pen had promised to get busy on the question. Somehow, the Heist Ladies would unravel the mystery and figure out how and why Cody got the money and what his motive had been in stashing it with Amber.

The elevator whirred almost silently to a stop on her floor. It always amazed her how much space the mega tech corporation used and how many employees must have occupied the various office spaces and cubicles. As a fairly newbie programmer, hers was just another in the cube farm, but she had personalized it with a small houseplant and some photos of family and friends.

Her favorite was of a beach in Bali where the Ladies had made a quick trip last winter when they nabbed a pseudo-religious couple in the process of absconding with a container load of money. She chuckled as she thought of the relatively tiny sum Cody had pawned off on her. Surely it would turn out that her problems were nothing in comparison.

"Hey, Amber," said a female voice at her cube opening. Carly Morse was an admin assistant she often ran into in the lunch room. "I thought you weren't coming back for a few more days—you met someone over there?"

"Change of plans."

Carly looked like she wanted to dish some more, but Amber ignored the eager look.

"And how was Europe? Dave seemed pretty excited about closing the Amsterdam deal."

"Yeah, he was."

"Come *on*—you've gotta tell me about Paris! I've never been. It had to be *so* exciting."

Amber sent her a polite smile. "Maybe over lunch later this week. I feel like I have to get back up to speed this morning."

"Oh, speaking of being up to speed. The latest around here is that the quarterly audit turned up some kind of discrepancy. They're being pretty hush-hush about—" Carly stopped in mid sentence as Vicky Salazar, a customer service rep, walked by.

Someone a row or two over called out to Carly and she hurried away, her heels clipping along on the tile floor. Amber set her computer bag down and took the machine out, glancing over the papers on her desk and remembering what she'd been working on when she left.

Two other programmers walked by and she caught, "… HR yet?" followed by "No, but they're talking to everyone."

A buzz ran through her, but she stifled it. Office gossip was always floating through the air. What Carly had told her and the random comments of a few others didn't have to be related. She needed to tune out the general noise and concentrate on the set of algorithms she'd been writing. She probably should have done more work during the trip, not so much R&R—romance and reading. It was going to take a day or more to get her head back into programming.

The morning flew by, and she managed to avoid Carly by eating a sandwich at her desk instead of going to the lunch room.

Chapter 12

Cody sat in traffic, gloomily mulling over the past few days. The con with Amber hadn't gone as planned. She was supposed to have breezed through Customs with the money in her bag and he would have met her a day later, figuring out a way into her home so he could find the bright purple bag and retrieve the cash. Now he had Pop pissed off at him, and Amber not answering his texts for the first time ever.

He would deal with all that. Somehow. Pop would be pacified once he saw how much more money there was. It just couldn't all be moved into the US right now. That needed to be a gradual thing, and one thing his father didn't understand was playing it low-key. He seemed to have this idea that money taken by computer transfer somehow just vanished into the ether, and since no one could find it, you just helped yourself and went out and spent it. Cody had to remind himself that although his father was a long-time grifter, he hadn't necessarily been a super successful one.

Pop's latest suggestion, made during the last few minutes Cody had spent at the track with him, was that Cody just show up in front of Amber, make nice, and get her to replace the cash. Well, that wasn't happening. Agents had taken the money. Plus, how was he supposed to admit to Amber he'd put the money in her bag, and secondly, to ask her to come up with it out of her own pocket. That wouldn't happen, and he wasn't about to call up some Jersey muscle to threaten her.

For now, he just wanted to get back to his job and see what was going on. Con games were interesting and, yeah, they could be lucrative, but he didn't quite have Pop's tolerance for being dead broke when they failed. He liked his electronic gadgets, his independence, and having some fun with cute girls. His wasn't a lifestyle that worked if you got down to your last few hundred and had to worry about where the next paycheck was coming from.

What he wanted was one big, final score, hopefully while he was still in his thirties, and he'd take off for someplace where you didn't have to do anything more ambitious all day than stretch out on a lounger under a palm tree. One with internet access so he could tinker with his latest programming brainstorm. When that succeeded, he could provide Pop with enough betting money to keep him happy (Woody Baker had a good enough eye for the horses that his habit was pretty close to self-supporting), and if Cody wanted to zip around the world and hang with the jet set he'd have plenty for that.

The cars ahead of his bus began to crawl along once again. He should have gotten an earlier start. His sleep patterns were still all messed up from the quick trip to Paris.

Now *that* had been fun. While Amber was in Amsterdam with those sales dudes, Cody had been watching the good neighborhoods in Paris, alert for a posh apartment with nobody home. A talkative doorman, an unattended door key, and he was suddenly the new 'owner' of a very cool place where he could take an American girl to impress her. By the time his little honey had arrived, he was all set up—his clothes in the closet, some wine in the rack, and a working knowledge of the nearby cafés, shops, and restaurants. It was as if he actually had lived there for two years, exactly as he'd told her.

He almost regretted some of the lies, especially when it became obvious cute little Amber was actually falling for him. Well, for his urbane, Euro-persona. He covered for his Jersey accent by telling her that's where he'd grown up (no lie there), and he'd changed his appearance by combing his hair straight back and wearing green contact lenses. If she ever ran into him somewhere else, it would take a minute to put it together that this was Cody Brennan from Paris. She would never know who Cody Baker from Newark really was.

The bus stopped a block from the office and he got out, knowing he was running late, not bothering to sprint the distance. Let old lady Spitz have a conniption if she wanted to. He didn't see himself long for this job anyway, since it was a short-term contract for only a few months. Spitz needed him more than he needed the job at this point. His skills were destined for bigger and better things. He pulled out his ID badge and put his glasses on before passing the downstairs security desk.

Chapter 13

Gracie was halfway to the supermarket when her phone rang and she saw that it was Mary. She pressed the button for hands-free talk. "Hey, what's up?"

"Just a heads-up," Mary said, keeping her voice low, as though she didn't want to be overheard in a crowded place. "That Detective Howard just came by the gym and questioned me."

"What?"

"Yeah, he's asking about Amber, her friends and connections, what kinds of things she might be mixed up in."

"So, what did you say?"

"The truth. I hadn't seen Amber in several months but as far as I knew she was just a young woman fresh out of school, who did her job and didn't have a huge social

life. When he asked how she might have access to large amounts of cash, I said I have absolutely no idea."

Except that Amber did know how to move money around and track it. She'd done so before. But, she had never siphoned off any that didn't belong to her, and she'd always been right there to help the Ladies take down the bad guys.

"So, if this detective came to your work, he's probably looking for me, too," Gracie said, pulling into the parking lot at Fry's.

"And Pen, and Sandy. I was surprised he knew all our names."

"Okay, thanks for the warning."

Gracie ended the call and stared toward the large market, thinking about her options. Her kids would be home from school in a couple of hours and she didn't really want the police showing up to question her in front of them. She fished around in her purse until she came up with the card Mark Howard had given her the night he'd taken Amber downtown.

Wait for him or be proactive? She dialed his cell number.

"I understand you may be looking for me. What can I do for you?"

She'd caught him slightly off guard but he recovered nicely. "I'm just working the case, tying up loose ends, and that includes speaking in person with friends and associates of Amber Zeckis."

"Well, if you've dropped by my house you've already figured out I'm not home. I've got some other business downtown in about an hour. I can come by the station first, if that works for you." *Better to meet the lion head-on in his own den than to invite him into mine.*

"I'll be there in twenty. If you get there first, you can

speak with my partner, Detective Marsh."

She timed her arrival twenty-five minutes later. No point in learning to read another cop or in going over the details Howard already knew. She inquired at the front desk and was escorted to a desk in a wide-open squad room. No privacy here.

Mark Howard was removing his jacket. He slipped it over the back of his chair, indicated that she should take the chair across the desk, and sat down with a sigh.

"Let's get right to it," she said, startling him. "What evidence do you have that Ms. Zeckis even knew that cash was in her bag?"

"I'm not going to discuss details like that with potential witnesses," he informed her, sitting straighter and aiming a penetrating gaze her way. "And I'll ask the questions, thanks."

He went into the same things he'd apparently asked Mary, and Gracie gave him a similar answer. "I've known Amber since she was eighteen. She babysat my kids, for heaven's sake. I just can't imagine—"

"Have you ever known Ms. Zeckis to use drugs?"

"No! No way we'd be friends if I learned something like that, and absolutely no way she'd spend any time with my kids."

He jotted something in a small spiral notebook. "Any mob connections, trafficking of contraband?"

"Absolutely not."

"Look, I'll be frank with you. That kind of cash isn't something any honest person just happens to have in their possession. It usually comes from an illegal activity of some kind—dealing drugs, trafficking weapons or humans."

"Seriously? You've seen Amber. She's like a lamb and you're sending her to the slaughter."

Again, he fixed that penetrating stare on her. "You'd be surprised. The innocent looking ones can be guilty as sin."

"But you need to have evidence. *What* is pointing you that direction?"

His desk phone rang and he flashed an irritated glance at it. "No comment," he said to Grace as he reached for the handset. She sat back in the chair while he went into something that sounded like a paperwork issue with whoever was on the phone.

The squad room buzzed with conversations and movement. Two plainclothes cops walked past her and paused beside the desk nearest Howard's.

"We'll need to get over to Blackwell-Gorse before the day is out," said the female cop, a no-nonsense type with dark hair pulled into a bun at the nape of her neck.

"Yeah, sounds like this could be something fairly big," the man in the brown suit said. He held a file folder open to some kind of report.

Gracie quickly shifted her gaze away when the woman looked directly at her. With a nod at her partner, the two moved away and Gracie saw them walk through a doorway at the far end of the room.

Howard seemed distracted after his phone call, so Gracie used the moment to excuse herself. "If you have any other questions, you have my cell number," she said, standing and heading toward the exit.

Blackwell-Gorse Tech was Amber's employer. Gracie felt her heart rate pick up. Something was going on and she had a bad feeling about this.

In the privacy of her minivan, Gracie picked up her phone with shaky hands and tapped Amber's number.

"If you're at work right now, give me a call when you leave."

"Uh, okay," Amber said, clearly puzzled.

"The sooner the better."

"I have a break coming up soon. I think I'll go out and grab a coffee at the corner."

Chapter 14

Gracie's call had freaked her out, so it wasn't a far stretch for Amber to tell her supervisor that she wasn't feeling well and wanted to leave early.

"The creampuff I ate on my coffee break must have been off," she said, completely sure that the sickly look on her face would match her story.

All the way back to her condo, the conversation ran through her head. "If there's anything incriminating on your computer or phone ..."

Amber couldn't think what that might possibly be, but the idea of having her emails and files searched felt so invasive. She'd seen enough movies to know they could construe anything to mean what they wanted it to, and her recent texts from Cody could easily have double meanings.

She whipped the Prius into her assigned parking slot in

the building's secure, residents' area, grabbed her computer bag and purse from the passenger seat, and practically raced up the stairs to the sixth floor. Her phone rang just as she reached the top step, showing one of the B-G extensions on the screen. She let it go to voicemail while she unlocked her front door.

Inside, she listened to the voicemail message: "Hey, Amber, it's Sadie. Sorry I didn't get the word before you left for the day … Someone from HR is trying pretty urgently to get hold of you, and she was kinda upset when I said you'd left. No idea what it's about, but don't be surprised if you hear from her. The woman's name is Greta something-or-other. There's all this rumor stuff about something in the quarterly audit and they're looking at peoples' computers, so maybe she just has some questions. Um, hope you get to feeling better soon."

Sadie Uphurst was her supervisor, a woman only a few years older than Amber and not someone who would normally call her when she was sick. There must be something to the office buzz.

She set her computer bag on the dining table, took the laptop out, and stared at it for a good, long minute. They were looking at the employees' computers. What would they find on hers?

Her intercom buzzer sounded, causing her to jump, sending her heartbeat zooming. Could she ignore it? Most people would think she was at work right now. Then her company cell phone rang. An unfamiliar number with a familiar prefix.

"Amber Zeckis." She forced her voice to remain steady.

"Ms. Zeckis, it's Greta Sash from HR. We're conducting a random check and I need to take your company computer and phone. It's probably only for a day or so."

"Uh, okay. But I came home sick this afternoon. I'll bring them to your office tomorrow."

"Actually, that's no problem. I'm here at your condo to pick them up. I just need you to buzz me in." The intercom buzzer punctuated her words.

Oh no.

"Oh. Uh, one second. I was just getting undressed." She ran into the spare room where she'd never quite unpacked all her computer gear. Somewhere, she had a portable hard drive. She rummaged into a box and got her hand on it. "Ms., uh, Greta, um, just let me get some clothes on. Can you give me two minutes?"

"Certainly."

Amber ended the call and raced back to the dining table. Her fingerprint scan brought the laptop to life, and with practiced hands she plugged the external hard drive into a USB port and started the process to copy the laptop's hard drive to it.

Two excruciating minutes went by, while the message on the screen said: **Approximately five minutes remaining …**

The door buzzer screeched insistently.

Amber ran to her bedroom and whipped off her work clothes, tossing a nightgown over her head. Back at the table, the screen said: **Approximately two minutes remaining …**

Buzzzz, Buuzzzzzzz

She walked to the intercom panel beside the front door and pressed the speaker. "Sorry, I had an emergency in the bathroom. Here you go."

She pressed the release button to allow the elevator to admit the visitor.

Approximately one minute remaining …

She messed up her hair and rubbed off her remaining makeup. The backup countdown kept going: **10 seconds remaining ..., 9 seconds, 8 seconds ...**

There was no time to do anything about texts or calls on her phone. She could only hope for the best.

1 second ... Backup complete. You may now remove the external drive.

She did. In one smooth move she unplugged the USB cord, closed the lid on the laptop, and dashed into her spare room to stash the portable drive at the bottom of a box of miscellaneous office supplies. She had provided her own computer bag, and she tossed it to the top shelf of the closet.

A sharp knock came at the front door. Amber took two deep breaths, hoping the flush on her face and uneven breathing could be explained by her so-called illness.

Greta Sash had an unfamiliar face, but that wouldn't be unusual in a company the size of B-G. She was in her fifties, with iron-gray hair in a severe bob and hard lines around her mouth.

"Sorry," Amber said, rubbing her temples. "I've really been feeling like crap this afternoon."

"I'll only take a minute," Ms. Sash assured her. "Here is a receipt, already filled out, for the company property in your possession. If you can just sign here and give me the items?"

"What's this about?" Amber asked as she signed the slip in duplicate.

"I'm not at liberty to say. There have been some irregularities and we're just following procedure."

Amber led the way and pointed out the computer and phone on the dining table.

"This laptop is warm," Sash commented.

"I told Sadie I'd try to get some work done from home. But I think I'd better just go to bed."

The HR woman gave her an appraising look. "That's probably a good idea. You don't look well."

Amber was never so happy to close the door on someone. She watched through the peephole to be sure Greta Sash actually walked away. Satisfied, she looked at herself in the mirror beside the door. Wild hair, glistening eyes, and a flush to her normally deep brown skin all gave credence to the story that she was ill, but there was no way she could tuck into bed and rest.

She paced through the condo for five minutes to calm herself down. She needed to talk to someone, but who? This wasn't the sort of news to share with the parents, and it seemed the rest of the Heist Ladies already knew of the heightened investigation. Eventually, she settled on calling Mariah Kowzlowski. Her lawyer really should know about this latest potential development. She picked up her personal cell phone and found the number.

The gruff voice greeted her, all business. "They gonna find anything on that computer? Anything that tells 'em you committed a crime?"

"No, I swear, I have not committed a crime."

"That wasn't the question. Could anyone have used your computer to commit a crime?"

Cody's face flashed before her, but no. Company computers were completely secure, requiring a fingerprint and several levels of encryption to get into anything remotely sensitive.

"No, the computer is good."

"And the phone—no personal hanky-panky stuff?"

"A few personal calls and texts, sure. But nothing illegal."

"Okay then. They have no proof. Sounds to me like they're on a witch hunt. Nothing for you to worry about, even if they come back and arrest you. A trial in court requires proof."

Amber saw about a million holes in that theory. *If they arrest you. And it's not like there aren't people doing hard time in prison, unjustly accused and unable to prove their innocence.*

The idea terrified her.

Chapter 15

Once again, Pen provided a grandmotherly shoulder to cry on. As soon as Amber called her, the older woman invited her over. Pen's hillside home on Camelback Mountain wasn't far away, and Amber needed the company. She needed to get outside her own four walls for a while.

She retrieved her car and pulled out of the parking garage, feeling almost immediately as if she was being watched. Was it the slightly edgy vibe of having lied to leave work, and now being out in plain sight? She chided herself—odds were extremely slim that anyone from the office would happen to spot her, and why would they care?

But, she reminded herself, the police still had her in their sights as well. She drove, eyes darting between her mirrors the whole way. Pen greeted her at the door of her spacious home, pulled her into a hug, and immediately offered tea. It was the most lovely thing about having a British friend—the tea would be hot and restorative.

"Let me just clean up here a bit while the kettle boils," Pen said.

Amber followed her through to an area near the large French doors where Pen had her easel set up.

"The light is perfect in this spot," she explained, picking up two brushes and setting them into a jar half-filled with some type of liquid. The canvas showed areas of brilliant color—blue in the upper third, the outline of mountains, and some undefined blobs in the foreground. "It's to be a landscape. I'm hoping to capture the shadows on those distant hills. I still feel so very new at this, but I must say I really do enjoy painting."

She wiped her hands and ushered Amber into the kitchen.

Sitting at the long granite breakfast bar, Amber let the morning's events pour out. Pen listened until she ended with the visit by Greta Sash and her frantic idea of copying the hard drive on the company computer.

"I didn't know what else to do, Pen. *I* know I didn't do anything wrong, but now that my computer's gone, I have no proof."

"No, it was a good idea to make that copy. If nothing else, if they should try to pursue you legally, you've got your own set of evidence."

"And if they find something on my computer that incriminates me?"

Pen thought about that for a moment. "Then you have a copy, and you'll know what to do. Forewarned is forearmed."

"I feel so helpless in all this. I can't just sit around and wait to be accused. I need to know what they're looking at and make a plan. Now."

"Shall we call the others?" Pen asked. "You know we are all on your side, and we have already committed to helping in any way we can."

Amber nodded.

"I see you brought your computer bag," Pen said, as she began composing a text message.

"With my personal laptop and the extra hard drive. I thought it might be a good idea to keep it with me."

"Good thinking." A ping sounded on Pen's phone, then another. "Oh, good. Mary and Gracie can come right over."

Amber busied herself plugging the extra hard drive into her computer and accessing the contents.

Within a half hour, Gracie pulled up in the driveway and Sandy had responded that she would join them as soon as she could get away from the bank.

Gracie immediately rushed to Amber's side and embraced her. "Mary and I were both questioned by the police," she said. "Didn't tell the detective anything. Don't worry."

Pen offered tea then had a better idea. "Perhaps I should prepare some lunch. Sandy will be here in a half hour or so, and we can compare stories once everyone is present. Gracie, would you like to lend a hand?"

Amber barely noticed their bustling about the kitchen or Gracie exclaiming over Pen's canvas. She was deep into the company files on the hard drive. Mary came in at some point, followed by Sandy, and soon the five women were gathered around Pen's dining table with a spread of sandwiches, fruit, and salads before them.

After a quick recap of the morning's events, Pen turned to Amber. "Have you found anything helpful on your computer? Or, for that matter, anything harmful?"

"Neither one—not yet."

"Okay then," said Gracie. "We need a plan, and I say it begins with this Cody. If he's the only one who had access to the suitcase with the cash in it, he's got to be involved. Has anyone done a background check on him?"

Amber gave her a withering look, and then immediately apologized. "Sorry. But, of course I did. You don't actually think I went off to meet a guy in Paris if I knew nothing about him."

"Many young women do things exactly like that," Mary reminded, then backtracked. "But you are much brighter than they are, and we're glad to hear you thought of it well in advance."

"Still," Amber admitted, "even being fairly sure I knew who I was dealing with, it really does look like he pulled one over on me. I was mainly intent on making sure he wasn't a rapist or murderer."

She pushed her lunch plate aside and pulled her laptop toward her. "Here are two online profiles I found before I met him. One is a simple social media account on Instagram. He doesn't post often. He said that's because he's just not into the whole scene of accumulating Likes and such. But what he did post all seemed to check out. The other profile is business, showing that he works for Omni, a multinational technology firm based in New York. I checked them out, and found his picture and resume on their site. He's got several degrees in computer sciences, programming, and a master's in computer engineering."

She showed them the two screens. "And here are a couple of selfies I took of the two of us on vacation. It's clearly the same guy."

Nods all around.

"It would seem so." Pen voiced the common opinion. "And so we must ask ourselves, what would he have to gain by using you in this way?"

"It seems pretty obvious that he wanted Amber to be the person to smuggle the cash into the US. If you'd succeeded without being caught he would have met up and figured out a way to get it back for himself. Since the cash was confiscated, he's disappeared." Sandy hadn't said much yet, but her analysis seemed spot-on.

Mary spoke up. "Amber, can you tell me ... because I know nothing about this stuff ... how easy would it be for someone to set up a fake social media account?"

"Simple. There's no proof required that you are who you say, so anyone could do it. Many people do. Don't you ever get those 'friend' requests from handsome men with gorgeous smiles but no history? You don't think they really exist, do you?"

"Right. So his Instagram account could be totally bogus. And what about the work profile?"

Amber began nodding slowly. "Sure ... yeah. It would take some real advance planning, but for a guy with his computer skills, probably easy enough to hack into a corporate website and add himself as an employee."

"And of course he'd give himself super impressive credentials," Gracie added.

"Yep."

Pen sat up straighter, setting her plate aside and resting her forearms on the table. "And what about those credentials? The various university degrees?"

"I'd need to ..." Amber began scrolling through the pages. "Hm. It doesn't say what universities he attended."

"But for a false identity to hold up well, he must have included that somewhere."

"Most likely."

"Let's divide up the tasks," Pen suggested. "University student records should be accessible. I can look into that."

"And I can call this Omni company," Sandy said. "It would be easy to say I'm verifying employment for a loan, doing a credit check, something like that. If he really works there, it will all check out. If not ... well, I'll just see what I can learn."

Mary spoke up. "And I'll be watching for this sucker, night and day, everywhere I go. And when I catch him, I'm going to kick his ass."

For the first time since she'd flown in from Paris, Amber felt herself relax a little.

Chapter 16

Cody sat in his cubicle, keeping his head down. There was a ripple of something going on. He'd received two calls from upstairs, which he ignored. It wasn't as if he needed this job—he'd rather be back with Amber, having a great time. Sure, the Paris gig had been fun but he knew it was the short con part of the long con. Ever since he'd come back to the States and talked with Pop, he'd been thinking of ways to twist this thing so he could join her instead of sitting here.

But, he couldn't quit the job too soon. The whole thing about being a successful con man, according to his dad, was to get in and out without even being suspected. Omni might have caught on to his having been behind the scenes in their website, beefing up his profile for Amber's benefit. Or maybe someone had guessed that his summer internship had technically ended months ago, so what was he still doing here? Most likely that's what the HR calls were about.

Still, better to be slippery than to get pinned down into answering questions. Only in his most private hours would Cody admit to himself that he was nowhere near the smooth operator that his dad was. He was a lot more comfortable at a computer keyboard than facing down an accuser and talking his way out of it. Woody would be disappointed that his chip off the old block was more of a fragment.

The intercom light on his phone flashed. Damn thing. He'd quickly figured out how to silence the buzzing on the stupid desk phone, but the flashing light always set him off. He took off his headset and logged off his terminal. He would claim needing a bathroom break. Let the caller leave a message.

Another message.

He left his cubicle and meandered toward the men's room. The 14th floor was such a sham. Technically, it was the thirteenth but buildings never had a numbered 13th floor. As such, it was the short-term hires who got stuck here. Would it kill them to paint the walls something other than dead tan, or replace the worn, unmatched cubicle dividers that had probably already done primary duty in better departments in their early years?

Shoving his shoulder against the restroom door, his critical eye took in this space as well. Beat-up tile and grout that had never been cleaned in its life. Two other guys stood at the urinals so he closed himself into a stall.

It wouldn't hurt to make some friends at work, he'd told himself. But then Woody's voice would intrude. "Don't take up with drinking buddies—ever. One day you'll have a little too much and you'll spill the beans. You gotta keep to yourself when you're around the same bunch of guys every day."

So he did. He heard a flush, water running in the sink, two paper towels being yanked from the dispenser. A second flush. Eventually the door whooshed open and shut twice. He peered out and saw the room was empty, so he peed, even though he really didn't need to. At least the stupid phone should have quit ringing by the time he got back to his cube.

He flopped into his chair again and thought back to Paris. A sigh.

With a furtive look around, he picked up his cell phone, connected to one of several virtual hotspots he'd created, and logged on to one of the foreign accounts. It was tempting to pull some more cash out. There was a hazy dream of getting back together with Amber and taking her someplace cool. Maybe with some of the money in the London bank they'd stay in a swanky hotel and have room service every day for a month. The French account was a little hot right now—it was from there that he'd pulled the hundred grand to send back to the States. But once things cooled off a little, he could grab some more and take her on a fabulous winter vacation to the Med, spend time on the Cote d'Azur or someplace like that.

Who would have thought—little Cody Baker from Jersey, hanging with the rich and famous. All it would take was a bit of research and putting on the Cody Brennan persona again. A smile settled on his face.

Chapter 17

Sadie Uphurst stopped by Amber's desk about five minutes after she arrived at work the next morning.

"Hey. Feeling any better?"

Amber was better at reading algorithms than faces, but her supervisor's concern seemed genuine. "Yeah, thanks. I guess it was just something I ate."

"Look, I hate to pile on anything more, but I need you to come with me. We have a meeting in HR this morning."

A rock settled in Amber's stomach.

Neither of them spoke during the elevator ride to the 22nd floor. Sadie stood aside and let Amber step out first. To keep her from pressing the button and making a run for it? Amber let the thought slide past. She could only guess at what this meeting was about, so she focused instead on thoughts of her parents' home in Santa Fe, with the wide open views toward the mountains on one side and the red-brown mesa where the chamisa would now be in full bloom along the roadsides.

The door to a private office stood open midway down the corridor, and Sadie again stepped aside for Amber to pass through first. She closed the door behind them.

At least, thank goodness, it wasn't Greta Sash at the desk. This was a woman in her thirties, with strawberry blonde hair worn shoulder length, vivid blue eyes behind stylish glasses, and a warm smile. The nameplate on her desk identified her as Melanie Banjo. Amber nearly chuckled, but quickly thought better of it.

"Amber, thank you for coming," Melanie said, indicating the two chairs in front of her desk.

As if I had any choice.

"I'm sure you are aware there is an investigation taking place within the company, something involving discrepancies in the quarterly audit. Often—actually, most times—these things sort themselves out and it's found to be a clerical error or some type of erroneous data."

Where was she going with this?

"As part of the investigation, we have been advised to check the computer files of several employees, including yours."

Amber wasn't sure what she was expected to say, so she filled the longish pause with, "Yes."

"I'm afraid ..." Melanie looked toward Sadie.

Sadie took the ball. "Amber, your work here has been exemplary, and please know that those up in the C-suite have noted and appreciated your programming skills ..."

Ball back in Melanie's court. She cleared her throat. "Unfortunately, it seems there were some irregularities with a few times you logged in."

"What?" Could this be about a mistyped password? "In what way?"

"I'm afraid I can't share details just yet, and believe me, this is all very preliminary still." Something in the woman's eyes shifted. It was a lie.

"Amber, we're being forced to place you on administrative leave until it's all sorted out," Sadie said.

"What does this *administrative leave* involve?"

"You're being sent home."

"And then?"

"For now, it's leave with pay and benefits intact," Melanie explained. "Depending on how the investigation goes, you may have your computer returned to you and be able to work from home until an outcome is decided."

"What type of outcome? I'm sorry, but I'm really in the dark here." Had they found out about the incident at Customs? And how could that tie in with what this woman was telling her?

Melanie put a rueful smile on her face, one she probably had practiced with everyone she had to fire. "I'm so sorry, but I'm really not at liberty to say anything at this point."

Some kind of signal passed between her supervisor and this deliverer of doom with the pretty face. Sadie stood up.

"I'll walk with you back to your desk," she said.

It turned out to be more than a simple walk to the desk. She stood by while Amber picked up her purse and the lonely houseplant, then accompanied her all the way to her car. As she turned to get into the Prius, Amber held out her employee ID badge. "I suppose you want this back, as well."

"Oh no," Sadie said brightly. "You're still employed."

She watched Amber's face begin to crumple, and her voice dropped. "Honey, I hope this all turns out just fine and you'll be back at your desk soon. Until then, I'd stay away. Your badge won't get you much past the front desk anyway."

Somehow, Amber held it together until she was out of the parking garage. She made it around the block before she had to pull to the curb and let out a scream.

Chapter 18

Well, that totally sucks," Gracie said. She'd been in the midst of gathering trash and flattening cardboard shipping boxes out in her garage when Amber drove up.

Amber gave a deep sigh and shrugged. Repeating the story had taken a little of the sting out of it. Very little. "Technically, I'm supposed to be at home right now. I'm on call to work if they want me to. It's part of the terms of my 'leave.' But without my company computer or phone what could I actually *do*?"

She offered to carry a couple of the trash bags.

"Is this related to the cash in your suitcase?" Gracie set the flattened boxes near the garage door and stacked the bags on top.

"I don't see how it could be. All they're saying is there was some irregularity in the quarterly audit. I have no idea what that means, but surely even an office this huge doesn't keep stacks of hundreds in cash. There's probably a coffee fund or a petty cash box somewhere, but not this kind of cash. Then again, the audit might have nothing to do with money—it could be some other thing. Maybe one of my programming algorithms went wacky."

Gracie chuckled. "Is that a computer term—wacky?"

Finally, a smile from Amber.

"Anyway, I figure as long as I have my personal phone with me and am willing to answer any work-related questions, how will they know I'm not physically in my home? Talk about solitary confinement. That's worse than being limited to the county."

Almost on cue, her phone rang. It was Pen.

"I hope I'm not disturbing your work, but I wanted to report my findings on your Cody's university degrees."

"No, this is fine. I'm not at the office." It hurt, saying those words, and she didn't go into the whole story.

"I've not had much luck," Pen said. "If you recall, the website profile we found shows only that Cody obtained certain degrees, but there was no mention of which school supposedly awarded them. So, I looked for alternate ways to find out. I did locate two men named Cody Brennan, each with impressive schooling. One, however, is a medical doctor—I was able to follow through and locate his practice. From his photograph, he is definitely someone else, a bit older, and he's located in California."

Amber was jotting notes of Pen's findings. "And the other?"

"He is in the correct age group. Attended City College in New York, but the titles of his degrees don't match up. So—I shall persevere and will report more as I know it."

When Amber thanked her, Pen evidently heard the

discouragement in her voice. When she questioned, the story of Amber's work situation came out.

"If I may make a suggestion?" Pen said. "It will be helpful for you to stay busy, and I could use some research guidance. Shall we do this together? Come to my place."

Amber felt her mood perk up at the suggestion. There was nothing to be gained by moping around. Gracie bowed out of coming along, so Amber headed for Pen's, stopping by her own condo to pick up her personal laptop on the way.

An hour later, they were side-by-side at Pen's table, comparing notes. Mainly, Amber was racking her brain for details, trying to remember if Cody had mentioned his university education while they were in Paris together. Nothing came to mind.

"You know, maybe we're spinning our wheels on this whole college degree angle," Amber said. "Our goal is to find him *now* and to figure out how to prove he put the money in my case so the law can deal with him."

"True. But I'd hoped we might learn his current address through an alumni association or some such."

"Actually, that's brilliant. Why didn't I think of it? I *know* his current address. I could take you there, to the apartment in Paris!"

Pen gave her a considered look. "But will he be there? He knows you were caught with the money. Wouldn't he pull up stakes and leave any place you could link to him?"

"Hmm, probably. I wonder how we could find out."

"Do you remember the street address of the place?"

"There were ornate metal numbers on the wall—12. But it was near an intersection that branched in several directions, and I don't remember the street names of any of them. That's no help at all, is it?"

"The neighborhood? Which arrondissement?"

"If I look at a map, I might be able to pick it out, based on some of the places we went nearby. At home I have a sack of little keepsakes—restaurant menus, cards, flyers. If I look through those I'll come up with names."

Chapter 19

Back at the condo, Amber set up her computer on the dining table and went into the bedroom for the items she'd mentioned to Pen. Things were still scattered, and it took a couple minutes of digging to separate the small gift shop bag from the rest of her accumulated travel junk.

"One of these days I need to get a desk and properly set up the spare room as an office for myself," she announced to the houseplant on the kitchen counter.

She liked that idea. It would be a project to keep her busy, as long as she was under orders to stay home anyway. She shook off the notion of settling into her little nest and complacently puttering around home all day. She was on a mission to clear her name and get her life back to normal. Still, before she dug into the bag of souvenir brochures and menus, her hand found itself clicking on an office furniture website, where she quickly chose a desk, a chair, and a bookcase. Click, click, click—they were ordered and set up for delivery later in the week.

"Ha," she said to the plant. "I can do both, settle in *and* pursue my case."

Exactly when she thought she would manage to arrange furniture and unpack the boxes that had sat in place for more than six months, she wasn't sure. "Hey, one thing at a time," she muttered to herself.

She spread the various flyers across the table. Here was the men's shop where she'd chosen a tie for Cody. She'd thought the poor man could use some wardrobe help, and the green silk looked stunning with his eyes. She flicked it aside. The shop had been miles from his apartment, a place they'd gone to via the Métro. The address was of no help, and she certainly wouldn't be shopping there ever again.

One of the restaurant menus sparked a memory. He had taken her there the first night she was in the city. But was it near his place? She couldn't say for sure, since she knew nothing of the city at that point. Same with a little café where they had eaten croissants the next morning. As she went through each of the brochures, the street names had a certain familiarity but she couldn't place them in her mind in relation to all the other sites they had visited.

"I need to see this laid out," she murmured.

She opened a map program on the computer and began entering the addresses, one by one. Little red balloon-shaped buttons appeared, and she started to see a pattern. Aside from the obvious tourist places, such as the Eiffel Tower and the Louvre, most of their eating and shopping had taken place within a fairly small section of the city.

She started plugging in the number 12 with a street name, pulling up photos of buildings. Some didn't exist at all, and she scratched those off her list. Others were obviously not the building she had visited—the street-level boulangerie might have residences above, but she knew they had not accessed his place that way. She eliminated a couple more.

The sun was setting, the room growing dim, when she realized she had been at this task for hours. She had two potential addresses. Both residence buildings were in the same neighborhood, both had the address No. 12, both had the familiar light-colored stone and black iron railings. Either could be the one.

A vague headache was forming behind her left eyebrow and she rubbed the spot.

"What am I doing, really?" she said to the empty room. "It's not like I can book a flight and go there and confront him. No passport. And Pen was probably right. He will have cleared out by now."

Had she spent the afternoon on a wild goose chase, or merely filled some otherwise empty hours with something that felt useful? The headache intensified.

"I gotta get moving."

The houseplant didn't respond.

Amber closed the computer and stood up to stretch. She was still wearing the business clothing she'd put on this morning, and that gave her an idea. Her timing could be perfect.

Chapter 20

Cody slouched into the corner of his bus seat. It had been a weird day and he didn't really want to wrap his head around all that was going on. So, when his phone erupted with the ringtone for his dad, just as the bus arrived at his stop, he picked it up.

"Hey, kid. How's it going?"

What to say? *I love my job, hate the company. I'm thinking about this girl all day, but she's in so much shit right now I can't reach out to her?*

"Fine. Just got off work, walking home from the bus stop."

"Well, I had a fantastic day at the track. I tell ya, kid, the ponies love me."

"Good, Pop. That's nice."

"Hey, you sound kind of down. It's not that chick still, is it?"

Cody stopped at a traffic light and pressed the button for the pedestrian crossing light.

"No. Well, yeah, kinda. Looks like it worked. She's the one taking all the heat about the missing money."

"Well, that's good. That's great! You can get on with other things now. Hey, I got this idea that maybe we could run the Russian Prince gig. You'd be so good at that one, and it could bring in a bundle."

"Pop, I think I need to keep an eye on this other situation a while longer. I mean, the money's out there, yeah. But I've got it spread in banks in three countries. It's making me nervous."

"You stop that right now, buster. We got no nervous-nellies in this family, you hear? We run the con, the mark takes the hit, we vanish. That's it."

The mark takes the hit. Amber could do prison time for this.

But he couldn't say that to his father, who would rant at him for being a wimp. If there was one thing Pop hated, it was a wimp.

Cody made some pacifying comments, meaningless agreement just to shut his dad up, and then ended the call. He crossed the intersection and strode the half-block to the side street where he'd rented a spare bedroom from some old lady who watched game shows on TV all day.

Doubts began to creep in. Could he do this to Amber, walk away and let her go to prison for something he'd done? Maybe he should go to the cops.

No. That meant he'd be the one going to prison. Couldn't face that, not at all.

Maybe an anonymous tip, an email sent through a fake email address and routed through a couple of VPNs.

He let himself into the house and heard the sounds of

Wheel of Fortune on the TV in the den. Mrs. Whatshername glanced quickly in his direction, gave a wave of acknowledgement, and turned back to her show. He let himself into his bedroom and closed the door.

The anonymous tip idea held a certain appeal, but he'd watched lots of cop shows. *NCIS* had forensic computer people like that Abby, who could backtrack anything. Phoenix was a big city, and they surely had all that stuff too. They'd find out.

He plopped into the worn armchair in the corner of his room and ran his fingers through his dark hair. His stomach grumbled. *Maybe I should have picked up food. I could order a pizza.* His stomach rebelled. He was tired of pizza.

Maybe Pop's right. I could pull up stakes, get out of here, fly back to England and draw out some more of the cash ... But Amber's face wouldn't leave him alone. The night they had dined at Restaurant Lasserre, the way her eyes shone in the candlelight, her full lips smiling at him, kissing him ...

He bolted from the chair and went into his bathroom for a cold shower.

Chapter 21

Happy hour was in full swing at Buster's Pub, the spot where some of the B-G employees hung out after work. These were the mid-level and newer staff, definitely not the supervisors, managers, or execs, but those weren't the ones Amber wanted to run into anyway.

She'd made friends with several of the girls in customer service, the ones who always felt in the middle—the company making policy and hammering on them to adhere, versus the customers who always wanted their jobs done yesterday and complained about being billed too much for what it took to satisfy their demands. These were the employees who needed a couple hours after work to vent, and by now they'd been at it for at least an hour already.

She edged into Buster's and stood against the wall near the door, checking out the room. After an afternoon alone in the quiet of her condo, the noise level in here hammered at her. She'd taken a couple of aspirin before leaving home, but the headache threatened to return. She ignored it and scanned the crowd.

The bar that ran along the opposite wall was filled, body-to-body. This was the flirting zone, the spot where dates were made, hookups arranged, even though B-G was fairly opposed to in-office romances. She spotted a few familiar faces, but the tables around the rest of the room were where most of her women friends were normally to be found. They had boyfriends or girlfriends already. They weren't interested in being hit on, only to unwind at the end of a stressful day before they went home to arrange dinner and put the kiddies to bed. Amber spotted Allison Porter with two other CSRs whose names didn't immediately come to mind.

She held her head high and walked over to their table.

"Amber!" The shock of seeing her in their midst was evident on all three faces.

"Hey, guys. How's it going?"

"I—we—wow, we heard ..." The news from the tech department had clearly made it to the Customer Service floor.

"Yeah, I know. Bizarre, huh?" She took the empty chair that put her back to the rest of the room. "I worked from home all afternoon. You know, it wasn't bad. If I could get that gig all the time, I might even get a cat or something."

Her nonchalant attitude threw them, she could tell. No one was sure what to say. She ordered a drink and kept up the pretense that all was normal and she was happy about it. Allison finally relaxed a little. The other two finished their drinks and declared the need to get home.

Once she had Allison alone, she pounced. "Okay, so

everybody knows. What are they saying? What does B-G think they have on me?"

"Uh, gosh, I don't think I should say." Allison stared at her glass, but it was still nearly full.

"Look, I don't want to put you on the spot, and I would *never* say where it came from. But I have to know what I'm up against. I've got a lawyer, and she'll do the digging. Just give me a clue where to start. HR wouldn't even tell me what's happened."

Allison scanned the room. People were starting to leave and the tables closest to them were empty now. The bar action had cleared by at least half. Conflicting emotions played out across her face before she spoke again.

"Okay, I can only tell you what they're saying. It's not my department, so this is just gossip."

"Dish."

"There's money missing. Something was off in the last audit."

"How much?"

"I don't know … Okay, I heard something like a half-million dollars."

"Holy crap!"

"Yeah. It's bad." Allison fidgeted in her seat, but she couldn't bolt without literally knocking over another chair or pushing Amber out of the way. "So, there's a rumor … you were stopped at the airport when you came back and there was a lot of cash …"

Amber stayed quiet.

"So, I think a few people are putting it together that somehow that cash came from the company …"

"How do they think I could have managed to do that?"

"Okay, I was about to walk in the break room and overheard two of the auditors who thought they were alone. Your name came up, and something about fund transfers to a bank in Santa Fe. That's where you're from, right?"

Amber felt her face go pale. This was bad.

"What else?"

"I swear, that's totally all I know. Like I said, most of that is rumor and speculation anyway."

Numb, Amber nodded and thanked her friend.

"Don't worry, I won't tell anyone we talked about this," Allison said, draining her glass in one long swig. "And don't you dare, either. I could be in as much trouble for telling as you are for asking about it."

"If anyone comments about seeing me here tonight, it was just the usual. I'm working from home these days, and I just popped in for a drink with friends."

"Got it."

"And, Allison? I didn't do anything wrong. I had nothing to do with money missing from B-G or the other thing, at the airport. I'm pretty sure I know how that happened, and let's just say it'll be a long time before I trust a man again. I was set up."

Allison nodded and reached for her purse, pulling out some cash. "I really gotta get home. I'm so sorry this happened to you, but I don't know how I can help. I feel for you."

"I know. Thanks, it means a lot. And you've already helped."

Chapter 22

Stomach churning, Amber pulled out the portable hard drive where she'd copied the company information and plugged it into her own laptop. Now that she had a clue what she was looking for she went into the drive's history.

She should have eaten something at the bar, or at least picked up food on the way home. One of these trips out, she really should bring in some basic groceries, now that she'd be spending more time here.

The portable drive opened with a long list of subdirectories and files. She entered a command and then initiated a search. Although the company system had her name, everything began with a login using her employee number, so she searched for that particular string of digits.

And there she was, in mind-boggling detail. Every day since she had worked for B-G there was a logon and logoff. And she'd entered her passcode multiple times a day, whenever she stepped away from her desk and came back. Every transaction began with codes for what she was doing at the time, and although she could easily read computer code, it was a mind-numbing load of data.

She stretched and walked into the kitchen, rummaging until she came across a packet of saltine crackers, two Cokes, five ice cubes, and some leftover fried rice. It would have to suffice as dinner. At least the food would help absorb the glass of wine she'd had earlier, enough to help her think clearly.

What had Allison told her? Money was transferred to a bank in Santa Fe. But she hadn't said when this happened. Amber set up a spreadsheet and began searching for bank routing numbers. Nothing stood out, most likely because in the course of her regular job she never entered banking information. Those numbers either hadn't come from her computer, or someone had disguised them.

Someone. Cody? He was the one person brilliant enough to know exactly how to pull this off. She still couldn't get over how well he'd fooled her.

How could she narrow down the search and come up with meaningful data, something that didn't involve going through every single day of her working career at Blackwell-Gorse. Ten and a half months, average twenty to twenty-five working days a month, logging on multiple times a day? Her head began to hurt again.

She picked up the plastic container of rice and began eating it, thinking. How to approach this? Her fatigue began to fade and the answer came, quick and clear. She had a friend in banking. She picked up her phone and said, "Call Sandy."

"Hey, kid," Sandy's cheerful voice said. "You must have

read my mind. I was just about to call you."

"I need some banking information," Amber said. "Can you find out the routing numbers for all the various banks in Santa Fe?"

A tiny pause. "I can, but I could do this faster from work, if it can wait until morning."

"I really could use the information now. It's pretty urgent."

"Okay, there's a way. Let me think." There was a pause and Amber could hear computer keys tapping in the background. "I don't have my ABA login info on this computer and it's not recognizing me. Let me see. Can you hold on for a couple minutes?"

It was closer to eight minutes, and Amber chafed a little as she finished her makeshift dinner and poured one of the Cokes over ice.

"I found an old copy of the printed version of the book. What's the name of the bank you need to know about?"

"I don't know, only that it's a bank located in Santa Fe."

"Um, okay. They aren't listed that way, but we can find some names to get started with." More computer keys, then Sandy spoke again. "I see some of the big ones. Bank of America, Wells Fargo ..."

"Let's start with those." Who knew whether the fraudster would use a big bank, thinking of the benefit of anonymity, or a small hometown bank, on the chance their controls weren't as strict.

Sandy went back to the book, read out some numbers, and Amber wrote them down. Midsize banks came next: Century Bank, Bank of New Mexico, Nusenda. She wrote those routing numbers down as well.

"There are several credit unions, too," Sandy told her.

"I doubt it'll be one of those, but we can always try them later."

"Glad to help. And, Amber? I really hope these give us a solid lead."

"Speaking of which … you said you were about to call me?"

"Ah. Right. I called his employer, Omni Tech, pretending like my bank is considering making a mortgage loan to Cody Brennan."

"Oh, that was smart thinking. Hopefully he hadn't spread the word around the company that he already owns a home or something?"

"He didn't. In fact, he doesn't even work there."

For a moment, Amber couldn't think what to say. "Why am I surprised? Based on everything else, I should have seen that coming a mile away."

"We all should have," Sandy assured her. "But he's a con man. Fooling people is what he does. You can't beat yourself up over it."

"I wonder if he ever worked there. He really did talk the talk."

"As most good con men do, he used tidbits of fact. He actually did work there once. I got through to his direct supervisor, who said he'd been hired last spring as a summer intern but he didn't last long. A couple of weeks into his employment they got around to checking with the university that had supposedly sent him for the job. The institution had no record of him. Supervisor told me she sent for him, hoping to straighten out the mix-up, and he had disappeared. Hiked his backpack up on his shoulder and told the guy at the next desk he was going to walk down to the corner for a coffee. He never returned."

"So he got a hint they were on to him and he bailed."

"Looks that way."

"And it explains why Pen wasn't having any luck verifying his university degrees."

Sandy mused, "He must have gotten into Omni just long enough to plant his photo on their website and post all those fake credentials."

"And yet his credentials didn't need to be faked. He knows his stuff."

"If he had already targeted you for this money scam, he may have also hacked into Blackwell-Gorse while he was at Omni. Is that possible? That he might have found out enough about you to get into their system and steal your credentials?"

Amber couldn't immediately see how he would manage it from another company's offices in New York or Paris. For that matter, did Cody *actually* live in either of those cities? He could operate from anywhere. Uncanny things could be done with computers and the right skills. She couldn't underestimate this man, and she couldn't rule it out.

Chapter 23

It was after midnight when Amber found the answers. Too late to call Sandy. She stood at the floor-to-ceiling windows of her condo, looking down into the neighboring residences around the courtyard. She'd been so engrossed in her search that she hadn't remembered to take Mom's advice and close her drapes after dark. She did so now, a little creeped out that she'd never thought of the openness of this place.

I suppose a person never feels like they're being watched, until they are. Damn you, Cody.

Closed inside her little cocoon now, she turned back to the numbers she'd tracked down, the places her own computer tied to her, the numbers that implicated her.

The money went to one of the bigger banks in Santa Fe, a nationwide one, and Amber could see that it made sense. Such a large amount would cause a stir at a smaller bank or credit union. She followed the lines of code and got the routing number, the individual account number, and a wire transfer code. That should be enough to get some information.

Amber drummed her fingers on the tabletop, impatient to be done with this thing. But although banking, in many ways, was a 24/7 operation these days, there were some things that should be handled during normal business hours. She would just have to wait. She shut down her computer and stifled a yawn as she turned out lights and headed toward her bedroom. It was hard to imagine she would get any sleep at all, but the next thing she knew daylight was showing at the edges of the bedroom curtains.

* * *

Sandy answered her phone on the first ring. "I thought about you half the night," she told Amber. "How can I help?"

"Well …" Amber gave out the bits of information she'd learned.

"I'm on it. As soon as I get to my desk at the bank, I'll make some calls. There's banker-speak that will get me a lot further down the line than you could get. Let me see what I can learn about this Santa Fe account you found."

"Call me the minute you know anything. And, Sandy? Thank you."

It was 9:17 when Amber's phone showed an incoming call from Sandy. She set a carton of yogurt in her market cart and answered it.

"Well, it's a mixed bag of news," Sandy said. "First off, there's a very small balance in the account now, less than a thousand dollars. *But,* some fairly big dollars have moved through it. The first deposit was a hundred thousand."

The round number set off Amber's alarm bells. Was it coincidental that it was the same amount found in her suitcase?

"Then there was ..." Sandy paused. "Maybe this is too much to go into over the phone. Can you stop by my office sometime this morning?"

"Give me thirty minutes." Amber tossed a couple more breakfast items into her cart, along with the frozen dinners she'd already picked up.

Nine minutes later she was out of the store and had stashed her food in the insulated carrier bag she always kept in the car. The branch of Desert Trust Bank where Sandy worked was only ten minutes away.

"Hey, glad you got here so quickly. I was just informed I have another appointment at 10:15." She reached for a manila folder, and Amber sat in the chair across from her.

"Okay, so this is a printout of the account information my contact sent me."

Sandy pushed a form across the desk. Pointing with her pen, she showed Amber the data.

"The account was opened with an initial deposit of five hundred dollars, basically just enough to get it established."

"Wait, who's this Blandishment Inc.?"

"The account was set up as a business. We'll need to check further to see who is behind it."

"But it's not me, and it's not Cody."

"Not personally. It's a Delaware corporation and there are—well, we'll just see, once we check it out." She pointed the pen at another line on the form. "A few days after the account was opened was when the hundred thousand was deposited. A wire transfer that matches the transfer number you gave me."

Amber's throat suddenly felt dry. She swallowed hard.

"Okay, that amount was almost immediately moved to a bank in Scotland."

"Scotland? Why there?"

Sandy shrugged. "Who knows?" She pointed again at the printout. "Two weeks later, came the big one. $423,890. Why such an odd sum? I don't know."

Amber was staring at the page. "And it looks like most of that also got transferred out?"

"Exactly. But not all at once. Three transfers to three different overseas banks, each for close to a hundred thousand, leaving the small balance that's in the account today."

"And no further transactions after that? It looks like all this happened more than six weeks ago."

"We need to find out who's behind this Blandishment Inc. and I'm also curious why no one questioned their moving such large amounts of money around."

"The plan to move lots of cash was probably a factor behind setting this up as a corporation. Businesses get a lot less attention when they move money. My guess is that when we investigate the company, find out where and why it was formed, it will be a fairly new entity with a stated mission of something involving high-dollar transactions— real estate would be a common one, but they could be claiming anything from a diamond wholesaler to an importer of some basic commodity."

Amber nibbled at her lower lip. "And what if my name is on that corporate paperwork?"

Sandy just shook her head. "That would be bad. Really bad."

Chapter 24

Cody could hear recorded announcements in the background when he picked up his phone. "Pop, where are you?"

"The airport. Come pick me up."

"Which airport? Pop, what have you done?"

"I'm here, in Phoenix."

"Okay, I'm not far away. I'll have to get an Uber. Wait at the north curb—there are signs."

He ordered the car, then picked up his backpack and walked out of the office. Nobody said a word. A few minutes later he was kicking back in the car, looking over Amber's social media accounts and wondering what he was going to do with his father. What had possessed the old man to hop on a plane? And how long did he plan to stay?

Amber's Instagram and Twitter accounts had seen no

action in days, so he switched over to looking for a nearby restaurant where he could take Pop. Over an early lunch maybe he could figure out how the rest of the visit would unfold.

"That's him," he told the driver when he spotted Woody's skinny frame standing near the curb. "Once he's in, we'll want to go to Café Miche."

"It's extra," the blonde girl said.

"Fine. Bill me." *What do I care—it's all going on a stolen credit card.*

Woody tossed a small duffle bag on the seat between them and climbed in. "Where's the fall weather? How the hell can it be ninety degrees in October? And palm trees—where's the beach? God, I never saw so much open sky."

"Yeah, it does have that. Welcome to Arizona, Pop."

They rode in silence for the ten minutes it took to get off the airport property and the next ten to the restaurant. Nothing they could discuss should be shared with a driver.

"I figured they didn't feed you on the plane. This place serves either breakfast or lunch." According to their Trip Advisor listing, anyway. Cody had never been there.

Catching the restaurant between normal meal times meant they were able to get a table in an isolated corner. They studied the menu; Woody ordered ham and eggs over-easy, while Cody opted for something called the Big Burrito. Despite the French-sounding name of the place, it seemed the food was all-cultures-included.

"So, Pop, this visit is a surprise."

"Don't know why. I've asked you more than once when we're getting the money, and I mean cash in my little hot hands."

Cody lowered his own voice. "Pop … don't you think we should slow this down a little?"

"Okay, so the last mark blew it and got caught. And why are you hanging out in this city to keep an eye on her? Move on, kid."

"That's not the only reason I'm sticking around a while. I got a job, a short-term gig to do some web design for a company, and I've rented a room. Which, by the way, there's no space for a visitor so we'll need to get you a hotel room."

Woody waved it off. "Whatever. You're not still chasing after the chick from Paris, are you?"

Well, I'm not admitting it to you. "Nah. I just haven't found the right person for the next trip."

"That's what you said on the phone. You shoulda had a new one lined up way before now."

Cody sighed and sat back while the waitress set their plates down and offered refills on the coffee. Once she was out of sight again, he spoke softly. "Pop, you know that's easier said than done. Takes time to get them trusting me. Girls don't just agree to meet up with a guy in a foreign country until they feel like they know you."

Woody was nodding as he cut into the generously sized slice of ham. "I get that. But time's wasting. Where all do you need to go, to round up this money?"

"There's still more in Paris, but I've also sent some to Scotland and some to England. We'll need to use somebody different for each country, unless I can find someone who's experienced at this and doesn't mind the risk."

"For a fee."

"For a fee," Cody agreed.

"How'd this get so complicated? In my day we just—"

"Get over this 'in my day' bit, Pop. Things are totally different now. Stuff gets tracked. I had the expense of setting up a dummy corporation so I could even do what

I've done so far."

Woody stuffed a wedge of ham, topped with gooey egg, into his mouth, while he waved off Cody's explanation.

"All's I'm saying is, I don't want our cash sitting around the world in other places too long. I like to be able to look right at my winnings."

"And that's the other thing, Pop. With wire transfers I could have it back here within a day. But that's traceable, and you're wanting cash money. It just takes time."

An elderly couple walked in and, as luck would have it, chose the table nearest theirs.

Cody leaned toward his father. "You win, I'll fly back to Paris. More on this later."

He cut into his burrito and kept his mouth full so he couldn't talk.

Chapter 25

Pen had her cover story clear in her mind before she placed the call. Best to stick fairly close to the truth. All successful liars know this.

"The Oakwood Group," said the voice at the other end.

"Hello," Pen said, giving the word the thickest of her British accent. "Is it the company that advertises setting up corporations? I believe the name in your advertisement was Biz Yourself."

"Yes, ma'am," said the young woman on the line. "Biz Yourself is one of our entities. Are you interested in incorporating your business?"

"Actually, I have some questions about how it's done. I'm a writer of romantic suspense novels, you see, and I've got a situation with one of my characters who needs to form a business very quickly."

"Suspense stories? Wow. What name do you write under?"

Pen always got this question when someone found out she was a writer, as if she'd never use her real name. "Penelope Fitzpatrick. And what's your name?"

"Ohmygosh, you're actually—" The voice went a little squeaky. "Wow, I've read *all* your books. I'm Lily Visionis, and I'm your biggest fan!"

She got this a lot too. "What was your favorite?"

"I just finished *Uncertain Destiny*. That's the newest one, right? But I mean, if you've got a newer one, please tell me. I cannot wait!"

"Um, actually, not yet. You're correct, that's the newest."

"You know, if you are ever in Dover, I will come to the bookstore and have you sign all my books."

"If you can answer a few small questions about the incorporation process, Lily, I will be happy to send you signed copies."

"Oh, wow! Okay, so what a person does is fill out a form. It's really a simple one—basically who owns the business, their address, and that kind of stuff. If they want a Delaware address, they can use ours. We actually have over two hundred businesses who list our street address as theirs."

"Really? They can do that?"

"Sure."

"Why would they not just list their real address?"

"You want some guesses, or do you want the official response? Cause I'm supposed to say that it's none of our concern what address they fill in on the form."

"But ... what's your guess?"

"Oh, all kinds of reasons. It's way cheaper and quicker to become incorporated here than most other states, maybe they don't want somebody back home to be able to check up on them, maybe they're doing something a little shady ..."

"Do you know of instances where that has happened? Something 'shady' or illegal?"

Lily paused. "Well, no. I mean I really can't say that it's ever happened. We don't ask."

"Doesn't the paperwork require them to state the nature of their business?"

"Oh, yeah, but it can be pretty vague. A lot of them just have something like, the purpose of the business is to buy and sell products. Or, the purpose of the business is financial."

"Ah, I see. And then when someone wants to look up information about one of those businesses, is it readily available?"

"Oh yes. By law. They can either call us or come by, or there's now an online search feature." Lily rattled off a website address.

"And once the person has set up their corporation ..."

"Oh, they can do anything that any other business does. Set up a store or office, open bank accounts, get a tax identification number. They're in business."

"Just that easy."

"Yep. Was there anything else you needed to know?"

"Well, I did come across a business recently that I was curious about," Pen said, deciding to keep young Lily talking. "It's called Blandishment Inc., and I do believe their advertising materials stated they were incorporated in Delaware."

"One moment, and I can tell you. Um, Ms. Fitzpatrick?

Is this going into a story of yours?"

"Maybe, someday."

Computer keys ticked away in the background while Lily kept talking, going on about her favorites of Pen's books. Within two minutes, she switched topics again. "Okay, here's what the official documents say about Blandishment Inc. Cute name, by the way. Doesn't it mean something like insincere flattery?"

Pen caught her breath. How appropriate for what Cody Brennan had done.

"Never mind," Lily was saying. "The principal officer in the corporation is a Woodrow Wilson Baker. Hm, why does that name sound familiar?"

"Woodrow Wilson was president of the United States at the time of the Great War," Pen said. "Actually, World War One."

"Really? Hm. I must have learned that in school."

"Is there other information on the paperwork?"

"Well, they did just what I was telling you about. Used our street address for the business. The purpose of the business is listed as Horses. Whatever *that* means."

"Anything else?"

"Nope. That's it. This Wilson guy is the only officer on the paperwork. He's president, secretary, board member, and contact person."

"And it's legal to do that?"

"A lot of states like to see at least two officers, but sometimes it really is just one person starting a business on their own."

Pen was feeling a bit stumped and was unsure what else to ask. "All right, then. Thank you so much for your assistance, Lily."

"Do I still get a signed book?"

Pen smiled. "Absolutely. Give me your address."

That accomplished and the call ended, Pen sat back in her chair and went through the conversation once again. She had learned something, but she was not at all certain what.

A scrap of paper on her desk caught her eye, the reminder that she was also to research Cody Brennan's university credentials and find out what she could learn from that.

Chapter 26

It was Gracie who called the meeting. Each of the Ladies had been on her own research mission. It was time to try and put some of the puzzle pieces together. Sandy offered to host them at her house, which was centrally located for all, and although she offered to cook, Gracie insisted on bringing a big assortment of takeout Chinese so they could focus on plans rather than cleanup.

Sandy's two black cats, Heckle and Jeckle, greeted each guest at the door and led the way to the dining room with excited meows, once they caught the scent of the chicken in Gracie's containers. Amber was the last to arrive.

"Sorry, last minute call from my parents," she told them. "Even when I explained I was driving, Mom couldn't stop asking questions. They still think I should pack up and get myself to Santa Fe."

"First things first," Sandy said, setting a stack of plates on the table. "Let's get our dinner while it's still hot."

No one argued with that logic.

Once they were all seated, with full plates, Amber was the first to report. "I cornered a friend from work, out at the favorite happy hour bar. Unless the rumors are way off base, the amount the company believes is missing matches pretty closely with what Sandy and I discovered from the bank transfers on my computer."

"This is not good," Mary said, swallowing a mouthful of Kung Pao Chicken.

"Definitely not good," Amber agreed. "It's not going to be long before an investigator follows the same trail of keystrokes from my computer and concludes that I'm the guilty party."

"What will they do? I mean, is this investigation going to stay within Blackwell-Gorse, or will the police become involved?" Mary asked.

Sandy spoke up. "My guess would be that the company will first try to determine if the theft came from within or was done by an outsider. Either way, they'll most likely turn it over to the police. If they can pin it to an employee," she said with a rueful look at Amber, "they'll terminate that person and press charges. And since it's a large enough amount to qualify as a felony, the police and prosecutor will pursue it as such. At least that's what I've seen happen at the bank."

Pen was nodding. "I believe Benton has told me of similar cases during his career. I think you're right."

Amber wasn't looking too well.

"But," Pen said, "we've been checking a number of avenues to catch this Cody person, and we'll have some ammunition for your defense. If it comes to that."

"Where do we stand with our various inquiries?" Grace asked.

Pen reported on the corporate name they'd discovered, Blandishment Inc., and her call to the Delaware firm that had set it up. "I'm not sure what connection there could be between Cody and this Woodrow Wilson person listed on the corporate paperwork but that's an angle we've yet to pursue. It may be completely unrelated, as the purpose of the business was stated as 'horses.' I've no idea how to interpret *that*."

"Using a long ago president's name seems completely bogus," Amber said. She was toying with an egg roll, dipping it repeatedly in sauce but not taking a bite.

"None of his claims of university degrees have panned out, have they?" Gracie asked.

Pen shook her head.

"But does that matter, really?" Mary asked. "Whether he went to a certain school or not—how does that help our case?"

"True. He's not in school now, not if he's living and working in Paris." Amber caught herself. "Or if he's *pretending* to live and work in Paris. He doesn't seem to be tied to academia."

"Well, his position at Omni Corp was a fake, or nearly so, taking a temporary job just to get in and establish an identity."

"So if he's no longer at Omni, where is he?" Sandy asked the obvious question. "Amber, do you believe he is still living in Paris?"

Amber shrugged. "I have no idea. He seemed so confident and at home there. So maybe yes, maybe he's been there all along, just as he told me."

"Perhaps a couple of us should go there and try to

track him down," Pen suggested. "I'll arrange—"

"I can't let you pay for tickets to—"

Pen laid a hand on Amber's arm. "It's a small price to pay to clear your name. Consider it a loan, if you must, but I insist on doing this for you."

"It would be a good opportunity to check on the money, as well. To see if the account there might contain the rest of what's missing from your company," Sandy said.

Amber slowly nodded. "And maybe I can work some of my magic, even from home, to see what I can learn about the movement of the money."

"Be cautious about that," Gracie said, reaching for the carton of General Tso's Chicken and scooping more onto her plate. "If the police are watching you, they could confiscate your personal computer too. They'd know every move you made."

Sandy nodded. "We all very well know that all computer searches leave a trail." She pushed some grains of rice around her plate with her chopsticks. "I'll tell you what—there's a brand new laptop computer at my office. Corporate ordered new ones for all our administrators, and we happen to be down one person right now so it hasn't been assigned to anyone. I'll loan it to you, as long as you promise to wipe out your browsing history when you've finished with it."

"Traces of things could still show up," Amber pointed out.

"But whatever scraps might be there would have no relation to the person who ends up with the computer later, for his or her job."

"Okay, it's a deal," Amber said. "Which brings up my next concern. I've had the strongest feeling, ever since I've been put on leave, that I'm being watched."

"The police?" Mary asked.

"No idea. When I left Buster's Pub after happy hour I even thought I caught a glimpse of a guy who looked a lot like Cody. I know—I'm probably losing it, thinking I'm seeing him around every corner. I'd feel a lot better, whether it's the police or Cody or just some boogeyman, if I didn't have the hard drive I copied from B-G in my possession. What can I do with it?"

"I can put it in a safe deposit box at the bank," Sandy offered.

"No, if it's discovered you did that for me, it could risk your job."

"Agreed," said Gracie. "We can't have all of us unemployed. Who's going to take Amber in when she becomes homeless?"

The joke kind of fell flat.

"I'll take the hard drive," Mary said. "No one would tie us together in this way. I'm not your banker or your lawyer, just a friend you meet for meals now and then. I'll carry it in my tote bag. It'll be in my locker at the gym when I'm there and under my mattress when I'm home. In the worst case scenario, if the cops bust in and demand a search of my gym gear, I'll toss it into a bin of dirty towels until they leave."

The image drew a laugh, until Amber spoke again. "Thanks, guys. This is the scariest crap of my life, having everyone but you guys believe I'm guilty. And I can't figure out a way to prove my innocence."

"We'll do it," Pen said. "Somehow, we shall get the evidence to prove your case."

Now to be certain they accomplished it before the police closed in and Amber faced a prison term.

Chapter 27

The flight to Paris took off late, which was the only reason Cody got a ticket, and it was a crappy seat at the very back, right next to the lavatories. When he and Woody had landed in New York was when the idea struck him. He'd cleared all his personal gear from game-show-lady's house, packing it into one suitcase and a backpack, leaving her with the bonus of an extra week's rent on the room. So why hang around, commuting out to Jersey with Pop, then having to come back to catch an overseas flight?

He quickly saw his father down to the commuter trains, looking up flights on his phone as they walked. Air France had one seat and he took it, realizing the flight was already boarding. It was a mad scramble through the JFK terminal, presenting his passport, pushing through security, and onto the jetway moments before they closed it.

He ordered a drink and leaned back with his eyes closed. Mentally, he tallied his resources. He had kept Pop out of the casino, pretending the idea of going to Paris was brilliant and the quicker the better. That gave him enough cash for the ticket and a place to stay once he got there.

He'd done a no-show at the job on the 14th floor. If his supervisor didn't like it, fine. Let 'em have it. Although he had to admit it would be fun to have planted a camera there so he could see just how long it would take anyone to notice he was gone. Part of his success as a con man, according to Pop, was Cody's ability to blend in, to disappear when he needed to, hiding in plain sight.

Seeing Amber outside that pub place a few nights ago was a prime example. He peered in the windows after he spotted her walking in there, saw her sitting at a table with some girls about her age, then he'd hung close by, meandering across the street, walking down the block and back. He watched the front door, unsure after thirty minutes whether she had got past him with the rest of the departing crowd. So he'd walked back and looked in the window again. She was gone.

Just as he was deciding what to do next, she'd come popping out the front door, not ten feet from him. Instinctively, he turned his back and knelt to tie his shoelace. She'd walked right past him.

"Sir, would you like another drink?" the flight attendant asked. "We'll be serving dinner in thirty minutes, then we will dim the cabin lights for the night."

She was pretty, a blonde he might have previously flirted with. But compared to Amber she seemed too pale, too dimpled. He shook his head and she turned to the passengers across the aisle.

So, Paris. Unlike Pop, Cody liked to have a plan in place.

He ticked off some items in his head. Get a place to stay. It didn't need to be fancy, like last time, as he would only be there a couple of days. Polish up his Cody Brennan persona and visit the bank to draw out the rest of the money in that account. *Cash money—God, Pop, this is so dumb.*

He fidgeted in his seat, wondering if he would get caught with it, the same way Amber did.

He could smell the food coming down the aisle, and his stomach growled. He couldn't actually remember the last time he'd eaten.

To take his mind off it, he went back to the plan. His last check on the Paris bank account showed a reasonably small balance, less than ten grand. So that would work. He wouldn't need to declare it. He could get to England before deciding how to handle the hundred-fifty grand he'd stashed there.

By the time the food cart reached the last row, the attendant apologized that the only thing left was the pasta. Would that be okay? At this point he could eat cardboard. He took it, and the ravioli actually wasn't bad. Stomach satisfied, he handed the tray back, slid down in his seat, and closed his eyes.

He didn't wake up until the breakfast announcement came. He got a croissant and cup of strong coffee out of that deal. He'd have to look for something more substantial once they landed. As soon as the person in the window seat raised the shade he leaned forward and stared out. There was nothing but white, and as the plane descended on final approach, he knew it would be a rainy, gray day.

Chapter 28

I love it that we get to fly business class," Sandy told Pen, handing her empty champagne glass to the flight attendant.

"Luckily, seats together were available on short notice." They were priced in the same neighborhood as diamonds, but Pen wasn't going to bring that up. And she most certainly wouldn't tell Amber the actual cost of this trip, should her young friend insist on reimbursing her.

The main thing now was to track the stolen money and get the local authorities to realize the importance of freezing the assets until the whole debacle of Amber's supposed involvement could be straightened out. Sandy's banking experience would be invaluable. And Amber's notes about addresses in Paris were going to save them a lot of legwork, assuming Cody still lived in the same apartment.

Amber had performed a search and found a nice hotel for them in Cody's neighborhood, hoping to make it easy for the ladies to get around to the important stops on their agenda.

They chatted through their dinner of filet mignon and roasted Brussels sprouts, toasted with another glass of champagne (the real thing, since they were on Air France), and snuggled into their reclining seats with their down duvets for a movie before sleep overtook them. When they woke it was to a gloriously sunny day, and Pen felt hopeful for their mission.

They checked into the Ritz, and treated themselves to a leisurely brunch before taking on the French bankers. One of the reasons Pen had purposely chosen the renowned luxury hotel was because it was near the bank where they had traced Cody's money transfer. They gathered their jackets and purses and set off through the lobby, stopping to get directions from the concierge.

"*Oui, madam*, it is an easy walk." The forty-ish man with dark, close-cropped hair pulled out a street map and drew a line. "From our front entrance, go to the right, *oui*? Then you will turn, just here, and two blocks more. There you will see the bank."

"After our meeting, we need to find this neighborhood," Pen said, pulling out her notes with the street names Amber had listed for her. "I'm not sure of the exact building, but it's an intersection where these streets come together."

He gave her an indulgent smile, being too well trained to be discourteous to a wealthy tourist. "If you are enjoying your walk, you would simply come back to this point," he said, indicating a spot one block from the hotel. "Then walk through the Jardin de Tuileries, cross the bridge here. It is several blocks, but today the weather is fine. You are lucky to come now. It is predicted to rain next week. Still, if you will be out several hours, I recommend you carry your umbrellas. This time of the year, things can change quickly."

"I suppose if the weather turns or we get tired, we can always get a taxi?" Sandy suggested.

"*Certainement.* Have a most pleasant day, ladies."

The man was correct, they discovered, stepping outside. The temperature was nearly sixty, the sun was bright, and the brilliant orange and red leaves on the trees gave the surrounding cream-colored buildings a colorful and festive air. They located the Banque Internationale without any problem, and asked at reception for Monsieur LeBlanc, the manager with whom Sandy had exchanged several emails before they left Phoenix.

A young assistant wearing an impeccable dark suit and silk tie led them up a staircase with elaborate iron railings to an office behind a heavy mahogany door. He tapped discreetly, waited for a response, and announced them in rapid French.

Sandy stepped forward and shook the hand of the man behind the ornate desk. He was nearly six feet tall, with graying hair, a sharp nose, and a ready smile. "I'm afraid my French lessons never went beyond high school," she said. "I was pleased to receive your emails in flawless English."

"It is all part of being an international banker," LeBlanc said. He turned to Pen, who introduced herself. "Please, sit. How may I assist?"

Sandy went through most of what she had already told him by mail, that they were investigating a theft from an American corporation and had evidence that the thief had transferred the money from a bank in Santa Fe, New Mexico, to his bank here in Paris. She had written down the series of routing and account numbers, along with dates and dollar amounts.

"We believe the account was set up either in the corporate name of Blandishment Inc. or in the personal name of Cody Brennan."

LeBlanc turned to a slim computer screen angled on the corner of his desk, as he pulled out a narrow tray that held a keyboard. Glancing at Sandy's notes, he entered account information and studied the screen, which was angled precisely to obstruct those across from him from seeing anything.

Two wrinkles formed between his brows. He looked back and forth from the note to the screen twice more, verifying his information.

"I see that you are correct. The money you have noted was indeed deposited, approximately three weeks ago. And it was entirely withdrawn yesterday. The account is closed."

"Yesterday?" Sandy's voice squeaked slightly on the first syllable.

"*Oui, madam.*"

Pen spoke up. "Can you tell how the money was paid? Dollars or euros? Cash or cashier's check?"

"*Oui,* of course. Normally, we would close an account using our own currency, the euro, but it appears the client requested dollars—in cash. After the conversion fee and transaction costs, the amount was ..." He tapped the digits on a small calculator Pen hadn't noticed before. "In dollars, $9423.12."

The women exchanged a glance. What was there to say? Cody could legally carry that amount on an international flight home, with no one the wiser. He'd beaten them to the bank by a day, but they might be able to catch him at the apartment before he could pack up and go.

They thanked LeBlanc for the information and left. It didn't explain the several hundred thousand still unaccounted for, but they didn't need to say so to the French banker.

Chapter 29

They walked the route on the map given to them by the concierge, strolling through the huge Tuileries and along the Seine into the neighborhood where Amber's notes seemed to converge. Once there, they followed a few false leads but eventually came to the building shown in one of Amber's vacation photos. Number 12. It was definitely an upscale building, with a burgundy awning and an elderly doorman standing guard.

Sandy showed him one of the selfies Amber had taken of herself and Cody.

"*Ce jeune homme? Oui, je me souviens de lui.*"

Sandy got a blank look and shook her head.

"He remembers Cody," Pen said. "Let me see if I can—" She paused, thinking. "*Il vit dans cet immeuble?*"

"*Non, c'était l'invité d'un propriétaire.*"

"Il est … là maintenant?"

"Je ne l'ai pas vu depuis deux ou trois semaines."

Pen turned to Sandy. "He was staying as a houseguest of an owner. At least I think that's what he said. But our friend has not seen him in two or three weeks."

Sandy nodded with a wry grin. "All I got from it was the part about two or three weeks."

Pen asked the doorman if there was a manager or someone who spoke English. "I'm running out of my knowledge of French, I'm afraid."

The doorman led them inside, to the first apartment on the ground floor, where he politely tapped the brass knocker on the door. A dark-haired woman answered, dressed as Pen imagined a housewife of the 1940s would, in a shirtwaist dress and sturdy shoes. She gazed suspiciously at them until the doorman explained in rapid French what the two strangers had been asking about.

"Do you speak English?" Pen asked. "I'm afraid my French is limited."

"Yes, some," came the answer.

"This young man," Pen said, holding up Sandy's phone with the picture on it. "We understand he was here as a guest of a resident? Is he still here?"

The woman sighed. "Most unusual. He come, he give the penthouse owner name. He have their key. Say something about watching their home while they are away."

She went into an explanation that included the word Barbados before she switched back to English. "I do not like this. But I no control what residents do." She gave a large, shoulders-touching-ears shrug.

"The young man—how long did he stay?"

The corners of the woman's mouth turned down, her eyes moving side to side as she thought about it. "A week?

Two week?"

"When was the last time he was here?"

Another shrug, more offhand this time. "Two weeks, maybe more."

The doorman had stood by, watching the whole exchange, and he nodded at this.

"Could you let us see the apartment?" Pen asked. "Accompanied by you, of course."

The woman took a step backward, looking as though she meant to close her door to them.

"We only want to be sure our young friend really did move out," Sandy said. "What if something happened to him in the apartment? What if he is up there—ill? Or worse."

The prospect of explaining that to a returning homeowner was apparently worse than taking the chance of letting these women see inside. The manager held up an index finger, asking them to wait while she found a key.

It was a very quiet elevator ride to the fifth floor, and the woman didn't speak as she applied the key to the lock. She stepped inside first, calling out a name, audibly sniffing the air. Pen supposed it made sense. If some harm had, indeed, come to Cody Brennan his corpse would be very ripe by now.

The apartment proved to be free of dead things. However, there were things seemingly out of place for a couple who had left on vacation. Dirty dishes in the kitchen sink, a robe thrown over a chair, a couple of takeout food boxes in the trash.

The manager's hands went to her face and she said something that probably meant, *oh crap, I'm in trouble now.*

Still, there was nothing to prove Cody had been the one inside the apartment. The place was, if not precisely clean, at least neat enough to indicate there'd been no wild parties, no trashing of the rooms or furniture. Pen and Sandy exchanged a look, then thanked the manager and left the apartment, beating a path to the street where they could speak more freely.

"Do you think it fits with Amber's story?" Sandy asked, once they were a block away.

"It could. I thought of snapping some photos to show her, but with the woman standing right there ..."

"Yeah, not cool to do that."

"Let's give our feet a break," Pen suggested. "There's a patisserie where we can sit down and get a coffee."

Sandy couldn't resist the macarons so Pen went along with the choice. With a cup of strong coffee and a cookie each, they settled at a table on the sidewalk.

"Well, we struck out all around, didn't we?" Sandy said after her first sip of the fragrant drink.

"He obviously beat us to the bank, and by such a short time. I wonder if he's still here in the city somewhere."

"Not staying at the same apartment, obviously." Sandy made a swooning sound when she bit into the macaron.

"No, and I suppose he could be nearly anywhere. If he knew his visit to the bank would be successful, he might actually be on a plane back to the US by now."

Sandy chewed thoughtfully. "This seems like a lot of extra expense and effort to remove money from a bank account. He could have done an online transfer in five minutes' time."

"But to close the account? Wouldn't he need to be there in person?"

"Some banks require an in-person visit, others don't. I should have thought to ask that while we were there."

"No matter. It's done now." Pen sat quietly,

contemplating the shops and pedestrians around them for a few minutes. "So, what now? We've come all this way for nothing."

"We still have the information Amber retrieved about the other deposits. There was money going to England and Scotland, as well. Maybe we can get to one of those before he clears it out. Wouldn't it be cool if we were there when he walked in? We could nab the sucker."

Pen laughed gently. "I'm not certain our authority extends to personally 'nabbing the sucker' but I'd be willing to give it a try."

Sandy set her cup aside and flexed her feet. "Meanwhile, I vote that we take a taxi back to the hotel, rest our bones or take a soak in the bathtub, and once it's a decent hour in Arizona we call Amber. She may have come up with some other ideas since we've been away."

"That's the perfect idea." Pen stood, adjusted the strap of her purse, and stepped to the curb where a taxi almost immediately pulled to a stop.

Chapter 30

Cody closed himself inside his hotel room at Orly and pulled off the fake eyeglasses. They always made him feel faintly nauseated, but it was important to keep the disguise intact as long as he could possibly be caught on the security cameras that seemed to be everywhere in the city now. The Cody Brennan look was especially important for his appearances in the banks.

Yesterday had gone smoothly, showing up at Banque Internationale, smooth talking a young clerk and her supervisor, walking out with his nine thousand-plus after chafing a bit at the exorbitant fees to convert it and hand it over in US dollars. And even though his flight to England wasn't until late tonight, he was fine with that. He had hours to do as he wished.

The temptation was to go back to his old neighborhood,

to enjoy a leisurely lunch at the street café where he'd taken Amber, to stare up at the penthouse apartment he'd used to impress her. One thing was certain—he didn't want to hang around a generic airport hotel room all day. But he was faced with the dilemma of carrying around nearly ten thousand in cash or leaving it in the room. Neither was exactly a safe option, considering the gypsies who freely roamed the streets, watching for tourists to rob.

He remembered a gift shop near the hotel's breakfast room. Donning his suit coat and the black-framed glasses once more, he rode the elevator down and set out on a mission. The shop carried all the typical things: outrageously priced packets containing one dose of aspirin, earplugs to drown out airplane noise, bags of snacks—both familiar names and strange ones. He found what he was looking for, a pouch to wear concealed under one's clothing. Precisely what he needed to stash the cash. He purchased it, along with two magazines and three bags of salty snacks. Pop had taught him to make his significant purchases less memorable to a clerk by adding extra items. Plus, he loved those mixtures of salted nuts.

Back in the room, he packed the money into bundles as flat as he could make them. Probably should have bought two of the pouches. But he got most of it in, leaving only a few hundred to spread out between his pockets and his wallet.

Then he changed from his suit to casual clothing—jeans, sneakers, and a bulky pullover sweatshirt—put the glasses in his inside shirt pocket, and arranged it all so the money pouch wasn't noticeable. In the bathroom, he ran his fingers through his neatly combed hair, mussing it stylishly and sticking it that way with plenty of gel. It took five or ten years off his age, looking trendy instead of business-like. Pop had taught him ways to pass for any age from seventeen to thirty, depending on how he dressed and how he moved. He smiled at his younger image in the mirror.

Backtracking yesterday's route, he caught a shuttle to the nearest Métro stop and headed toward the city center. He was having fond thoughts of Paris, he discovered, almost as if he actually had lived there. It would be fun to revisit some spots, to catch a couple of the famous sites he had not visited. It wasn't as if he would ever come here again. If he were to skip out of the US, it wouldn't be for a city that turned rainy and cold in the winter; his ideas were far more tropical.

The Métro deposited him at the Louvre-Rivoli stop. He and Amber had popped in at the famed museum but had covered a bare fraction of the exhibits. He could go there again. But he decided not. Art wasn't really his thing—he'd gone with her because it was a thing all tourists did, and he had been playing the local guy who wanted to show his visitor around. It was a quick walk to the Tuileries Gardens, romantic with your arm around a girl, no big wow to somebody who didn't care about linden trees or old statues. So he ended up just walking the streets, window shopping at the places they'd gone together.

He strode right past the Vuitton shop, in case the clerk who had accepted his bribe to have Amber's carry-on bag modified should spot him. That had been somewhat of a challenge, using Google Translate to put together enough French to communicate the idea of what he wanted. He'd used the app to come up with a repertoire of phrases to get him through whenever he was out with Amber and wanting to impress her.

He crossed Place Vendome and walked facing the one-way traffic that was coming around the rectangular loop around the old fashioned bronze statue in the middle. In front of the Ritz, two women were getting out of a taxi, one tall and stately with gray hair in a smooth bob, the other shorter and blonde, a little on the pudgy side. Nothing about them said French—they were either American or British, and he guessed the former. He turned sideways and pulled out his phone, looking like every other twenty-something who couldn't stop staring at a screen.

From the corner of his eye he saw that they went inside the swank hotel. A chill went down his spine, the kind of premonition Pop would call bad juju.

Chapter 31

The furniture delivery men had set the larger pieces in place late yesterday afternoon. Now it was up to Amber to create some kind of order and make the spare room into her home office. She stood in the middle of the space, staring at the boxes and equipment she'd basically done nothing with since she moved in here.

"Well, it's time," she declared to herself and the houseplant, which she'd brought in to take better advantage of the light in here and to brighten her desk.

She started by placing her laptop on the desk and her new chair behind it. Those simple moves made the concept feel more real. Over the months, she'd already dug into various boxes, so she began with those which held her most-used supplies. Books and her few paper files could come later. She'd come to a large zipper bag of pens and markers, half of which she knew were so old they should have been thrown away ages ago.

The phone rang and she saw that it was Pen's number. "Hey, you're not back already, are you?"

"Oh no, this is just a report. Sandy and I are kicking off our shoes in the hotel room, then we plan to enjoy the spa facilities until we have to leave for our flight to London."

"Any luck?" Amber grabbed a scratchpad and began going through the writing instruments, scrawling large doodles, tossing the first marker when it didn't work.

"I'm afraid not," Pen admitted. "It seems Cody got to the bank ahead of us. We changed our flight—it was meant to be tomorrow—in hopes we can get to the British bank before he does."

"Do you have all the information? Account numbers and such?" Amber asked, trying a blue gel pen next.

Pen apparently had put the speaker on because Sandy piped up. "Yep, we did fine at the bank here, as far as identifying the account. It was just that Cody got here a day earlier and had already closed it."

"How is everything there?" Pen asked. "No more calls from your employer?"

"Quiet. Probably too quiet," Amber admitted. She rummaged through the cardboard box at her feet and came up with an old souvenir mug she liked to keep the pens in. "But I'm using my time well, getting my home office set up. And of course my parents are still checking in every day. Dad thinks I should be out applying for different jobs. Mom doesn't get it that I can't just pack a few things and go stay with them."

"No word directly from Cody?" Sandy asked.

"Nothing. It's so weird. He was so attentive in Paris, and I really had begun to think we had something. I guess it really was just a fling."

"That's okay," Sandy said. "Better that he vanishes than to be around if he gets you involved in some illegal shenanigans."

Amber laughed at the old-school word. "You're so right. I think if I were to see him today, I'd ... I don't know. I'm tempted to say I'd kick him where it hurts or throw a drink in his face, or something like that. But I don't know if I'm the type."

"I doubt you are," Pen said, "but it might make you feel better."

"What would make me feel better would be to get myself out of this jam, to stop worrying that the police are watching me, and to catch whoever has caused me all this trouble. And if that turns out to be Cody, well, I don't think I'd have any problem watching him go to jail."

"Good for you," Sandy said.

"Well, our spa appointment is in ten minutes," Pen told her. "I'm going to soak my aching feet, get a massage, and then sink into my seat for the flight tonight."

"Have fun and call me if you need any other info," Amber told them.

She turned back to her task and made good progress with the bookcase and desk drawers. By noon she had a stack of boxes to flatten and take down to the complex's recycling bin. Her printer was set up and working, and she'd checked in with each of her social media accounts where she posted chipper messages about how great it was to work from home. What she left unsaid was the simple fact—she was bored.

She called Mary and Gracie to see if anyone was up for a shopping trip or needed help with anything or was dying for a happy hour together, even if they only did it on Zoom. She drummed her fingers on her new desk then picked up her phone.

Chapter 32

The hotel in London wasn't nearly as elegant as the Ritz. "Apologies that I was not able to get us in at the Savoy," Pen said. "Sometimes a hotel truly is full, and even a bestselling author can't angle her way in."

Sandy plopped her bag down on one of the twin beds in the smallish room. "It's fine, really. Mainly, we just need to get decent rest so we can be at the bank first thing in the morning when it opens."

She indulged herself in a moment of regret—while Pen put a few items in the bathroom—that she'd not seen more of Paris. The City of Light had been a lifelong dream of hers, and Sandy knew she would figure out a way to go back sometime. And although she wanted to lecture Amber (just a little) on the fact that she'd taken up with a man she barely knew, Sandy now saw the allure of the beautiful city and how a romance there could easily bloom.

She sighed and hung her jacket in the small wardrobe just as Pen emerged, face scrubbed clean and dressed for bed.

They were standing outside the HSBC Bank at Woodstock Terrace at five minutes to ten the next morning, waiting for the doors to open.

"At least this time we don't need to worry whether the manager speaks English," Sandy joked. "Even if he throws out British idioms, you can translate for me."

The *he* turned out to be a *she*, and the manager's well-dressed assistant led them directly to an inner office. As before, Sandy provided all the numbers needed to find the account and Ms. Love looked it up. Pen knew they were in for a disappointment when a frown crossed the woman's face.

"Oh dear, I'm afraid it looks like this account has been closed."

"When?" Sandy asked, dreading the answer.

"Well, yesterday afternoon. It seems the account owner came in just before closing time and withdrew all his funds."

Same scenario. Cash converted to American dollars. Only this time the amount was more than two hundred thousand.

"You had that amount of US currency on hand?" Sandy asked, incredulous.

"Well, we had to pull from several sources," Ms. Love admitted. "One of our branches services a major American corporation and the currency was meant to fill their order. We had to transact an urgent-request transfer from the central bank, but managed to shift all the money to the proper channels on time."

"You would go to those lengths for just anyone who came in off the street?" Pen asked.

The banker shifted slightly in her seat. "Normally, no. We would insist they give us at least twenty-four hours to make the arrangements."

"But …"

"Apparently, he had put in the request in advance using our online banking service, and once we checked the account credentials, we really had no choice." Her mouth tightened slightly. "Plus, I understand there was something of a dustup between the client and the assistant manager who was helping him. He wouldn't seem to accept no as an answer."

Sandy wondered if that was typical of Cody Brennan, and she realized how very little they really knew about the young man. They thanked the woman behind the desk and left.

"I cannot believe this," Pen said once they reached the street. "We are seemingly right on his trail and yet he manages to always get there first."

Sandy felt her frustration grow. They started walking in the direction of a park their taxi had passed on the way to the bank. "So, what next? It's hard to believe there's a man walking around with well over two hundred thousand …" She lowered her voice and looked around to be sure no one was close enough to overhear. "… in cash, on his person. What can he be thinking?"

"And what can he possibly do with it?" Pen mused.

"If he plans to go back to the States, he's going to have the same problem Amber did—how to get it past Customs without being caught and arrested."

"Perhaps he has no plans to go back."

"Or he's out here, looking for another young woman

to woo and convince to do this *favor* for him."

"It would be fairly sketchy to just choose someone he has never met, to entrust her with that amount."

They paused under a maple tree with brilliant red leaves and looked straight at each other. "Unless he's already chosen someone. He could be pulling the very same thing he did with Amber!" Sandy said.

"My thoughts exactly. How did she say they met? The internet. They became chummy over time and he pretended to live and work in Paris … What would be so difficult about setting up the same story, using London, convincing another American young woman to meet him here?"

"Or more than one," Sandy suggested. "Surely he knows he lost the hundred grand that Amber was carrying. He might try another tactic. Two women, each carrying fifty thousand."

"He has more than two hundred with him."

"All right, four women. Or ten women, each carrying twenty. Or twenty women, each carrying ten—"

"Which would be legal, and he wouldn't run the risk of losing it."

Sandy thought about that, her eyes focused on a bed of chrysanthemums in shades of orange and purple. "It makes sense, in a way, but where is he going to find twenty women, all traveling from here back to the US at the same time—assuming he wouldn't want to drag the operation out too long. There's too much risk of losing track of everyone."

"And he would surely want to be close by, on the same flight, if possible, or following no more than a day behind."

"As he claimed he was doing with Amber. Remember, she said he was supposed to be on the next flight."

"How would one man manage to do that?" Pen asked,

staring toward a duck pond in the distance.

"With a tour group. Could he somehow have targeted a group? I'm thinking mainly young women, since he seems to have a certain charm that might not work so well with men. They would need to be young. Older folks are going to be suspicious and more likely to know the laws."

"If this were one of my novels, I should have to place the characters where I wanted them at the precisely right time," Pen said. "But I don't have a clue how a person could set that up in real life."

Chapter 33

Cody felt conspicuous on the street, pulling a wheeled suitcase. When his phone rang with Pop's ringtone, he ignored it. The old man was starting to get on his nerves, and he had enough worries already. Most of them caused by his father. Seriously? *Why* did all this money need to be in cash?

He passed an alley with a name—Montlake Wynd. Whatever that meant. But it was dim and wound out of sight, and he didn't like the idea that some thug could come popping out of such a place and rob him in a flash. He needed to get off the street.

He'd slept fitfully last night, and when he learned his hotel didn't offer room service he'd decided to bring his suitcase along while he got some breakfast. He had a ticket for the train north to Edinburgh this afternoon, but what to do in the meantime? Well, he hadn't officially checked out of the hotel yet, so he might as well go back there. He could spend some time online and see what Amber was up to. If she'd been arrested for the embezzlement, it would surely make the news back in Arizona.

He glanced over his shoulder to make sure no one was following him. A cop gave him the eye, a guy with a day-glo green vest on. Silly looking, and why did the cops here all have to be named Bobby—seemed stupid. Cody hurried on. His hotel was on the next block, just past a park with an iron fence around it and a duck pond in the middle.

Then he spotted her, the tall woman with the gray hair. A jolt shot through him. It was the same woman he'd seen outside the Ritz in Paris. Had to be. She was wearing the same jacket and there was a shorter, blonde woman with her. They were standing near a big leafy tree, talking intently. Shit!

He couldn't very well stop here to tie a shoe or stare at his phone. No way was he taking his hand off the suitcase. He turned to his left and jaywalked to the other side of the street. The cop's whistle chirped, but Cody ignored it and dodged to a cross street. The moment he was out of sight of the cop and the park, he broke into a run as well as he could with the damn bag bumping his heels. He would have to circle the block and hope his hotel had a rear entrance.

It did and he ducked inside. Who the hell *were* those women? It was beyond weird that he'd seen them outside the bank in Paris, then near the luggage shop where he'd purchased Amber's bag, and now in London. They had to be cops, but they sure didn't look like anybody named Bobby. Plus, that wouldn't work in Paris and here, both. They had to be undercover.

And if that was the case, how many more were there?

He'd only spotted these two. Maybe the US Customs Service had a greater reach than he'd ever imagined, and maybe they'd sent agents here to track him down. He forced his breathing to slow as he approached the elevator, scanning the lobby before he stepped inside.

The maid was cleaning his room when he arrived, so he gave her an extra tip and said she could quit with what she'd already done.

"You don't want me to hoover the room, sir?"

He had no clue what that meant, but he said, "Nah, it's fine. I've got some work to do so I need to be alone."

She flashed him a smile as she carried her bucket of cleaning products out. For a nano-second he wondered if she would be someone he could approach about transporting the cash back to the States for him. No way, he decided. He'd checked out Amber pretty carefully, and look how that turned out. He couldn't take a chance with the rest of what he'd worked so hard to get.

He locked the bolt on the door and set the suitcase on the bed. What *was* he going to do with all this? For probably the twentieth time he cursed his father. Then cursed himself for listening. Sure, Pop was the pro, the guy who'd pulled jobs all his life, but the old man didn't live in the modern world if he thought flashing cash all over the place wouldn't raise some eyebrows.

Cody realized he would either need to take the chance on having more than two hundred thousand on him after he finished in Scotland, or he would have to recruit somebody—several somebodies—he could trust. Or he would have to electronically transfer the money.

He got out his laptop and set it up.

Chapter 34

Pen and Sandy strolled through the theater district, meandering their way toward Covent Garden.

"I can't believe I'm here," Sandy said. "All the history ... these places I've read about in novels, all my life. I wish we could stay a month."

"This was one of my favorite places to visit as a child," Pen said, pointing out the stalls, with their wide variety of goods for sale. "Of course it has changed dramatically. All these high-end designer shops, and the restaurants. Look, there are themed ones now—*Harry Potter, Game of Thrones.*"

Sandy gave them a glance but found her eye drawn to a pole with some flyers stapled to it, in the more traditional market section. She walked toward it, and Pen followed.

"We wondered where Cody might find a group of American women traveling together and heading back to the US soon—look at this." Sandy gripped Pen's arm and pointed toward a poster.

Women's College Football Playoffs – Britain vs America in the Finals!

The photo showed a soccer player in midair, making an astounding kick, and the smaller print said the big game was this afternoon at 2:00.

"Football," Pen said. "Even at the college level it's immensely popular here."

"So ... if Cody knew someone associated with the American team ..."

"Or if he could talk his way into something such as becoming their luggage handler or something ..."

"He might even pretend to be an airport official, if he could get hold of credentials that looked somewhat convincing," Sandy said.

"We need to investigate further." Pen stared out toward the street.

"But how? Even if we knew what hotel the teams were staying at or could somehow get into the game at the last moment, how would we get the chance to speak with their coaches, to warn them?"

"What we really need is to get near enough to spy Cody with them, hanging near the edges or such."

Sandy gave her friend a sideways look. "Again, *how*?" Then she began to bounce on the balls of her feet. "Wait—what about this? There's surely a pre-game press event of some type. Could you talk your way in there as a writer?"

"Journalists need credentials, badges."

"Okay, you are who you are—international bestselling novelist—and your next book is going to be about women's soccer leagues, and you're doing research."

Pen laughed. "It might just be audacious enough to

work. Now, how do we go about being in the right place at the right time?"

"You'll want to speak with the American coaches, or even the team ..." Sandy pulled out her phone and did what everyone does. She Googled it.

* * *

The small press room at Wembley Stadium was jammed when they arrived. Almost immediately, it became apparent Pen would not get a chance for any kind of meaningful exchange with their targets from their standing-room-only spot at the back of the room. She nudged Sandy.

"At this point, let's just learn their faces and what they are wearing. We'll have to catch up with them later," she whispered. "Meanwhile, if we get very lucky, we might spot our true quarry, Cody, somewhere nearby. Keep a sharp eye."

Sandy agreed. Crammed in here with more than a hundred sports reporters from all over the world, there was no way a novelist had any standing whatsoever. But it didn't mean theirs was a lost cause. She edged her way along the wall, vying for a spot closer to the front from which she could study faces, watching for Cody's. Pen would wait near the exit, doing the same thing when the press conference broke up.

As it turned out, the crush of bodies was simply too much. Sandy did manage to tug at the sleeve of an American assistant-assistant coach who was standing at the sidelines and pull her aside long enough to ask if they could have a word, just a few questions, please.

Because of her lowly position, most likely, the young woman actually met her eye and smiled. "It's insane right now," she told Sandy. "If you need to talk to the head coach, tomorrow is going to be best."

"Who handles the luggage for the players, going back home?"

"What—gosh, um. The girls mostly handle their own, but I help out some."

Those at the front table, the coaches with microphones bristling toward them, suddenly stood and the head coach gave a sharp little whistle aimed at the woman Sandy was talking to.

"Uh, sorry. Gotta go."

"Can I catch you later?" Sandy called out.

The woman shrugged. "You can try."

While the important people filed out through a doorway at the front of the room, the reporters all made for the exit, presumably to take up their assigned places somewhere at the field where they would broadcast the action, to their heart's delight.

Sandy caught up with Pen at the back door. "Any sign of him?" she asked.

Pen shook her head, continuing to watch the last few departing faces.

"So now what? If we can hang out through the game, I do at least have an in with that coach I was talking to."

"It's probably worth a try," Pen said. "Are you a sports fan?"

"I suppose I can become one."

Chapter 35

A mber Zeckis?"

Four flattened cardboard boxes flew from Amber's grip at the sound of the unexpected male voice.

"Sorry, didn't mean to frighten you. Detective Mark Howard. Remember me?"

"Of course."

She walked the last ten feet to the recycling bin concealed in an enclosure in the parking garage and tossed in the three boxes she hadn't lost. He picked up the dropped ones and followed her.

"I have some more questions. Would you rather we speak here or downtown?"

Dumb question. Who in their right mind *wants* to get caught up in the maze of a big government building? On the other hand, did she want to invite him into her home?

Was there an answer like, C, none of the above?

"Here's fine."

A white-haired man, a resident, walked up carrying a bag of household garbage and excused himself as he had to pass close by to access the dumpster.

"Are you sure?" said Howard after the man had walked away. "It's not very private and voices do carry."

She held her ground.

"All right. In that case, can you tell me the last time you logged in with your Blackwell-Gorse Technologies employee credentials?"

Amber felt her confidence slipping. Had he somehow found out about the copy of the hard drive? "I've been on administrative leave for a week."

"I'm aware of that. It doesn't answer my question."

"What's this about?"

"It's been reported that the company is missing a whole lot of money, and your login information is all over the transactions. Amber Zeckis, you're under arrest for embezzlement."

While he snapped handcuffs on her wrists and recited her rights, thoughts flew through her head—she had nothing with her but her house key. He guided her up the ramp from the garage and into a squad car waiting at the curb. Her mind went blank. She couldn't remember anyone's phone number but her parents. And she was wearing grubby clothes after a day of house cleaning.

The next two hours were a blur of photos, fingerprints, and questions. As she sat, stony faced and silent, she forced herself to calm down and clear her mind. Finally, Gracie's phone number came to mind.

"I want to call my lawyer," was the first thing she said.

Gracie called Mariah Kowzlowski, who showed up

forty-five minutes later. She took a seat on the same side of the gray metal table with Amber. Detective Howard sat across from them. Howard explained the charges to the attorney. "This time it's more serious," he said. "Embezzlement, grand theft of nearly a half million dollars."

$423,890, to be exact. Amber forced her face to remain neutral, thinking of butterflies, unicorns, the last good book she'd read ...

"Where's your proof that my client had anything to do with this alleged crime?"

"Ms. Zeckis is in a position, in her job at Blackwell-Gorse, to have access to the computer codes and information necessary to carry out the banking transfers. And a forensic search of the company computer issued to her, shows that her login information was used to gain access to the company bank accounts and transfer the money out."

The bulldog lit on him. "Blackwell-Gorse is a huge corporation, with more than two thousand employees worldwide. Any one of them could have carried out this alleged crime."

"Using her private password that she alone knows?"

"My client's company computer was taken from her possession a week ago and she has been at home, completely without access to anything related to Blackwell-Gorse. Whoever has accessed this latest withdrawal most certainly wasn't Ms. Zeckis, and it's most certainly the same person who made the earlier withdrawals."

"Are you sure that's true?" Howard responded. "There's evidence that a copy of the company computer's hard drive was made, early on the day Ms. Zeckis turned the computer back to them."

Amber swallowed hard and hoped he didn't notice.

"All of that is a matter for the court to determine, whether your so-called forensic evidence is valid. Meanwhile, I am here to take my client home. She was already released on the earlier charge, and she's under mandate not to leave the county. If you have further questions for her, they can take place at my office." Kowzlowski started to gather her papers, as if to leave.

Amber held her breath but Howard didn't cave. "Nice try, Ms. Kowzlowski, but the judge will have to decide in the morning."

Mariah's mouth pinched into a tight line, but she didn't respond to the detective. "Amber, hang in there and don't say anything. I'll see you tomorrow."

* * *

The courtroom in the downtown judicial complex was no more than a quarter full, people sitting in the gallery, conversing quietly as they waited for whatever reason the judge would call them. Gracie looked around, wondering— since this was criminal court—what those various reasons might be. It could become an interesting hobby, hanging around a courtroom such as this just to see the various dramas unfold.

Kowzlowski nudged her elbow and nodded toward the first row of seats. "We're second on the docket, as soon as the judge gets back from his *coffee* break. It's Rheingold, and I swear the man has a bladder the size of a peanut. Always a lot of recesses during his trials."

As if he had heard her (and maybe he had—her voice wasn't exactly a whisper), the bailiff stepped forward, calling order and announcing the judge. Gracie took a seat next to Amber's new attorney. The judge did all the usual moves—tapped his gavel, told everyone to sit, glanced down at papers in front of him, and called the first case.

Gracie was a little stunned at how quickly it happened. A man accused of second-degree murder stood beside his lawyer, pled not guilty, was denied bail and sent back to jail. The young lawyer beside him made no attempt to argue. He gave his client what he must have hoped was a reassuring look as a deputy led him through an ominous door at the side of the courtroom.

"Next case!" A bang of the gavel. "The state of Arizona versus Amber Zeckis. Is the attorney for the accused here in the courtroom?"

Mariah stood and stepped forward. "I am, your honor."

The judge motioned her to pass through the bar and take a place at the defendant's table. Amber came in, cuffed and wearing jailhouse orange, looking as though she hadn't slept three minutes all night, which was probably close to the truth.

"The charges are grand theft, embezzlement, and failure to declare a large amount of cash at US Customs. How do you plead?"

Gracie didn't even hear Amber's timid "Not guilty." Her ears were ringing with the words grand theft and embezzlement. The words sounded so ominous.

Her attention went back to the front of the room as Kowzlowski presented her reasons why Amber should be allowed out on bond. Upstanding citizen, no prior record, no solid evidence against her.

A man at the prosecution table took his turn next. "Your honor, the accused was caught coming into the country with a large amount of undeclared cash. Upon investigation, it has been discovered that her employer,

Blackwell-Gorse Technologies, has been the target of a large embezzlement. Ms. Zeckis is in a position, in her job there, to have access to the computer codes and information necessary to carry out the crime."

The bulldog lit on him. "Your honor, Blackwell-Gorse is a huge corporation, with more than two thousand employees worldwide. Any one of them could have carried out this alleged crime, and there is nothing yet to suggest that my client had a part in it."

"She's a flight risk," the prosecutor insisted. "She has demonstrated that she can leave the country on a whim and has the means to do so."

"My client surrendered her passport willingly and will stipulate that she will not leave the state of Arizona until her name has been cleared."

Bang went the gavel. "So ordered. The passport stays in police custody and the accused will post bond of $100,000. Next case!"

Mariah gave Amber's hand a reassuring squeeze as the bailiff led her out through a side door. She turned to Gracie and said, "Paperwork takes a little while. We'll meet you downstairs."

Gracie was waiting in the lobby, her expression clearly relieved when she saw Amber and Mariah coming her way.

"Come on, let's get you home," she said, putting an arm around Amber's shoulders. "You've got to be starving. What would be your dream meal? My treat."

"I'm not hungry. I just want to go home and have an hour-long shower." She slumped in the passenger seat of Gracie's van and stared out the window the whole way to Scottsdale.

Back at the condo, they opened the door to find the whole place in disarray. There was a copy of a search warrant lying on the back of the sofa.

"They searched my home, without me even knowing it." Amber's voice was on the edge of angry tears.

Gracie stood stock still. "Let's get inside. I'll help you straighten up everything."

Amber rushed to her home office, where the chaos was most evident. Every drawer of her desk, every book on the shelves, had been pulled out and dumped. Her bedroom was slightly less disturbed, although when she looked in her dresser drawers it was evident someone had pawed through all her clothing.

"What were they looking for?" Gracie asked, from the doorway.

"The hard drive." Amber instantly regretted voicing this aloud. What if they had planted a listening device?

Chapter 36

The high-speed train had Wi-Fi and Cody put it to good use. He'd dumped his bag and computer case on the seats across from him so no one else would take those spots, and he set up his own little mini-desk on the table between. Now that Pop's instructions were out of his head, he had a clear path to follow and he was making good headway.

Through his login information for Blandishment Inc., he had set up six more online banking accounts—three in America, three in offshore tax havens. Already, he'd moved money in small uneven increments to each of them.

The old man had sputtered when Cody told him this was how it was going to be, but he decided, screw that. Let him stew. This wasn't the 1960s, and Cody knew what he was doing. The conversation rankled a little, still. And there would be a lecture when he got back to Jersey.

For now, he just had to figure out how he would deal with the cash he'd already collected in Paris and London. It was stupid of him to have listened to the old man this long. He put that out of his mind while he checked one last thing.

A week ago, he'd set up one final automatic transfer from the B-G corporate account, all done with Amber's credentials, of course, and now he saw it had gone through seamlessly. He had to admit he'd held his breath on that one, knowing she'd been caught with the cash in Customs, but most likely since this final transfer had already been in the system, no one was the wiser.

He wondered what she was doing now. He'd tried a few tentative texts, but she hadn't responded. He had to assume she was royally pissed if she figured out he was the one who'd put the cash in her suitcase. Surely, the cops had taken the money away, and that would be the last of it. Maybe another week or two for her to cool off and he'd try reaching out to her again.

Or not. Maybe Pop was right about that part of it. A mark was a mark, and you didn't get personally involved with them. Do the con, leave 'em hanging, get on to the next thing. And his next thing, right now, was to get this money spread out without leaving any kind of clear trail that could tie it back to him. Layers, lots of layers. He and Pop would each have a little to live on for a year or two, and then he could gradually start to access the bigger accounts.

A train attendant came by, offering drinks and snacks, and he took the little tray she held out. A beef sandwich and some kind of salad he didn't recognize. He asked for a Coke even though he'd rather have a Scotch. But he needed a clear head for his last few moves. He could relax once he reached his hotel in Edinburgh.

He thought about the two women he'd spotted in Paris and London. Where were they now? He had hung back at the train station, watching the crowd in case they had somehow figured out his plans, even watched most all the other passengers board before he stepped on. No sign of them. Maybe they hadn't actually been following him at all? Maybe they were simply tourists? That was good—one less worry for this final leg of his trip.

Waverly Station was bustling, even at ten p.m., and he found the information desk where he inquired about the distance to the Hilton. A chuckle from the man and a rapid explanation, which Cody had to ask him to repeat twice. It was going to take a little while to adapt his ear to the Scottish accent. It turned out the hotel was around the corner and a block down.

He hoisted his backpack and grabbed the handle of the wheeled bag and set off walking, hoping like hell this was a safe city at night. Five minutes later he was walking through the front doors of the castle-like building. The lobby was teeming with tourists (German, from their conversations) and he waited in line while tour guides collected room keys for them. All he wanted was to disappear in a big and bustling place, and it seemed he'd found it.

It was nearing midnight by the time he finished his shower, flopped down in a chair in the small room, and switched on the TV. Maybe a half hour of some mindless talk show would make him drowsy enough to sleep. He had banking to do in the morning, and with luck would be out of here soon.

The default channel on TV seemed to be international news, but before he could decide whether to switch upward or down on the channel numbers the banner running along the bottom of the screen caught his eye.

Tech giant Blackwell-Gorse hacked.

Cody turned up the volume and had to wait for two other stories to be talked to death before the commentator got back to this one.

"In breaking news from America," the pretty blonde began, "tech giant Blackwell-Gorse seemingly has been hacked. Money from the corporate banking accounts is missing, and at the center of it all is an employee. The young woman was initially questioned nearly two weeks ago when she returned to the US on an international flight and a large amount of cash was discovered in her luggage."

So far, all the video was of the front of the corporate headquarters in Phoenix, signage of the corporate B-G logo, and some generic footage of office workers in cubicles that could have been taken anywhere. But Cody knew exactly who they were talking about.

"After an extensive investigation by authorities, including the confiscation of the employee's computer and cell phone, Amber Zeckis was arrested today in Phoenix, Arizona. Corporate officials are saying nothing, and our business correspondent theorizes they will continue to maintain silence on the subject." The blonde turned to an equally blonde man at the desk beside her. "That stance would be typical for a multinational corporation, wouldn't it, Ian?"

"Most definitely. It's a source of embarrassment for a business to admit that an employee might have accomplished something like this," the thirty-something guy said. "And of course, unless the amount is in the hundreds of millions, it's most likely a drop in the bucket, so to speak, for a company of this size."

They immediately went on to another story, a dip in

the price of the Chinese yuan, and Cody realized he'd been sitting bolt upright. He leaned back in the chair again.

Amber. He felt a moment's regret that she'd actually been arrested. Her job hadn't seemed so important, or the dollar amount so large, that he thought anyone would notice. As Pop said, those big businesses wrote off more in paperclips and lost ballpoint pens every year than what he'd taken.

The first time. But then there were the other cash transfers, including the most recent. Did they know about those yet?

He needed to finish moving this money, burying it deeper under layers of various names. And soon.

Chapter 37

"Well, that was a complete waste of time," Pen said, as they turned over their luggage to an airline worker and headed toward the gate for their flight to Edinburgh.

"I did learn a lot about the rules of soccer," Sandy said. There really was no other way to positive-spin the fact that they'd spent half a day on a false lead.

Pen gave a somewhat impatient look but checked herself. How could they have known what Cody would do next? And the idea was logical, that he would be looking for gullible women to carry the money for him ... well, it might have worked out. She couldn't blame Sandy for the decision.

The assistant coach they'd spoken with vowed that no one had approached them about handling their luggage and adamantly stated the sponsors and chaperones with the young women would never let them be taken in that way.

Pen wanted to tell them what had happened and the fact that it had happened to a pretty savvy young woman, but there was no point. All they could do was keep going forward. That's when her phone rang and she saw it was Gracie.

"Not good news, I'm afraid," Gracie began, hardly saying hello first.

"Arrested!" Pen immediately lowered her voice, although the terminal was so noisy no one would have noticed if she'd shouted it.

"I'm going to stay at her condo with her tonight," Gracie said. "She's scared and a little overwhelmed. The police searched the place, and I'm going to help her clean up."

"Oh, that's dreadful." Pen saw Sandy was watching her closely. When she ended the call with Gracie, she passed the news along.

"Could this day get any worse?" Sandy moaned.

"Don't invite it," Pen said. "We are about to board an airplane."

It was far too late to visit the bank by the time they arrived in the Scottish capital. They told an accommodating taxi driver they needed a hotel near that address, and he recommended the Hilton. A half hour later, the two women fell into their beds, exhausted. Decisions and chases could wait until the following morning.

Full sunlight came streaming into the room and Sandy rolled over with a groan, shocked to see that it was well past nine o'clock. She'd apparently forgotten to set an alarm. In the next bed, Pen breathed softly. Sandy got up and carried clean clothes into the bathroom. A shower would surely wake her up. When she emerged fifteen minutes later, Pen was up and heating the kettle.

"What do you think about our odds of catching up with the money today?" Sandy asked, accepting the basket with coffee and tea choices Pen handed over.

"I'd like to think we've finally caught up and are in the same city, and perhaps we'll actually get to the bank first this time." Pen glanced at the clock. "However, I'm keeping my hopes in check. The entire trip has proven frustrating."

"Beyond frustrating," Sandy agreed.

The kettle clicked off and Pen poured the boiling water into their mugs. "Do you think a telephone call might work as well as a personal visit?"

"The visit is probably better. I doubt they'll share account information, but I want to show the photos of Cody and see if they'll admit he's their customer. At least we'll know if this is still the right track."

Pen carried her tea into the bathroom where she carefully applied minimal makeup and dressed in the suit that usually impressed bankers and other business types.

Ultimately, it was the same story. The account they were inquiring about was now closed. The crusty old man behind the desk yielded few details, although he did admit that the dark haired young man in the photo was the one who was here this morning when the bank opened.

Sandy gazed over at Pen. So close. Again.

"You understand, I'm certain, it's a privacy issue," the banker said. "You have no warrants and no law enforcement credentials. I canna tell you about another customer's accounts."

"Can you at least tell us this—did the young man withdraw the balance of the account in cash? Specifically, in US dollars?"

The man clamped his mouth shut, but a slight shake of the head told them that was not the case. With a sigh, the ladies stood, thanking him.

"Well, at least we could spend the day sightseeing," Sandy said as they walked out of the manager's office. "I wonder how far it is to the castle. It could be a nice walk."

A twentysomething blonde girl sat at the reception desk outside the manager's office. She spoke up. "It's not far at all. Would you like me to point the way for ye?"

She was immediately on her feet, circling the desk, and taking Sandy's arm.

"Erm, yes, thanks," Pen said.

Together, the three walked to the bank's main entrance on Princes Street. "If we step out here, I can show you what you're looking for," the girl offered.

She pointed toward the west. "I heard what you were asking my manager in there," she said, keeping her voice low, continuing to gesture with her hands. Anyone watching would believe she was giving directions. "That Cody Brennan you were asking about, he was here the moment the bank opened this morning. But you're wrong about the type of transaction. He brought cash, a whole lot of it, and deposited it in an account with the company name Blandishment."

"Your manager said the account was closed," Sandy said.

"Technically, that's true. But there are some other transactions, and it's what I was working on when you came in."

"Go on," Pen encouraged.

"The money is to be split and transferred to several other accounts."

"Also in the name of this Blandishment?"

The girl shook her head. "I really shouldn't say."

Sandy gave her a pleading look, and the girl named two American banks.

"That's not actually what I wanted to tell you," the girl said. "I'm to finalize these transfers and close the Blandishment account, and Mr. Brennan said he would come back this afternoon to verify it all and sign the documents."

"He'll be back?"

She nodded. "Hearing what you said to my manager, I took it that you were most interested in speaking with Mr. Brennan, more so than wanting his personal banking information."

"What time will he be here?" Pen asked.

"Two o'clock." The girl glanced anxiously over her shoulder. "Sorry, I really must get back inside. The castle is directly up this road, and just follow the pathway. Enjoy your day!" She uttered this last a bit more loudly as she pulled open the door to return to her work.

Pen and Sandy walked a block before they spoke.

"This is exciting," Pen said with gleaming eyes. "We are very close to catching up."

"And then what? We confront him, although we have no power to arrest or detain? Or do we try to get local law enforcement involved?"

Pen sighed. "You're right. I'd hoped we could catch up with the money, find evidence that leads to his being responsible for Amber's predicament. But to deal with Cody himself … I'm not quite certain where to turn."

"True, but if we can get our hands on him, we can drag him to the authorities. This is where it would have been good to have Mary along on this trip."

At least that picture drew a smile from Pen.

They walked five minutes in silence, making their way up the narrow lane that led to the imposing castle on the hill. At the sturdy iron portcullis was a ticket booth.

"Before we go inside, let's think of the best ways we could be spending our time," Pen suggested. "Maybe we can set a trap? I suggest we call Amber."

"It's the middle of the night at home."

"She won't mind. This is important. We should see if she can lure Cody into thinking he's meeting her."

Chapter 38

Cody bought his ticket and stood with the group he'd been assigned for the 10:30 tour of the castle. Twenty or so people, milling around the upper parapet that looked out over the sprawling city below as they waited for their tour guide. With a few hours to kill, this was at least more interesting than hanging out in a hotel room.

He was feeling lighthearted, relieved, after his meeting at the bank today. The manager had been a gruff old coot, but his secretary was a cutie and she'd smiled when he flirted at her desk. She assured him she could take care of the details—depositing the cash he'd brought into the various accounts he'd already set up.

She was the one who suggested he come back later in the day; he was the one who proposed that he take her out for a drink afterward. He couldn't remember whether she actually agreed. The main thing was that he would see her again. And this time he didn't even need to recruit her to move any cash for him.

Pop would just have to live with the fact that the money was not the green sort.

A woman in a straight skirt and blue blazer stepped out to the wide overlook and called out, "Blue tickets! The 10:30 tour group! Please assemble here with me."

Cody meandered over, fitting himself instinctively into the middle of the group. They moved toward a doorway in the thick stone wall, and he was determined to relax and enjoy a few sights of the ancient city. The good news was that he hadn't caught sight of those two American women for more than a day now. If they were tailing him, he'd shaken them off at last.

"Follow me, please, as we enter the castle, which has been a military fort, a royal residence, and a prison during its history."

They passed through the Great Hall, a cavernous room that could serve a whole stag to thirty knights, most likely, when his phone dinged with an incoming text message that echoed through the huge space. The tour guide shot him a look. She had requested that everyone turn off their cell phones for the duration of the tour.

He glanced at the screen. Amber? She hadn't responded to a message from him in nearly two weeks.

"Sir?"

"Sorry." He made a show of switching off the phone and putting it away. "Sorry."

Amber's message: Miss you. Can we get together?

His mind spun with possibilities. And it looked like he would have another forty minutes to figure out how to answer.

Chapter 39

Sandy listened, enthralled, to the tall young tour guide who called them onward toward the Great Hall. The tours were well organized, with small groups, well-informed guides, and a ton of information about the history, which dated back to the Iron Age, and the enticing bit that this was where Mary Queen of Scots had been imprisoned for a short while.

A previous group was exiting the great hall at the other end as the Red Group entered.

Pen seemed a little distracted. Of course, she had grown up amid the history of the United Kingdom and had probably visited this very castle a dozen times. In the shuffle of movement from the rest of the group, Sandy murmured her thoughts.

"No, it's not that. I'm just eager to hear back from

Amber, to know whether Cody is responding."

"Do you think he'll buy the idea that she's now here in Scotland?"

It seemed farfetched, now that they'd had time to consider the plan. But there was only one way to find out. They trusted Amber to figure out what to say.

The large hall seemed dim and cold to Sandy and she wasn't particularly interested in the displays of suits of armor, but the guide entertained them with fun bits of trivia.

"We'll shortly make our way to see the Honours of Scotland, otherwise known as the crown jewels," he said as they made their way out the door at the far end of the large hall. "It may be a bit more crowded in there, as the room isn't large, and our visitors tend to want to stay longer there. But never fear, everyone will have a chance to see the lovely crown and the scepter and sword. And you'll marvel at the story behind the Stone of Destiny."

The guide was right, the room with the crown jewels was more crowded, with visitors clustered around the display behind glass. And although the room itself was dimly lit, to showcase the priceless items, Sandy's pulse jumped when she looked ahead and spotted a familiar face. She reached back and touched Pen's hand.

Cody Brennan stood at the glass, staring at the sword in the display.

"It's him," Sandy whispered. "What now?"

Pen didn't have time to answer. Cody looked back and spotted them. Now there was no doubt he knew they were tailing him. He bumped a woman in front of him and edged his way roughly toward the exit door.

Chapter 40

What. The. Hell? Cody had no time to think. The two women knew he'd seen them, and a glance over his shoulder told him they were pushing their way through the crowd and coming after him. He didn't even bother to apologize as he elbowed through a cluster of teenage girls and ran along a corridor that looked as though it might lead outside. *Why didn't I pick up one of the tour brochures and memorize the layout?*

A little late for that regret now.

He heard a female voice behind him, around a curve. "He went this way." American accent. It had to be one of them. He tried an ancient-looking handle on a door, but it was firmly locked. Same with the next, on his left. Crap, where did this hallway come out? He should have followed the tour path when he first got out of the crown jewels room, but he'd assumed that would lead to more crowds.

Ahead, he spotted a green Exit sign above a door that looked more modern. He ran full-out for it, rammed it open, and immediately faced a wall. More signs directed him to the left, and in a few seconds he felt the rush of cool air and caught the scent of rain. He rushed in that direction, but he could hear the two women behind him. They'd just come through the same exit door.

Outside now, he realized he was in an enclosed courtyard. There was a small scrap of lawn and a pathway running along the edge of the stone building on his right. He didn't even know if that was still the castle itself or some other edifice. The guide had said the grounds contained military barracks, an armory, and a prison. Not to mention there had to be modern day offices and facilities.

He dashed along the skinny path and came out in a larger space with a stone floor—at home, he might have called it a deck—surrounded by a low parapet. Several heavy black cannons sat there, large muzzles facing out through cutaways in the rock. It had begun to rain and people were milling about, bringing out their umbrellas, staring around as if unsure what to do next.

Cody spotted a sign for a men's room and knew he could duck out of sight there. But he saw the two women emerge from the same archway where he'd been. They would see him go into the restroom and although they wouldn't follow, they could simply wait outside. He would have to come out at some point.

Instead, he eyed the low wall. In jeans and a light jacket, he could leap it. The women weren't dressed for wall-jumping. He ran toward it, hoping none of the castle guards would try to stop him. He had his hands on top of the three-foot wall, ready to vault over, when he gave a good look on the other side.

It was a straight drop, hundreds of feet, to treacherous rocks below.

Chapter 41

Sandy watched in dismay as Cody ran for the parapet on the far side of the large overlook. Pen was gripping her arm. "Don't follow. It's a deadly drop from there." She had pulled out an umbrella and was holding it above the two of them.

Cody's body was nearly on top of the low wall when he realized his mistake. Before the women could react, he'd pivoted and dropped back on this side of it and had taken off running again. His feet slid a little on the stone flooring but he was away.

"My shoes will have no traction on this," Pen said. "Go!"

Sandy wasn't in a much better position to follow someone fifteen years younger while wearing ballet flats, but she ran anyway. Cody had headed back toward the main entrance of the castle, and by the time she rounded the turn he was out of sight. She kept going. Behind her, Pen had folded the umbrella and was doing her best to keep up.

The rain was coming down harder now, making the surroundings gray and blurry, and people were dashing for cover everywhere. There was no way to pick out one person on the run among all the others. Sandy stood there, drawing the hood of her jacket over her head, but having no luck at spotting their quarry.

Pen caught up and raised the umbrella again. "Did you see where he went?"

There were gift shops and a pub or two lining the narrow roadway leading down the hill toward the city. He could have ducked into any of them.

"Or he may not have left the castle at all," Sandy said, finishing Pen's thought. "There's a little path that says it goes to the dog cemetery, and that sign points to bathrooms ..."

"And there are dozens of doors, any of which might happen to be unlocked."

They felt discouraged, having been this close.

"At least we know where he'll be at two o'clock," Pen reminded.

"We do. Meanwhile, how about if we find a warm spot to dry off and get a cup of tea?"

Chapter 42

Cody couldn't take the chance of going back to the bank, he realized. He'd taken a taxi to another part of the city, desperate to put more distance between himself and those women. He still had no idea who they were, and cursed himself for not having the presence of mind to snap a photo on one of the occasions he'd seen them. He might have been able to identify them through social media or something, and figure out why the hell they were right behind him everywhere he went.

The taxi dropped him at a big mall where he could calm down and think about his next moves. If these were cops on his tail, he would abandon the things he'd left at the hotel—although losing his computer would be a major setback. But if cops had gotten his computer with all the data it contained, he was toast anyway. Best to stow away on a ship and lose himself on an island somewhere if that were the case.

But these weren't cops. They didn't have the look. Their whole method of chasing him was too disorganized. Real cops would have called in local law enforcement in each country where they'd spotted him.

He could abandon the few thousand dollars he'd left in the Blandishment bank account here. Most of it was now moved to other accounts, but he didn't like the idea that he would be fresh in the mind of the girl at the bank. It couldn't be every day that an American walked into their bank with stacks of cash to deposit. And it had been plain dumb of him to let her handle the movement of that cash through the Blandishment account and out to the others. She knew too much. He had to do something about that.

But what? He felt stumped, and being without answers wasn't something Cody Baker ever did.

He made his way to the mall's public toilets and used the air hand dryer to get his jacket, shirt and hair dry. The jeans were clammy feeling, even after several rounds under the hot air, and his shoes were hopeless. He dug into his pockets and came up with enough cash to buy a new pair. With dry clothing and a plan, his mood brightened. Hey, you could get anything you needed in a mall.

But when the shoe clerk explained that they didn't accept American cash, his mood fell again. A trip to an ATM gave him what he needed for the replacement shoes and a meal. It also left a paper trail, which he wasn't happy about. But there was no way around it. It wasn't as if authorities couldn't figure out he'd been to Scotland— there were plane tickets and passport scans.

He cast off his worries, along with the soggy shoes, and went to the nearest restaurant. The pastry and coffee he'd had early this morning had long since worn off. Over lunch, he thought about his dilemma. He needed to stay out of sight, finalize the banking transactions, and get on his flight back to Jersey.

Shepherd's pie and a big glass of ale helped clarify his thinking. He had to get to the girl from the bank. By the time he finished his meal and walked the length of the mall, to an exit door, the rain had stopped, the sun was peeping through the clouds, and he knew what he would do.

He hung around the mall, checking his phone. There had been Amber's message to him, but nothing more, even though he'd responded. Quick math told him it was the middle of the night in Arizona, and he felt a moment's hope that she was sleepless and thinking of him.

But no such luck. He went back and asked for another ale, nursing it and waiting until he heard the boom of the One O'Clock Gun, a cannon-fire tradition the tour guide had mentioned, one that had been in place every day except Sunday since 1861. He didn't want to call the bank too early and give the girl a chance to turn him down, or too late when she would already be pissed at him.

Her name was Aileen MacPherson. In the tradition of Woody Baker, Cody never let a pretty one get away without getting her name first. He called the bank at 1:53 and said he couldn't make his appointment. Would she be able to break away and bring the close-out documents and cash he'd requested? She agreed.

He had already missed the checkout time at his hotel and since he was paying for another night anyway, he suggested the lobby as a meeting place. It was near the bank, a public space that wasn't right out on the street, and who knew—if he thanked her with a sincere and winning smile, he might get lucky.

Aileen showed up at exactly 2:05 with a slim portfolio tucked under her arm. She was every bit as pretty as he remembered, and he led the way to a quiet alcove beside the hotel bar, a grouping of chairs and small tables.

"Thanks for meeting me," he said. "I'm afraid I ran into a time crunch between two other meetings. My colleagues from New York insisted on my being here at 1:30 and that meeting ran over."

"It's no problem," she assured him in her delightful accent. "I was due a break anyway." She reached into the portfolio and pulled out the forms he needed to sign. "Were those the ladies who inquired at the bank earlier? Your meeting?"

Cody froze. "What?"

"Oh, I shouldn't have said. It's none of my concern."

"No, the meeting was with someone else." His mind was churning. Those women were doing more than tracking his movements between countries. They knew something about the money.

Aileen spread the papers out and prattled on about what each form was for, indicating where he should sign. He scrawled an unreadable signature on each line, not paying attention to any of it. How was he going to handle this with the banker? Say something, making it memorable in her mind? Or say nothing and hope for the best?

He opted for his tried-and-true method. Handing the pen back to her, he made sure his fingertips brushed her hand. "Say, would you be interested in extending your break a while longer? Have a cup of coffee or a drink ... There's a well-stocked minibar in my room upstairs ..." He stroked her hand as if it were a soft kitten.

She blushed deeply. "I ... erm ... it's very tempting, Mr. Baker."

"Cody."

"Cody. And if my manager were out for the day I would be ... well, I would be interested. But he watches us like a hawk and I've already some explaining to do about leaving for this meeting. Afraid I've really got to go back."

"Tonight, maybe? We could make drinks right after work?" Even as he said it, he realized he would need to be at the Edinburgh airport for his London flight, or he would miss the connection to New York.

"We'll see," she said. "Text me later?"

He walked her toward the front doors, giving her a long and desirous look, in case she might change her mind about staying. She sent a regretful glance over her shoulder as she left.

Good. At least the last thought on Aileen's mind wouldn't be about the women who'd come looking for him earlier. He decided to pack his stuff and head for the airport, even though it was a few hours too early.

Chapter 43

Sandy nudged Pen and pointed across the street at the bank. Cody Brennan was to have been here at two for his appointment, but they'd seen no sign of him. At 2:01, the blonde girl who'd spoken with them earlier walked out, a portfolio under her arm.

"What do you think?" Sandy asked.

"You follow her. I'll wait here to see if Cody shows up. It could be his business is with the manager, not with her."

"Good thinking." Sandy stayed on the opposite side of the street, crossing only when the banker made a left turn. She stayed back and watched until, one block later, the girl walked up the steps and into the Hilton hotel.

Interesting.

Sandy pulled sunglasses from her purse and a collapsible hat she'd carried as rain protection. Tucking her hair mostly into the hat, she hoped she'd disguised her appearance well enough. She strolled along the front of the hotel, browsing the window displays set up by the retail shops inside. Behind her dark glasses, her eyes were busy looking into the lobby.

The blonde walked up to a man waiting near a pillar in the large space. They shook hands and she held up the portfolio. The man was Cody—Sandy was ninety percent sure of it, although her sunglasses and the reflection from the hotel's large windows made it difficult to see for sure. The pair moved out of sight.

Sandy felt a moment's hesitation. What to do? *Well, I'm not going to know what he's doing if I stay out here.* She walked up the steps, pausing at a tourist brochure stand just inside the front door. One of the larger publications was some sort of magazine, real estate listings or some such. She picked it up and pretended to give it her attention as she moved into the lobby.

Cody and the woman had moved to the far end of the lobby where groupings of tables and chairs sat outside the formal confines of the bar. They'd taken a table and had their heads together in conversation, as the woman pulled papers from her folder. Neither one looked up as Sandy strolled toward the elevators. She turned and stood behind a huge potted plant, but she was still too far away to hear anything they said.

The best way to stay unnoticed while in plain sight was to be using an electronic device. She tucked the magazine into the side pocket of her bag and pulled out her phone. A quick text let Pen know that Cody was here. No point in waiting for him outside the bank. Careful if you come through the lobby—he could see you.

Thx got it.

Sandy moved to an armchair in the main part of the lobby and checked her email and messages while keeping one eye on the little bar table forty feet away. There seemed to be some flirting, now that the paperwork had been put away. Got to give this guy honors in the department of wooing women quickly, she decided.

Anger flared for a moment. This was becoming less about tracking the money this guy had probably stolen and more about protecting Amber. A thief *and* a cheater. This Cody guy needed to pay a price for his behavior.

There was a message from Amber. It must be early morning in Arizona by now. Suggested to Cody that we meet up. He asks if I'm back in Paris. Surely he knows I'm not?

Probably testing you to keep up the ruse. String him along.

While she was typing the text message, the couple across the room had moved and Sandy was startled to see them walking in her direction. She turned in her chair, hoping her hat brim concealed her face well enough.

The girl from the bank sent a regretful glance over her shoulder toward Cody just before she walked out the front door. Sandy sneaked a peek and saw him give a little wave, but the moment the girl was out of sight he straightened his shoulders and walked toward the elevators.

All at once, his eyes widened and he went into motion, bypassing the elevators and heading down a corridor that led to a series of meeting rooms. Sandy did a double-take. Pen had just walked into the lobby.

"Pen, over here!" Sandy shouted.

Cody took off at a run.

Sandy nearly tripped over the magazine that had fallen at her feet, but she recovered in time to see Cody yank open the door to a conference room and disappear inside.

She followed.

Chairs, set in neat rows, filled the darkened room and there was a man at the front whose PowerPoint presentation was now being ignored as heads turned to see what the commotion was about. Sandy nearly slammed into a table of water glasses before she realized she was still wearing her sunglasses. She pulled them off and saw a Cody-shaped silhouette disappear through another door at the far end of the room.

"Sorry, sorry," she murmured as she rushed to follow.

Somewhere behind her, she heard the door open, the one she'd just come through, and Pen's calm reassurance to the crowd that everything was fine. Pen caught up with Sandy and they stepped into a lit service passageway that ran behind the meeting rooms.

"Which way did he go?" Pen asked.

Sandy looked both directions but there was no sign of Cody. Then they heard a metallic crash.

"The kitchen must be that way," Pen said, pointing left. "There has to be an outside exit there."

An angry guy dressed in kitchen whites—formerly white, now covered in something shockingly red that must have been a sauce—fumed at the wreckage of a metal serving cart and the spillage from two large kettles that now lay on the floor.

"Sorry," Pen said. "Did a dark-haired young man come this way?"

The response was a string of unintelligible Gaelic and wild hand gestures that neither of the women wanted to confront. They backed away and returned to the corridor.

"I think we must admit we've lost him."

"Again." Sandy's discouragement showed.

"I suppose we could go back to the desk and see if he's

registered here at the hotel. Must admit that's a thought that never occurred to me," Pen said.

Sandy could only nod. They made their way back down the corridor, listening for voices, avoiding the room where they had already disrupted someone's meeting. At the desk, the male clerk said there was no Cody Brennan registered. When they described the young man who had just rushed from the lobby minutes earlier, the young man said he'd been away from his post and hadn't noticed. Sorry.

As they waited for the elevator, Pen rested a hand on Sandy's shoulder. "We've done our best. Time to let Amber take over, assuming he will agree to meet with her."

Chapter 44

Amber stared at her phone screen while her first cup of coffee brewed. Could it be that Cody had no clue she was on to him and the scam he'd tried to pull with the hundred grand? He was certainly persistent for a guy who'd broken the law and tried to lay the blame on her. He must not have put it together.

And what about the embezzlement charge against her? He certainly didn't seem to know she'd been arrested, and she wondered how long she would need to keep him in the dark about that. She flipped back through the most recent texts between them.

He'd asked if she was back in Paris, but he had to be aware she wasn't. She'd responded that no, she was home in Arizona.

What about you? Your company planning to transfer you

back to US?

Maybe. I've asked. Want to be with you.

But your office is in NY. Do they have anything in AZ?

No response to that yet. His declarations of interest were still puzzling. What was he up to?

The phone vibrated in her hand, startling her. Pen's name showed on the screen.

"Hey, where are you?" Amber pulled a mug from the upper cabinet and poured the coffee.

"I didn't wake you, did I? Sandy and I are at Heathrow, waiting to board our flight. Thank goodness it's direct. We're both feeling a bit knackered."

"I'll bet. So, what's the word?"

"On your Cody, nothing. Well, I should say we've lots to report, but none of it means he's been caught. The man is as slippery as an eel."

"I'll keep it in mind. You do know he's started texting me again?"

"Yes, right. And how is that going?"

"He's playing along as if he's still working in Paris, says he's still interested in me enough to put in for a transfer with his job so we can see more of each other."

"Do you believe it?"

"Not unless you can confirm he still lives there."

Pen told her of the visit with the building manager in Paris and her assertion that Cody was merely visiting friends there. "But then we also heard that he was using the apartment of a couple who were away on vacation somewhere else. How he managed to get their key, no one seemed certain. He apparently is expert at bluffing his way through nearly any situation."

"Including fooling a young woman about his romantic intentions."

"Be careful, Amber. He'll say anything."

"I know." A pang of sadness at the thought, but she knew Pen was right.

"Here, say hello to Sandy quickly. They've called our flight, so we're boarding soon. We'll be home by eight-ish your time tonight."

"Hey there," Sandy said when she came on the call. "Just wanted to give you a little warning. Cody is definitely on to me and Pen. He spotted us twice in Edinburgh and knew enough to run both times, so I'm guessing he had previously figured out we were asking questions. Maybe in Paris, maybe in London. We aren't sure. Anyway, if he gets in touch with you be careful not to let him see pictures of us together and don't mention us. It could be that he only knows our faces, but don't underestimate him. He could know our names too."

"Good advice. Thanks." She wished them a good flight.

Amber was halfway through a bagel when a new thought hit. Had she ever posted pictures of herself and the other Heist Ladies on any of her social accounts? Yikes—that could identify everyone and blow their entire mission.

Chapter 45

Cody sat at the old family breakfast table, staring at the two slices of overcooked toast his father had set down in front of him. What was it about parents, thinking you always wanted to eat the minute you arrived? During the long flight to Newark, Cody had stared at a stupid screen through two movies and stewed about the trip all the way back. Right now he was sleep deprived and grumpy, and burnt toast wasn't cutting it as breakfast food.

"Let's go out," he said. "Get some eggs at Joey's or something." The nearby diner had been their go-to place while he was growing up.

"What, you don't eat toast anymore?"

"Pop ... don't start with me."

"This is about that chick, idn't it? You still going around all wound up over her? Told ya, you can't get involved with a mark."

"Drop it. I didn't say I was involved, did I?"

"You're letting your little head do the thinking for the big one, son."

"*Pop!* Don't talk—" But it was probably true. He needed to get over this girl and move on. He knew what topic would distract his father. "Hey, tell you what. Let's get some breakfast and then we'll go down to the bank."

Woody grumbled a little more, but Cody could tell he was pleased. The subject of money always brightened the day for the old man.

"I don't want none of that *app* shit where I have to get a fancy new phone," Woody said as they picked up their jackets and headed toward the door. "Give me a checkbook."

"We'll just do an ATM card. You can get cash that way."

"Yeah, okay, I can deal with that."

Cody explained the way he'd set up the various bank accounts, and the reasons neither of them would have access to large amounts of the money right away, as they walked the three blocks to the diner.

"Yeah, yeah, I know. You think I ain't done this before?"

Then why were you talking like I should bring you a suitcase full of money, the last time I was in town? But he didn't say it out loud. He just wanted some food, to get this money business out of the way with his dad, and then see what he could do about getting together with Amber again.

Joey's Diner sat in a cinderblock building stuck between two others on a block where more than half the businesses were shuttered. The place was run by a decrepit old guy who shouted insults at his customers (what, you want *more* coffee?) while he shuffled toward their tables to pour for them. But the plates were piled high and the prices were something out of the 1960s, so no one cared that the walls smelled like grease and Joey was such a curmudgeon. It was a neighborhood clientele who'd known him for decades, and in their own way they all loved him.

"Woody! Hey, you old coot. Weren't you just here yesterday?" Joey shouted it across the long, narrow room. "And this is your boy, all grown up now?"

Woody grinned and nodded. "Cody. He's just back from *Europe*."

"Ooh, *fancy*." Several of the old timers laughed at Joey's comeback.

Cody did what was expected of him, ducked his head a little and played shy. Just like he'd done as a kid.

Woody led the way to his favorite booth, which happened to be the only empty one, and called out to Joey to hurry it up with the coffee. Their banter was like an old vaudeville routine, predictable and yet somehow funny to most everyone in the place.

While his dad made the rounds and said hello to everyone he knew, Cody studied his phone screen, re-reading the conversation thread with Amber.

Hey I'd like to see you, she'd said.

Are you back in Paris? As if he were kicking back in that big apartment, ready for a visit.

I wish. Was hoping you finally made it to PHX

Emergency callback to work. Hoping to get there in a week or so.

Would be great to see you. Was that a wistful tone on her part? He felt a blush rising, but Woody was on his way to the table. He put the phone on the bench seat beside him and fixed a neutral smile on his face.

"So what're you having?" Woody said, not bothering to pick up one of the one-page menus from the little prong holder at the end of the table.

Joey sent a waitress over, a biddy who had been as much a fixture here as Joey himself. She wrote down Cody's order for two eggs over easy, ham, potatoes, and white toast. Woody just asked for his usual, which obviously the woman already knew.

While Woody went on about various people in the diner, Cody sneaked peeks at his phone.

There were two texts from a co-worker, asking where he was. Bob, their supervisor, was more than a little pissed that Cody hadn't called in. He sent a quick note back: Family emergency. No time to call, but tell him I'll be back by the end of the week.

Almost immediately came a reply: You tell him, dude. Enough shit's going down around here. I'm not covering.

Cody deleted the messages. What he didn't know couldn't come back to bite him, right?

He read through Amber's last two texts again. Was it true that she was still interested? She wasn't acting like she knew anything, no clue he'd been involved with the cash that got her stopped at the airport. Of course he wasn't admitting he'd heard she was arrested either, and a little stab of guilt hit him over that.

He shushed his mind. He'd known perfectly well he was using her login credentials to pry into her employer's site and to work out the details to get the money. Yeah, that was before she'd slept with him, before he'd actually even met her. It didn't count when you didn't know the mark, right? Whatever a guy did was about nothing more than scoring.

But once you met her, started to like her?

He hated this, getting a conscience.

Chapter 46

So Cody was back in her life. Amber wasn't sure how she felt about that as she went back through her photos of the two of them during their romantic week in Paris. Meals at Chez la Vieille, a selfie with the Eiffel Tower in the far distance, his smile as she ruffled his hair. It had all seemed so genuine.

She wanted to think she could read people fairly well, but maybe she'd spent too much of her life buried in computer code. Pen and Sandy—and her parents, for that matter—all had so much more experience. She should listen to them. But it was hard to ignore the chemistry she had felt with him.

Swiping the screen to move away from the photos on her phone, she opened Instagram. Sandy's warning was valid. If there were public photos of Amber with the rest of the Heist Ladies, it could ruin their chances of catching Cody and learning the real story behind the money. She couldn't risk it.

She carefully went back through all her posts for the past three years. There was only one picture, a shot of the five of them together on a trip to Bali right after Christmas. They'd been wrapping up their last investigation and doing a little celebrating on the beach when a local girl offered to take a group photo of them. They all had wide smiles, windblown hair, and colorful bathing suits. With a sigh, she deleted the post, but not before checking the names of everyone who had liked it. No Cody. Thank goodness.

Snapchat—same scenario. Twitter, the same, although she rarely added pictures there. Still, it was worth the time to check. She rarely posted anything on Facebook, but wasn't sure if the others did. She browsed through all of their posts and saw that both Gracie and Sandy had shared the same photo. She shot a quick text off to each, letting them know to delete it.

Hopefully, the social media links were now gone. She was fairly certain Cody had not yet made the connection between her and Pen and Sandy, but from what Sandy had told her, Cody knew their faces. It wouldn't take much for him to add it up. They would need to be extra careful from here on, or they would run the risk he'd simply vanish.

Her coffee mug was empty. She refilled it and carried the steaming brew to her new desk. Two computers were set up now—her personal one, which she still used for her own banking and social accounts. She needed to be sure her online presence seemed as normal as possible, in case the police should confiscate and examine it.

The second machine was the loaner from Sandy, the one she was using for all things related to tracking Cody.

Once they had nailed him, she would run the hard drive through a program that would triple-delete everything on it.

And there was the matter of the other hard drive, the external one she'd used to copy everything from her B-G computer. Mary still had it, had assured Amber just last night that it was in her gym bag, which rarely left her sight unless it was locked away. Amber prayed that was true; she had to trust that Mary would never let her down.

Amber leaned back in her chair, gently swiveling it slightly from side to side as she tried to decide what she could do *now* to work on solving this thing. Pen and Sandy had done their part, trekking around Europe. Now on the plane heading home, they couldn't do anything. Mary was guarding the hard drive. She'd offered to kick Cody's ass if they ever caught up with him, but this was all she could do for now. And Gracie—who could ask for better emotional support than Gracie had offered by bringing her home from jail and staying that one night with her? Right now, Amber felt it was up to her to come up with the answers, and her strength was right here in front of her. Computers.

She slid the chair closer and booted up the borrowed laptop. She couldn't help thinking that something tied back to Cody's brief internship at Omni. Why would he have bothered to put his profile up on their website, unless he wanted it to be seen? Maybe there was something about his job there, something high-level which would bolster his resume.

She started with the corporate website and learned who their web developer was. A couple of false leads, but eventually she was into the back channels she needed. Internal corporate memos began flooding onto her screen.

"Whoa," she said to the plant on her desk. "Lots of

stuff here."

She paused the endless string of messages, long enough to figure out how to search for specific words. Entering Cody Brennan's name narrowed the search to practically nothing. There was one memo when he was hired, a few during his limited time there, and a couple more when he'd apparently just ghosted the job. After several days without an appearance in the office, according to a manager, they'd terminated his internship and sent a notice off to the university to inform them.

That there was no reply from that particular institution didn't especially surprise Amber. The Ladies had already determined that Cody had never attended classes there.

She went back to the long list of interdepartmental memos, debating what search terms to use next, when a familiar phrase caught her eye. Misappropriation of Funds. It was fancy-speak for embezzlement, and she knew this because the cop and her attorney had bandied it about a little when Amber was being questioned.

Oh-ho. She searched that term among the memos and found it no less than sixty-three times. Top management and HR were discussing the fact that an internal audit had revealed money was missing. A chill went straight through her.

Oh shit. I cannot be caught with this information about Omni in my possession. She quickly backed out and deleted the entire browsing history.

Her mind whirled. What did this mean?

Whatever it meant, it couldn't be good. She called Gracie. "We need to meet."

They decided the best way to get the whole team together would be for Amber, Gracie and Mary to be at the airport tonight to meet Pen and Sandy's flight.

"I'll call Mary. I need to get that external drive back from her," Amber said.

Itching to do more before this evening, Amber hid the borrowed computer, shut down her own, and headed down to the parking garage. She had research to do, research that would be better not showing up on any computer in her own home.

Chapter 47

Pen and Sandy walked through the frosted glass doors that deposited them out of the realm of international travel and into the everyday world of the bustling Phoenix airport. They seemed both surprised and delighted at the sight of their three friends.

"I know you thought I'd be picking you up by myself," Gracie said, offering to take the handle of Pen's suitcase. "But we've had some exciting news."

"Well, I don't know about exciting ..." Amber said.

"Somewhat juicy, anyway," Mary added.

Sandy seemed somewhat weary from the flight, but her blue eyes brightened at the idea of juicy news. "Tell us."

They walked through the terminal, making their way via Sky Train to the parking garage where Gracie's minivan waited.

"It's Amber's to tell," Gracie said, stowing the bags in the back and inviting everyone to find seats.

"Okay, bottom line is that Cody's former employer got embezzled," Amber said, her face animated.

Amazed expressions all around. "And you've proved he did it," Mary said.

"Well, not really. I got into a series of internal memos about it, and the dates lined up with when he worked there. He quit without notice, just didn't show up one day, and it was right about the time the money disappeared."

"Do we want to know how you got hold of internal memos at a company on the east coast?" Mary asked, handing over the B-G hard drive.

"No. You do not." Amber gave a significant glance toward Sandy. "I deleted my entire browsing history the moment I got that far."

"Thank goodness," Pen said, from the front passenger seat.

"I spent the afternoon at the library, using public computers, to look up news stories about the Omni case. Unfortunately, very little was said—almost exactly like what happened to me at B-G."

"Because big corporations don't want their vulnerabilities broadcast to the world," Sandy said.

"Do you think Cody Brennan was behind both of these?" Mary asked.

"It seems like something that would have been easy for him," Amber told them. "If he was successful taking money from Omni, he might have figured out how to get into the system at B-G ..."

"Could you have done it?" Pen asked. "Once you were far enough into Omni's company records, could you have gotten into their banking accounts?"

"I hate to admit this, but yes. Easily."

"So, Cody could have done the same thing."

"He's every bit as good with computers as I am."

Gracie steered the van up Pen's hillside driveway and pulled into the circular loop at her front door. Pen turned in her seat to face those in the rear. "Be extremely careful, my girl. You cannot let yourself be drawn into his misdeeds."

Amber nodded.

"At this point we do not know who we're dealing with or who is behind him. A young man such as this Cody Brennan may only be the fingerprints on the keyboard, so to speak, and there could be a much darker mastermind behind him."

Amber looked solemn. "I hadn't thought of that."

"We all must keep it in our minds." Pen walked to the back of the van and took her suitcase. "Good night, all."

Gracie got into the driver's seat and started the van, heading back down the hill. "Mary and I should take any further surveillance," she said. "He'll know the rest of you."

"I wish we knew where to surveil him," Sandy told them. "We had leads as long as we knew the banks where he had moved the money, but that has all changed. At the last bank we visited in Scotland we were told, on the down low, that he'd moved a lot of cash and the entire account balance into a multitude of other accounts. At this point we don't know whether he's still somewhere in Scotland, on continental Europe, or even back here in the US."

"I still have a connection," Amber said. "It's skimpy, though. He has texted me a few times." She leaned back in her seat with a huge sigh. "I don't know … It just really is starting to feel hopeless."

Gracie spoke up. "For now, just use the texts as a way

to string him along. Keep flirting, make him believe you're interested. Try a video chat like Facetime or something—maybe you'll be able to spot some clues in his surroundings."

Amber nodded silently. "That's a good idea, Gracie. But we don't even know for sure who he is. None of our searches for Cody Brennan have turned up a real person with a history. There's just the fake job, the probably fake social media."

"We'll keep working on that," Sandy said, laying a gentle hand on Amber's arm.

"I'd like to box his pretty little face," Mary said, punching at the air and hoping to lighten the mood.

"You're my next stop, Amber," Gracie said. "Unless you want to keep riding along for the company? You can always come home with me and spend the night if you'd like."

But Amber's eyes had taken on a new spark. "No—home is fine. I just got an idea."

Chapter 48

Cody sat at Pop's breakfast table, the same metal and Formica thing that had sat in the very same spot since he could remember. If he were to look under the edge, he'd bet that wads of his old bubblegum would be stuck there. He resisted reaching underneath now to check. Yuck.

Instead, he scrolled through the text messages from Amber. It would be after ten p.m. in Phoenix now, and he remembered she told him in Paris that she put her notifications on hold at night. Otherwise, she'd never get any rest.

"What's that?" Woody's voice was right behind him.

Cody jumped and nearly dropped the phone. He tried to hide the screen but the old man was quick, snatching it from his hand.

"Jeez, boy. You still hung up on this?"

Think fast. "Pop, I'm playing her along to see what's going on back there. She got arrested for taking the money."

"Exactly as we planned." Woody set the phone down on the table, a little too hard. "That's what we wanted. We get the cash; she takes the blame."

He saw the regretful look cross his son's face.

"Hey! Don't you start that!" Woody's expression grew dark, his temper rising. "You know how this thing works. You pick the target who's best for your purpose. This *Am*ber chick is computer smart and she's cute. You played up to that, appealed to her vanity. But you don't get involved. Use 'em and skip out."

He shook his finger, and Cody felt every old lecture from his childhood roaring in his ears.

"You want a woman in your life—fine. Get yourself a nice girl from the neighborhood, one that'll cook and clean and give you some kids, but she don't ask questions and she don't get a share of what we earn."

Earn? When we steal everything we have? "Oh, like you did with Ma, huh?"

Woody drew his arm back and Cody squeezed his eyes shut, waiting to get belted across the mouth. But it didn't come. He peered through his lashes and saw his dad across the room, staring out the dark window above the sink.

Cody stood up and pulled his backpack from the hook near the back door. "Here's your damn checkbook," he said, pulling out a packet of starter checks. "I'm outta here."

He stomped down the wooden steps to the sidewalk and took off into the night, not looking back. His mind whirled. As a kid he'd been oblivious to what his dad did, only that Ma and Pop fought a lot. By his teens, Ma had long since left the house. He got birthday cards from an address he recognized as his aunt Sally's house in Rochester. Was Ma really sending the cards, or did Sally just take pity on a kid? He never checked and he never knew.

Pop took it for granted that his quiet son who'd rather sit in front of a computer than go to the racetrack would just love the life of the con man. And for awhile it was a heady feeling, watching digital numbers move across the screen and knowing that it was real money, moving from somebody's account into one of theirs.

Pop was right, though. He should have never let his feelings develop for Amber Zeckis. She was the girl he'd pick if he'd done what Pop said, choose someone to settle down with. Except Amber was way smart and way too savvy. She'd know, within weeks, what he and Pop were up to. Somehow, he knew it wouldn't sit well.

He reached the end of the block and turned toward the bus station. He could get the shuttle to the airport and be in Phoenix by dawn. Would he be welcomed back at the job he'd walked out on? He had no idea, but he knew he wanted to be in the same city with Amber.

Chapter 49

Punch his pretty face. Mary's statement was the last thing Amber heard before Gracie dropped her off at her condo. *Face*. That was the answer.

Within five minutes after unlocking her door, she was on the computer—the borrowed one. Facial recognition software was available, although the highly rated ones weren't cheap. They were designed for retail stores and governments that needed to catch flickering shots and identify criminals. Her needs weren't quite that tricky. She had good photos. The challenge would be to get a program that would interface with official databases. She needed his real name.

It was nearing midnight when she found what she wanted. She did a gulp as she entered a credit card for the purchase, and then began the download to install the new software. Partway through she wondered if this would have been easier if she'd just turned over her pictures to the cops and let them do the searching. But it was a done deal now.

Plus, she didn't know what would turn up. Until she cleared her name, she had no way of knowing if the police wouldn't just believe she and Cody were in this embezzlement thing together. Especially considering how happy she and Cody looked in these photos.

While the software installed and the computer updated, she seriously considered, for the first time, exactly how she was going to match his picture to something that would officially identify him. She'd already searched for him on social media and found Cody Brennan to be exactly who he'd said he was. And that made sense if he were building a false identity to scam people.

She needed the truth.

She started with an online forum, a place where hackers hung out, a somewhat dark place she had only visited once. To get in she had created a fictitious user name—badkitty. Everyone else on the site was using similar pseudonyms, and she pictured them as those loser guys you saw in the movies, the ones with a man-cave in their mother's basement. Badkitty had only remained on the forum fifteen minutes on that visit. Scary stuff was being discussed.

But she knew it was where she could find a lead for what she needed now—a way to hack a government database.

It was nearly two a.m. and the room was crowded. She watched silently for a half hour, getting a feel for the topics and the characters. She had a hard time thinking of drdoom or madmax4 or whatsurgame as real people. At last she spotted a thread where someone was asking about getting into the FBI. Another user posted a link.

Seriously, guys? You think the FBI isn't going to have a way to watch you?

But then there was another, less threatening one. The Department of Motor Vehicles for the state of Texas. That could be useful—not Texas, in particular, but a driver's license photo would be a great way to match a person's picture. She hoped.

Whatsurgame posted an answer. It seemed a little complicated, but Amber read the lines of code and figured where she could insert the name of any other state. She copied the code and sat back.

Now, in which state would Cody have likely gotten his driver's license? He had claimed to work for Omni, a company in New York. But lots of New Yorkers didn't drive—public transportation was everywhere. Still, it was likely he'd gotten a license at some point.

She went into the computer's operating system and inserted the code she'd copied, gave a few other commands, and eventually came to a website. It required a password. Great.

Back on the forum, the other user had obviously run up against the same thing, and had come back to whatsurgame for the answer. He gave what he claimed was a generic default entry name. Amber took her chances with it. It worked.

From there it was a matter of figuring out how to get her new software to search for matches with photos. Dawn was showing at the edges of her drapes by the time she'd set up the thing to run automatically. Far cry from the way they show it on TV, she thought, rubbing at her burning eyes.

Pictures were flicking across the screen at a dizzying rate, and she decided it was time for a break. She stood and stretched, checked the screen again, and knew there would be time for a shower and clean clothes. When she emerged from the bathroom, the program was still merrily whizzing through photos. Okay, then, coffee.

She toasted a bagel and spread it with cream cheese, walked around the condo as she ate it, drank a second cup of coffee, debated whether the floors needed vacuuming. Each time she looked in on the computer, the same thing was happening—nothing.

Finally, two hours later, from the kitchen she heard a *ping*.

"Yay," she said to the houseplant. "Answers!"

Her optimism was unfounded. A box in the center of her screen said **No Matches Found**. Well, rats.

"Okay." She paced the width of her little office, muttering. "Where else? Just because he worked in New York doesn't mean he lives there. So—neighboring states. Maybe he's from Connecticut or New Jersey or Delaware ... or even Pennsylvania."

This could take a very long time.

At least her movements were quicker this time. She repeated the steps of revising the code, entering the parameters, and starting a new search. Connecticut took slightly less time, but the disappointing answer was the same. No matches. She retried, setting it up for New Jersey and thinking she should have gone back to the forum and asked if there was a way to do this for the entire country at once.

But there was a nagging little something in her mind, the worry that if badkitty spoke up she would be noticed and could be caught. She was in enough deep doo-doo with the law already.

She went into the living room and picked up a novel

Pen had loaned her, stretching out on the long sofa in the half-hearted belief that she might actually be able to concentrate on it. At least it was a way to pass the time. Three paragraphs into the first page, she fell asleep.

When she woke up the angle of the sun told her it was midafternoon. Feeling draggy, she rolled off the couch and stood up to stretch. Her computer search! She hurried into her office and woke up the darkened computer screen.

There was a match.

Her hand shook as she picked up her phone to call a meeting of the Heist Ladies.

Chapter 50

"His real name is Cody Baker," Amber told the group who'd gathered at her condo. "And I got an address in Newark. In general, it fits with his schooling and work history."

"His *made-up* history," Gracie reminded.

"True. But it's harder for a kid to fake the info on his driver's license. He received his when he was only eighteen, and probably had to provide his birth certificate at the time, so most likely the address is, or was, his childhood home." Pen pointed out those details from the computer screen Amber showed them.

"So, do we jump on a plane and head there?" Mary had an eager gleam in her eye.

Sandy seemed more pensive. "Baker .... Baker ... Where do we know that name?"

Gracie held up an index finger in a Sherlock Holmes ah-ha gesture. "The corporation. Blandishment Inc. Its registered agent with the Division of Corporations in Delaware was listed as Woodrow Wilson Baker."

"I guess I was so focused on the odd use of Woodrow Wilson that Baker didn't click with me," Amber said.

"Another alias of Cody?" Mary suggested.

"Maybe. Could also be a relative, or someone else's alias," Pen said.

"Do you think the woman you spoke to in Delaware would recognize Cody's photo as the person who set up the corporation?"

Pen gave it no more than a moment's thought. "I doubt it. She said they do hundreds of these a year."

"That might not be terribly important," Gracie said. "The crucial details are that we have already connected the money missing from Amber's employer with this Blandishment Inc. Now, if we can connect Cody Baker to this other Baker person, surely the police will have to listen when we tell them."

Sandy had another question. "Amber, could that program of yours locate this Woodrow Wilson Baker? I'm wondering if Cody could have set up multiple identities for himself."

Amber sat in her desk chair again and turned the computer screen so the others couldn't see. It was best if they didn't know exactly where she was when she logged into the New Jersey DMV. "This could take a few minutes. Do we want to order some take-out? I haven't eaten since—I don't remember exactly."

"You still have those menus in the kitchen drawer?" Gracie asked, taking the hint and leading the others from the room.

It took a slightly different pathway to search for a name rather than a photo, but Amber quickly figured out how to do it. By the time Mary and Gracie returned with a bag of barbeque sandwiches and various salads, she was able to join them at the kitchen counter with a report.

"I found this Woodrow Wilson Baker guy," she said. "The good news is that an unusual name comes up pretty quickly. The bad news is that he's dead."

Amber held out a printed page, a copy of the driver's license of Woodrow Wilson Baker. It pictured an old man whose age at the time was well into his eighties. "Obviously, this isn't an alias for Cody. Unless he's got an expert makeup artist and someone within the DMV who would let the proof of age requirement slide."

The women passed the printed image around, studying it. "Hard to tell if there's any resemblance to Cody. They list the same eye color, but I don't see much else," Sandy said. She had carried plates in from the kitchen and set them on the table. "Do you think this guy would have had the know-how to set up such an elaborate con?"

Pen was studying Amber's face. "There's more?"

"The weird news is that he died two years before his name was signed to the paperwork for Blandishment Inc."

"What?"

"This man couldn't have set it up."

"So, that means … what, exactly?" Mary asked as she passed out sandwiches and set out containers of potato salad and coleslaw.

"I'd like to know why no one checked to see that the identity of the person forming the company was a dead man," Sandy said.

Gracie answered. "The woman on the phone told me that the whole process is quick and simple. I could call her back and ask more, but I got the feeling nothing really has to stand up to scrutiny."

"Maybe we can locate some other relatives of Cody's? See if one of them is the man named in the paperwork?" Mary suggested.

"Baker is a pretty common last name. We could be spinning our wheels for a very long time," Gracie said.

"Not with computer searches," Amber said. "I can give it a try. We do have an address."

"Good idea," Pen said. "Now, what else can we check? Do we need more information on this quickie corporation of his?"

"I'll volunteer, if there's travel involved," Mary said, raising a hand.

The others laughed. "You're just eager to get away to somewhere that really feels like autumn," Sandy teased. "I would have traded a drenching in northern Scotland with you."

Amber had polished off her sandwich and seemed eager to get back to work. "I had another thought. Even if we do locate other Baker relatives, we still have to keep our eye on the goal of getting our hands on Cody." She blushed a little. "Well, not literally. Getting him in sight so the cops can grab him."

"Precisely. What do you have in mind?" Pen asked.

"I've texted back and forth with him a little, as you know. He's hinting that he is still working in Paris, which we're pretty sure is pure b.s., so I've been thinking of ways to figure out where he really is."

"And?"

"I'm going to suggest a video chat. He has Facetime. We used to talk quite a bit before we ever met in person. I'll suggest that and see if I can pick up any clues about where he really is. For sure, if he's back in that Paris apartment—"

"He won't be," Sandy assured her.

"Most likely not. But I might recognize something else. I'll suggest we each pick our favorite outdoor café and have a virtual lunch together. I can make it sound romantic but really it will be research."

"I like it," Pen said.

Chapter 51

Cody stared at his phone messages, torn about accepting Amber's idea. Although they were in different cities, she suggested, they could each go to a favorite outdoor café and have a video lunch together. Hadn't she hinted that she might return to Paris if he wanted her to? How was he going to fake a Parisian backdrop from here? He chewed on a dry cuticle and debated how to phrase his answer.

There was a lot going on right now. Watching the various bank accounts daily, making certain he was happy with where he had stashed the money, including what was in the account he'd given his dad. It appeared Woody was spending some, but he hadn't drained the account or anything.

He was keeping an eye on the news reports. Nothing

more had come out about Amber's arrest, although clearly she had either been questioned and released or was out on bond. She couldn't very well be offering up a restaurant lunch if she were behind bars, and she probably wouldn't have her phone with her either. He felt torn. If she'd gotten away with it, that was a good thing. But it was still a big unknown. A video chat could be a good way to quiz her for more information.

Then there were the calls from work. Why couldn't his manager just drop it? *Because you're the sharpest programmer he's had in his department in a very long time. He doesn't want to go through the hassle of finding someone else.* Well, that wasn't happening. Too risky. Staying on the move was better right now.

He reread Amber's latest text. He really wanted to see her. Surely he could find a French restaurant around here somewhere. This was a big city. If there was one thing he did well, it was bluffing his way through different situations. He texted back a yes. He had until tomorrow at noon to find the right spot.

First though, he needed to line up a better place to stay. Even the cheap motels were eating through his cash and he was trying not to leave a trail with credit cards, at least until he could get some new fake ones set up. He called his old landlady, the one who watched game shows all day, and she said sure, his old room hadn't rented yet so he could come back. What the hey, he decided, it was cheap and she had decent Wi-Fi, and it was handy to the bus line so he could get around.

He went there now, taking the express bus away from downtown and walking the final few blocks to the house. Doing this bothered him a little. He needed to break the habit of reverting back to his old haunts. That's how guys got caught. At least no one knew about his living quarters—he'd given the landlady a fake name and he paid in cash. She wouldn't say anything, most likely wouldn't even if a cop showed up with his picture in hand. She liked the money.

Back in his old room now, he set up the laptop he'd been carrying everywhere in his backpack. It still recognized the household Wi-Fi and he was online right away. He searched first for French restaurants, anywhere along the bus line would do.

Chapter 52

Amber stared at her image in the mirror. *What am I doing?* She'd applied way more than her normal eye makeup, and her deep brown skin looked radiant. Even her hair was behaving today. She had debated trying to fool Cody into thinking she really had flown back to Paris to be with him, but decided it was just too much effort. Realistically, he expected her to be in Phoenix at her desk. Life was just a breeze, right?

On the other hand, she had chosen an outdoor café with a French look about it. The point was to make him believe this was a romantic lunch, and she planned to order wine with her food. But she also remembered his genius computer skills and wouldn't put it past him to know a way to track her exact location.

With that in mind, she would drive across the city to

Tempe, miles away from her home. After the stunt he'd pulled, she thought it only fair that she keep the upper hand this time around. She gave a final tug to an unruly curl and turned away from the mirror. Taking a deep breath she walked down to her car and proceeded to coach herself on acting romantic. Although she was no actress, she couldn't blow the mission now.

Le Petit Parapluie, the restaurant she'd chosen, was an old favorite from her college days, one that was a little too pricey for everyday meals, but she'd been there a few times on dates. The onion soup was a favorite. She arrived twenty minutes before noon and asked for a table in a corner. It would be tricky enough, this acting gig, in front of Cody. She really didn't want to invite an audience.

While she waited for him to come online, she flipped over to her weather app and looked up the weather in Paris. Rainy. Interesting. If he really was there, would he still opt for an outdoor venue? Doubtful. Just then the Facetime tone alerted her—it was showtime.

She had to remind herself that she was the one who'd suggested they get together, so she put on her brightest smile as she answered the call.

"Hey—wow. I'm so glad you were able to do this," she said.

"Me too. I've really missed you."

His facial expression seemed genuine—longing, maybe some regret? She tried hard to read him and keep up her perky, friendly attitude.

"So, how are things? Work going okay? Paris still having gorgeous weather?"

His eyes cut to the side. "Yeah, uh, well, you know. Work is same old, same old. Weather's not bad. Getting a little colder."

"Aim your phone around the room," she asked. "I want to see. Are you at one of the places we went together?"

"Uh, no. This is a different one. And it's really nothing. Kind of a dive, actually. How about you? What kind of restaurant did you choose?" Smooth way to change the subject.

"Well, French, of course." Her waiter showed up just then, carrying a tray and carefully setting a bowl down. "I've ordered the onion soup. Even though it's not exactly genuine, and nothing like eating it right there in Paris, it's the thought that counts, right?"

Cody didn't appear to be eating anything. She used the distraction of cutting through the cheesy topping on her soup to focus her attention on his surroundings, but it was hard to tell much. Clearly, he was in some kind of public place. People moved behind him in the distance, and there were general noises—conversations, dishes, maybe something like a TV in the background. She listened for Jersey accents but the clatter was too chaotic.

"Hey, I … I don't know whether to bring this up or not," he said, looking a little uneasy, as if someone else might be there judging what he said. "I heard you were arrested."

Amber dropped her spoon before she remembered she was supposed to believe he was in Paris. "All the way over there?"

"It was on the news. Nothing very specific. Are you okay? I mean, obviously you're not—"

"No, I'm not. I have a good lawyer."

"Is it going to be all right? This lawyer, he'll get you off, right?"

"Let's not talk about this." She watched his face carefully as she cut off the topic. He seemed relieved.

"Okay—you're so right. I wanted this to be a romantic lunch. I hope it works out for us to be together again soon." He sounded sincere.

But, she reminded herself, all con men sound sincere. It's what they do best. Establish empathy and make their victims believe anything they say. She'd recently watched an interview with a woman who pleaded, with tears in her eyes, for the release of her sweet innocent son who was wrongly accused. Anyone watching the show would believe everything she said. Later, the son confessed to two murders and gave all the details, including the fact that his mother had watched while he carried them out.

Suddenly, Amber had no appetite. "Look, I've got a really full afternoon. It was great to see you, and maybe we can do it again sometime?"

"Sure. I really want to." Just as Cody spoke a couple in shorts and t-shirts passed behind him. The guy's shirt had an ASU logo, and Amber caught a scrap of their conversation. The woman was describing the location of a mall that was no more than ten miles away from where Amber was sitting right now. She quickly cut off the video call, her heart pounding.

Could it be that he was this close? And why? How?

Her hand was shaking too much to manage her soup spoon. She tossed her napkin down and left some money on the table. She had to get out of here.

Chapter 53

"Okay, I didn't actually believe he would be in Paris," Amber told Gracie a half-hour later. The Nelson's house was the first place she could think to go that was a fairly short drive. "But it never occurred to me he might be right here in this city."

Gracie knelt in front of a flat of bedding plants, pansies and petunias, which she was planting in pots for her front porch. The upcoming cooler weather would be ideal for them, and she'd decided to take advantage of the couple of days Scott was away on business. She paused with her small spade in midair. "You mentioned a snippet of conversation you overheard. Was it enough to *know* he's somewhere in the Phoenix area?"

"There were just lots of clues. He sat at an outdoor table—I could see large plants in the background. All the voices—yes, they were indistinct, but they were American accents. There was no French being spoken. There was the ASU logo on someone's t-shirt. People were wearing shorts! Right now it's raining in Paris, and it would be dark."

"He's from New Jersey or New York …"

"Where it would be pretty cold for shorts and t-shirts this time of year."

"Sounds like good detective work on your part," Gracie said, scooping potting soil around the four small plants she had just placed.

Amber let some of the tension flow from her shoulders. "Thanks. Maybe that's what I needed to hear."

She knelt on the porch step. "Gracie, can I tell you something that I don't really want to share with the other ladies?"

"Honey, sure you can."

"In some way I think I really still wanted him to be genuine. I still don't know for a fact that he's the bad guy, I mean, yeah there was the cash in my suitcase. But I … he … well, I thought in Paris that we really had something."

"I know."

"Could I be that bad a judge of character, so bad I would be with a guy who lies and steals?"

Gracie's mouth crooked upward at one corner. "Hormones at work." She laid one palm on the edge of the terra cotta pot. "Hey, we've all been there, gotten mixed up with the wrong guy, fallen for somebody totally wrong."

Amber's lower lip trembled.

"But, hey, I don't know this Cody. Maybe he's working for someone else, and is in over his head. That can happen too."

Amber shook her head, reaching for a second cookie.

"Possibly. But is *that* the sort of guy I want to get involved with? No."

"Then we're going to chalk it up to the hormones. You just haven't met the right guy yet. Someday you will. And meanwhile ..."

"Meanwhile, I have to clear my name, get another job, and get on with my own life."

"Right."

"And I need to be looking over my shoulder. If he's really watching me ..."

Gracie was silent for a minute. "Absolutely. I get the feeling this whole thing is coming to a head. Do you think he knows where you live?"

Amber shrugged. "I have no idea. I had no idea he was within a thousand miles of me."

"Would you like to stay here until he's caught?"

"No, that's asking too much. You've seen my building. It's really secure. I don't buzz anyone up unless I'm expecting them, and I never answer the door without looking."

"That's good. Keep it up." Gracie set her spade down. "I think it's about time for another visit with that detective. I'll see if I can find out if they've got any new evidence. He still seems to think I'm an associate of Mariah Kowzlowski, so I'll play that up."

"And I'll get out of your hair. I had a few ideas of things I can check out online."

Gracie saw Amber over to her car, then she went inside and called Detective Mark Howard.

Chapter 54

I was practically on my way out the door," Howard said. "I've got questions for your client. I can go to her or she can come to me."

"We'll come there. How's three o'clock?" Gracie said.

At least he still believed she had a right to be there when Amber was questioned. She debated calling Mariah next, but they would learn more if the lawyer wasn't there shushing them every other minute. She called Amber instead.

"I know you're not even home yet ..." She explained the detective's request.

"I'm turning around. I'll come back to your place and we'll go together."

"Meanwhile, we need more ammo for this meeting," Gracie said. "We can do some research from my computer."

They spent an hour on a website that purported to locate the criminal record of anyone. After paying the small fee, they browsed into the life of Cody Baker's brushes with the law since the age of nineteen. Officially, there were only two.

"A traffic violation ten years ago?" Gracie seemed disappointed.

"Yeah, but look at this one. An arrest for fraud when a woman filed a complaint that young Cody had pulled the old pigeon drop scam. The case went before a judge, who ruled that Cody pay back the victim's money, do thirty days of community service, and pay a fine of one hundred dollars." Amber studied the details. "Isn't this proof that he understands scams and isn't above taking money?"

"I agree. Unfortunately, I don't know if the police are going to think this is super relevant. Cody was barely twenty. Lots of young guys go through a wild phase, and a little brush with the law like this is what sets them straight."

"Sounds like what his lawyer would say," Amber said. "What if it's true?"

Gracie turned away from the computer screen. "On the other hand, we *know* Cody didn't quit after that little infraction. We're ninety-nine percent sure he stashed the cash in your bag. And we know there's more. You found a lotta, lotta banking transactions that add up to way more money than a guy like him earns. Sandy and Pen chased him all over the UK to figure out what he did with it. Do those sound like the actions of a totally innocent person who learned his lesson way back when? I'm thinking, no."

"You're right," Amber said with a sigh.

"One thing I've learned about con men, such as the time my mother got roped in by the fake movie producer, is that they don't generally learn their lessons and they don't often change their ways. They depend on the victims not to report the crimes because it's usually the victim who is embarrassed that they got taken in."

"True that. I don't want to admit this time it was me."

"Hey, we'll figure this out." *Somehow.* "Let's go talk to the cop. We'll see what we can learn and we won't tell him we're working on our own. Right?"

"Got it."

Howard escorted them into an interrogation room. Gracie found it hard to read his mood. He was carrying an evidence bag and a folder of papers, but she couldn't tell what the bag contained. Once they were seated, he laid it on the table.

"Is this your cell phone?" he asked Amber. The phone's case depicted a piece of art that Marianna Zeckis had painted. She'd had the cover custom made for Amber last Christmas. "The phone belongs to Blackwell-Gorse Tech. The case is mine. I'd like it back."

"Later. This phone was issued to you by your employer?"

"Yes."

He set the printed pages on the table and spread them out slightly. "This is a transcript of the text messages found on your company phone."

"People send lots of text messages during the course of their work day," Gracie said.

"The ones highlighted in yellow seem more personal," Howard told them. "These particular ones were sent between Ms. Zeckis and one Cody Brennan."

He turned the pages one-eighty degrees, so the printed text was visible to the women. Their eyes immediately went to the highlighted lines.

"There are a lot of references to cash," the detective

said, pointing. "This one in particular, where Mr. Brennan talks about 'big money' and your response says 'got away with it.' Care to explain that?"

"I've never seen these!" Amber was nearly out of her chair, and Gracie set a gentle hand on her thigh to get her to sit back down. "Show them to me on the phone."

"They're on there," Howard said. There was no trace of warmth in his eyes now. "The phone itself will be brought out at trial. I assure you, these pages are an accurate transcript."

"We'll need copies of these pages," Gracie said, her heart pounding as she tried to maintain a cool air.

Amber was trembling, practically ready to leap across the table and grab the evidence bag. Gracie's grip on her knee tightened.

"Have you questioned the other party, this Cody Brennan?" Gracie asked.

"Not yet."

"Do you plan to?"

"We've been unable to locate Mr. Brennan as yet."

"Our own investigators have learned that his real name is Cody Baker," Gracie told him. "He has a driver's license issued in New Jersey. I can give you the address."

Howard showed marginal interest. "We'll check it out. Obviously, that's quite a ways out of our jurisdiction."

"But since the alleged crime occurred using a cellular connection, it's really in no one's jurisdiction, is it?" Gracie wondered how she'd come up with something so logical sounding while her own nerves were on edge like this.

"Back to my questions," Howard said. "What, exactly, were you referring to in the message about 'getting away with it'?"

"Ms. Zeckis has answered that. She did not send the

message and has never seen it before. And we're done here."

She'd always wanted to say that to someone. She was frankly amazed when Howard handed over the transcript papers and stood up.

"These are a copy," he said.

"Come on, Amber. We're going home."

It took a triple brownie hot fudge sundae with extra nuts at Cold Stone Creamery to calm Amber down enough that Gracie felt at ease leaving her at the condo by herself. She'd seemed in a daze as they left the police station and kept mumbling "how did he do it?" as they drove away in Gracie's van.

Chapter 55

Amber knew she wouldn't sleep tonight. Her stomach was way too full of ice cream, and Detective Howard's revelation still had her mind churning. Gracie had dropped her off, promising that she and her husband would get Amber's car back to the condo. There was no way she wanted Amber driving, as upset as she'd been.

She'd gone through the printed sheets of text messages a dozen times. The frightening thing was that many of the messages were real. She remembered correspondence within the department, and messages from coworkers. Even some of the notes between herself and Cody were real. But the damning ones were those that referred to cash, the ones that made it seem as if she and Cody had plotted something together.

The guy was clever. She had always known it. But to

figure out a way to hack her phone, to plant messages and make them fit—after the fact—the theft of the money from B-G and the cash in her bag coming back from France. He'd made it look as if she'd texted him from the airport after she'd cleared security in Paris, knowing there was illicit cash in her bag.

How? How had he done it? The question ricocheted through her head constantly.

She paced her condo restlessly, closing the drapes at dark, feeling like a caged animal. Her thoughts wouldn't leave her alone.

Okay, she finally decided. *How do I solve things? I go online. I look it up.*

It was after ten p.m. when she settled at her desk. The texts were on her company phone. There had to be some way he'd hacked it. She sat in front of the borrowed computer from Sandy and began searching. Once again, the computer nerds in that same online forum provided an avenue to try.

Little miss badkitty asked how a person might plant texts on someone else's phone. She took a little razzing about what her love life must be and a few suggestions that she was trying to take out a competitive lover, but she went along with it lightheartedly.

Hahaha. Yeah. So what would you guys do?

She actually received some good suggestions, but they all involved getting into the account for the phone, and that was Blackwell-Gorse.

"Okay. Let's just give this a try."

The houseplant didn't respond.

Of course her old password and employee credentials were no longer valid. That came as no surprise. She tinkered with a few of the options the forum nerds had provided, hoping like crazy that B-G had not updated its security systems. She finally hit upon the one that got her into their system. From what she knew when she worked there, even though data itself was encrypted, there were no overall sweeps that would detect someone signing in through this one particular channel.

She had two goals. First was to figure out how Cody had framed her. If he could plant fake messages on her phone, could she figure out a way to make them disappear? Secondly, she needed to find out exactly how much money had been taken. That was more of a curiosity at this point. If her case ever went to court, it would surely be a highlight. But, if the thing she had in mind proved to be true, and if she found a way … the dollar amount would be important.

It took more than two hours of running into dead ends before she admitted that she couldn't figure out how to get into anyone's company cell phone, including her own. That appeared to be a function of the cellular provider, and that was a subject she would work out later.

Internal company memos seemed a promising way to find out more about the missing money. She located the account of the corporate comptroller and began reading emails that had gone out during the weeks leading up to her arrest. She'd just found the thread when the computer sent out a *ding*.

Hmm. It wasn't the signal for incoming email—she'd never configured this machine with an account. She toggled away from the browser tab she'd been working on and looked to see what the new message might be.

The facial recognition software had picked up something.

Hm, puzzling. Amber didn't remember having left the program running. She didn't remember shutting it down either, so she clicked the icon to bring it up to full-screen size.

There was a photo of Cody Brennan. Side by side were one of the pictures she had loaded from her phone, and the match found by the software was an employee badge.

Cody Brennan was an employee of Blackwell-Gorse Tech.

Holy crap!

Chapter 56

Like an avalanche reaching the bottom of the mountain, everything fell into place. Chaotic, destructive, yes. But so many things now made sense. Amber slapped the surface of her desk so hard the houseplant flinched.

She raked her fingers through her hair, unable to take her eyes off the screen. What the hell, what on earth, *what the f—* was happening? She turned away for a moment and then looked back. It was real, all right. He'd been working in the Phoenix office, right in her same building. Her leg began twitching.

She stood up and paced to the kitchen, staring around. She strode the length of the living room, back to the hallway to her bedroom, making a circle of her home. Had he been watching her all along? Targeted her specifically? How long had this been going on? She trotted back to her desk and took a closer look at the badge. His date of employment began four months ago.

When had she first heard of Cody Brennan? Three or four months ago.

Had he moved here from the east coast specifically to spy on her? A creepy feeling washed over her. How much watching had he done? Could he have even come to her condo and placed bugs or cameras?

Paranoia was quickly followed by anger.

"If you're listening in, Cody, I have one thing to say: Watch out!"

She reined herself in. Wait a minute. This isn't how Pen would handle it, not the way any of the Heist Ladies would. They would play it smart, set a trap, gather their evidence, and then get angry. No, not get angry—get even.

The boiling anger inside her settled into something else. Cold, hard determination.

"You don't mess with my heart, and you don't mess with my livelihood, you rotten little creep."

Except he hadn't been a creep—he'd been handsome and romantic and *so* gentlemanly. The perfect con man.

The walks, the dinners, the kisses under the linden trees, the single pink roses—it was all nothing more than a means to a goal. She felt tears prickle her eyes, but she blinked them back. She had to keep her wits about her. This was war.

She picked up her phone to call the Ladies. It was 1:56 a.m. She couldn't wake everyone now. It wouldn't be nice. But she could work out a plan and call them together later in the morning. For now, she needed to delve deeply into the code behind the company screens and figure out exactly how Cody had pulled off the scam.

From the facial recognition program, she printed

the page with the two images of him. She would begin gathering every scrap of evidence she could put together for the police. But she had no intention of turning it over to Detective Howard just yet.

First, she had a score to settle.

Chapter 57

Cody woke up in a cold sweat. At first he couldn't figure out if the landlady had left the thermostat set too hot or too cold. He kicked off the covers. His skin felt clammy.

He'd been dreaming, and this one was real, exactly what had happened seven months ago. He'd been back in Jersey, where it was bitter cold. An ordinary day in late winter, one of those where everyone was ready for spring but yet another cold front was pushing through. A buddy from school called, suggesting Cody come out to Arizona for spring break. Except he wasn't still in school, and there was no such thing as spring break when you worked at Omni.

"Hey, man, the winters here are nothing. Some rain for a couple weeks … you might put on a sweatshirt once in a while. It's gorgeous here right now and I'm sitting by the pool in shorts. Dump that gig and come on out here."

At that moment the power went off. It stayed off for two days, as the whole Eastern seaboard was shut down by an ice storm. Three days later, once planes began flying again, Cody was on a flight westbound.

He smiled now at the memory, but there was something more. He couldn't remember the ending of the dream, but it felt ominous, like a warning of some kind. And then he knew. Amber had figured out his lies and knew he was now in Arizona. He knew it when something in her expression abruptly changed during their video chat. He reached down and pulled the blankets back over his body, suddenly unable to stop shaking.

Chapter 58

"I want to catch him and I want to wring his neck," Amber said through gritted teeth.

Gracie was the first of her friends she'd been able to raise this morning. Once her two kids were off to school, Gracie suggested, they should meet for breakfast at their favorite place. It was the two of them now at Brennan's where the eggs Benedict were heavenly.

Pen had said she could join them later. She was on an early call with her editor in New York. It was Mary's turn to take the opening shift at the gym, and Sandy had management people in from her bank's home office. They had all requested updates from Amber as soon as possible.

"But before I kill the slimy worm, I need to clear my name."

"We need to figure out the best way to do that," Gracie

said, stabbing a fresh strawberry that had come with her meal. "And just to be clear, you don't actually get to kill him."

"I know. Dammit."

"Trust me, you don't want to. There's always way more blood than you expect, and then there's the life sentence in prison. If you thought embezzlement was serious ..."

Amber actually chuckled, which drew a stare from a severe looking woman at the next table.

Gracie lowered her voice. "But secretly, I agree."

Amber cut into her eggs and ate a generous forkful.

"So, how do you propose to clear your name?"

"I say we steal the money back. Remember how we did with Pen's stolen necklace? Well, we just figure out how to gather up all the missing money."

"And then what?"

"I'm not sure. Haven't got that far with the plan yet."

"You do remember what Pen and Sandy told us, that Cody redistributed the funds to a bunch of different accounts. It doesn't sound like it'll be easy."

"Nothing worth doing ever is."

"And we can't forget, if we use Pen or Sandy in parts of the action, Cody most likely will recognize them. They'll have to stay out of sight."

"Right. We can figure out all that."

Pen walked in just then, elegant as always in a lavender shell and slacks with a black blazer and pumps. She kissed Amber on the forehead and took the empty seat across from Gracie. "I understand you had a rough afternoon yesterday," she said.

The server, seeing a newcomer, approached and offered coffee. "Just some tea, please," Pen said.

Amber quickly filled her in with the basics of both the

detective's revelation about the fake text messages and the bombshell identity revelation that had come across her computer late in the night.

"Wow, I must say, it's been eventful."

"And now she's ready for revenge." Gracie glanced toward the neighboring table, but the eavesdropper had left and no one sat there now.

"I think we need to first steal the money back," Amber said. "But we have to do it in a way that pinpoints Cody as the real crook."

Pen nodded and accepted the small teapot their server brought over. "And how do you propose we do that?"

"Do you have a list of the banks where he transferred cash? I think you said a young banker told you something about that?"

"At the Bank of Scotland? Yes, I believe Sandy has that information. Earlier in the chase, in London and Paris, I'm afraid I don't know."

"Didn't you say he withdrew cash from at least one of those?"

Pen nodded. "That's right. He took out cash and then deposited cash in Scotland."

"I wonder if it was all of it?"

Pen shook her head. "No idea. The young woman we spoke to was rather nervous, just sharing the bank names. She gave no details about the money amounts."

Amber focused on her water glass for a minute. "Okay, at least that would be a start. I can try getting into the banking records."

"What can the rest of us do?" Gracie asked.

"Sandy may be able to help with the banking aspects," Pen suggested.

Amber shook her head. "Can't risk her professional

status. We need to move money around without Cody's knowledge, and most likely those accounts are in his name."

"Or the name of that company we discovered, Blandishment Inc."

"Right. I'm thinking it's legally iffy for us to do that."

"You *think*?" Gracie's mouth formed a wry grin.

"Yeah, well, it's something we don't want Sandy involved with. She could lose her whole career over it."

"Whereas ..."

"Whereas, I have nothing more to lose." Amber said it nonchalantly, but the others knew she was deeply upset over the whole mess.

"All right. Moving the money will be a top priority," Pen said. "And Amber, you will handle the details. Equally important, to my thinking, is that we need to find out where Cody actually is."

Gracie brightened. "Exactly. Once everything is in place, if the police won't chase him down, we will."

"Mary will. She's already promised to kick him into the next universe." Amber filched a strawberry and gave an evil grin as she bit into it.

Chapter 59

The first thing Amber wanted to know was whether Cody was still employed at B-G and whether he'd reported back to work after his recent jaunt to Europe. She accomplished that with Sandy's help, again saying her bank was considering Mr. Baker for a loan and needed to verify his employment.

"Strange answer," Sandy reported after making the call. "They said 'technically.'"

"He's *technically* employed there?"

"When I asked the woman to clarify, she simply said yes, he is."

"So, as a banker wondering if the man has a job, how would you decide his loan application?"

"I'd turn him down. The job does not sound like a certainty."

Amber chafed. "I wish I still had access to the building.

I'd scour that office, floor by floor, and see whether he's at a desk."

"Well, that sounds like a whole lot of work. How about just hanging within sight of the entrance at quitting time?"

"That's easier. Good idea."

And so Amber found herself at the little spot across the street from the B-G building, where she used to pop out for a latte when she simply needed to get out of the office. She'd pulled her hair up under a floppy hat and traded her chic rectangular sunglasses for a pair with large round lenses. Now she sat at a table that faced the windows, without being right up against them. She could see the big glass doors that led into the lobby, but it was impossible to monitor the entrance and the parking garage at the same time. If he parked and drove out the west exit, she'd have no way of knowing.

On the other hand, if he'd actually ripped off the company for hundreds of thousands and managed it so Amber took the blame, why would he still be working here? Maybe that's what the HR department had meant by 'technically.' He was on the payroll but not showing up any more.

She avidly scanned the faces coming out the door. The bus stop was a half block up the street, and that's where many of the employees headed. There was a massive push between 4:00 and 4:10. Once the bus glided away, no one wanted to stand around until the 4:45 bus arrived, and Amber found herself staring at the normal street traffic.

It was a good time to check out the traffic from the parking garage, so she picked up her phone and the paper cup of latte and strolled out. At the end of the block, she took up a post leaning against a building diagonally from the corner where the garage ramp discharged its cars.

Right away it became apparent she couldn't see faces very well behind the tinted glass most Arizonans used on their windows. And she had no idea what type of car Cody would be driving. He'd never mentioned one. She tried snapping discreet photos of a few cars that emerged, but that proved a waste of time. Between the distance and the glare on dark glass she couldn't make out the features of anyone in the vehicles.

"Okay," she said out loud, releasing a breath. "What am I really doing here?"

A passing man in a business suit turned to look at her, and a homeless guy who'd been shuffling up the block stepped up his pace. Amber turned in the opposite direction and crossed the street. She could accomplish more with an afternoon online.

She got in her car. With plenty of time to think, considering the crawl of rush hour traffic leading away from downtown, she brainstormed ideas.

Yes, it would be good to catch Cody in person. She had no faith that the cops would follow through, even if she did supply his name. Detective Howard had certainly been noncommittal about tracking him. But ... wasn't it more important to get the money back first? If Cody caught on that they were after him, he'd figure out a way to move the money yet again. And it was already a known fact that he wasn't above cashing out and filling a suitcase with the green stuff.

So, she would make the money her top priority. Cody would come later, when she handed him a big dish of revenge, served cold.

Her mind began to formulate a plan and her fingers itched to get to the keyboard.

Chapter 60

Cody hopped the bus and rode downtown, more out of habit and wanting to get away from the four walls of his bedroom, where the theme music and wildly excited shouts of game shows were a constant background. Since their Facetime chat he'd been thinking about Amber, trying to figure out why she'd suddenly gone cold and abruptly ended the call.

Last night's dream and the chill he'd felt—was that connected somehow? He realized his upbringing hadn't exactly prepared him for the deeper questions of life. If you couldn't make money from it, Pop wasn't interested. If you couldn't program a computer code to make it happen, Cody hadn't a clue.

Somehow, his move to Phoenix had been a turning point, and from the moment he'd spotted Amber and learned where she worked, fate had been set in motion. He leaned against the bus window and the rocking motion sent him thinking back to his arrival here.

His buddy was a student at ASU and had probably assumed Cody would enroll and they'd hang out together, drinking beer and consuming pizza instead of studying. But Cody and Josh were on different wavelengths. After a few afternoons of scoping out the girls on campus and looking through his friend's Snapchat connections, Cody was bored.

Even though he'd never earned a fancy degree, from the moment he talked Ma into getting him a used MacBook when he was twelve, he wanted to know how it worked. Ma. She held out hope that her influence—get a good education, get a good job, be an upstanding citizen—would outweigh Woody Baker's constant preaching about finding the easy way out, latching onto people you could use to get what you wanted. Find those rich cats with money and take 'em for all you could.

Cody borrowed library books, found used college textbooks online when he could, and taught himself the ins and outs of programming. When his school friends were all gaga over homecoming or prom or making first string on the team, he was already writing sophisticated programs. Well before they graduated high school, he'd found his first job, a company filled with the super-bright techies. He copied everything he could learn from them. He used Omni to create his online presence, and that credential to get him in at Blackwell-Gorse.

Pop had nearly exploded. He'd done his level best to teach Cody the tricks of all the con games he knew; achieving those things with the use of computers was beyond him. But Cody was still his father's son, and he saw the potential. And when he saw Amber Zeckis in the lobby of B-G on his first day at work there, the plan was sealed. He had the means to tap the huge resources of a major tech giant, and he had the innocent looking girl who would steer all suspicion away from himself.

He used his Cody Brennan online presence and proceeded to woo Miss Amber into doing what he wanted. Soon, he and Pop would be wealthy.

He just hadn't counted on actually starting to fall for Amber.

The bus came to a stop in front of the B-G building. With eyes open for every detail, Cody stepped down and entered the lobby, scanning his employee badge at the security point before pressing the elevator button for the 14th floor.

Two weeks ago, he'd bailed, with attitude, and now he wondered. Would he have a job here still? How much more could he skim off before they wised up? Or should he just erase his tracks and get out while suspicion was still directed at Amber?

Chapter 61

Amber knew it needed to happen all at once, the money movement. If Cody spotted cash disappearing out of his accounts, she knew he could most likely stop her. His programming abilities were amazing. She didn't dare try to outrun him in that way. It was going to take all her skills to set this up perfectly.

She was staring at the screen of the borrowed computer, which now had the external hard drive attached with all the Blackwell-Gorse info she had copied from her company machine. Using his employee ID, she found the maneuvers he'd used to move B-G money into the various foreign accounts. The Ladies knew about those already. But then he had taken cash out and redeposited it elsewhere. The whole thing was either a masterful genius plan or a convoluted mess.

Pen and Sandy had brought back valuable information when they learned from the Scottish banker that Cody had sent the money off to other accounts. Amber had spent the evening devising untraceable searches for his various names and the name of his shell corporation. But now that she was actually ready to press the keys and start the money moving around, she was having second thoughts. There was no room for error here.

She called Sandy, posing some theoretical what-ifs. As a banker, what red flags might come up? What would catch their attention and prevent the transfers from going through?

"The biggest thing you're going to run into is the waiting time. You know, the few days between the funds moving and when the customer has access to them. If Cody notices something wrong, or if the banks themselves become suspicious of the transactions, they could put a hold on it and stop the whole thing."

"That's not good."

"No, it's not. Can you think of a way to keep Cody from monitoring his accounts for two or three days?"

She could think of one way. But knowing what she knew now, there was no way another languid week in Paris would happen. She'd be forced to murder him in his sleep. Which, of course, was another way to keep him from checking on his accounts ...

"I'm pretty sure he's here in the Phoenix area somewhere," Amber said.

"Right. Gracie mentioned what you said about your Facetime visit. So, let's think about this. How can we get him away from his phone and all computers?"

Amber nearly laughed. "Getting a guy like Cody off all electronics isn't going to be easy."

"Let me send a text out to the Ladies and we'll come up with ideas. Maybe we can all get together tomorrow sometime?"

Amber felt a stab of impatience, but this was not the time to rush. She knew this. She took a deep breath and told Sandy to proceed.

Chapter 62

Cody spent the morning tucked into his cubicle, trying to be as inconspicuous as possible, acting as though he'd been in this spot all along, and hoping no one made a big deal of the days he'd missed. Mainly, he needed to create the perception that he was diligent about his work and hadn't a care in the world.

Just because Amber had been arrested on the embezzlement charge didn't mean they weren't still digging around. They might think she had an accomplice, and Cody needed to know if that finger was likely to point toward him.

No matter what his father said about finding a mark, using her, and then disappearing, Cody knew Amber was brilliant when it came to programming. Even if the company didn't yet know he was behind the disappearance of the money, Amber might have figured it out. And she could have talked her little head off to the cops. He needed to be on the inside at B-G to get an idea what was going on.

Meanwhile, he'd received another not-entirely-welcome call early this morning. Woody was on his way out for another visit. Pop had his eye on a racetrack in the northern part of the city. Apparently the old man couldn't keep his money in his pocket. He talked like he could just stay with Cody and they'd spend their days at the races. He obviously still had no concept how large and spread out this metro area was, nor did he realize Cody didn't have a car. The bus lines and light rail were good, but they were limited in how well you could get around.

With his programming module open on one screen, Cody flipped over to another to check out hotels near the racetrack. If he could put Woody up there, that would solve a big problem with how he would entertain the old man. Since it looked like the visit would last a week or more, he reserved a rental car at the Alamo desk at the airport.

"Hey, dude." The voice startled him and he looked up to see Josh, the other intern on the job. "Where were you last week?"

"Why? Were they asking?"

"Well, *yeah*. Bob was about to split a gut. I told him what you said, family emergency. Everyone okay?"

"Yeah, it's all fine, but my dad's coming out here. I need him where I can keep an eye on his situation. He's getting older, you know."

Josh launched into something about his own grandmother and how she was having some dementia issues these days. Cody just nodded, letting him believe Pop's case was similar. He picked up enough facts about the condition he could spout them back at Bob if the supervisor came around asking.

That didn't happen for nearly an hour, but soon Bob was standing there at Cody's cube, wanting an explanation. Cody put on a serious expression and gave a bunch of useless details he'd created on the spot to explain how much attention his father needed these days.

"That may be," Bob said, "and I'm sorry to hear it, but interns don't just have carte blanche around here. If you can't be on the job consistently, we'll need to get someone else."

Cody thought of all the money he'd set up for himself and Pop. What did he need with this job anyway?

"Fine by me," he said. He erased his recent searches, shut down his terminal, and picked up his backpack. "Have a nice life, Bob."

The supervisor sputtered a little, clearly thinking Cody would toe the line or at least give a week's notice. But Cody walked right past him and got into the elevator. As the doors whooshed shut, he overheard Josh make some kind of comment to Bob, along the lines of, *so now I'm supposed to take on all his work too?*

He chuckled as he exited the building. Bob hadn't even thought to demand his employee badge back. Not that Cody had any intention of using it and creating a trail they could follow. The fact that security hadn't stopped him boosted his mood—clearly, they weren't at all suspicious.

Chapter 63

Amber almost decided she could get used to being unemployed. The days felt amazingly long and free of commitment when she wasn't having to jam in a personal life around a ten-hour-plus workday. But she also knew her mortgage payment would come due next week and a month after that, and a month after that. She'd saved some, but not enough to live on forever. And there was no way she would go to her parents for money. Having the job at B-G had been a huge source of pride, being completely independent for the first time since her college days, and she didn't want to let go of that.

Pen had suggested they all meet at ten o'clock at her house where they could talk privately. Sandy made up a client meeting to explain her absence from the bank; Gracie was nearly always free at that time of day; Mary said she'd handed off her spinning class to another instructor, a guy who frequented the gym often, one whose name seemed to make Mary blush. The Heist Ladies were ready to plan their next actions.

Amber drove the short distance to Pen's, amazed that the city streets weren't *always* jammed with bumper-to-bumper traffic. Yes, there were definite benefits to being unemployed.

The other vehicles were already there, arrayed around the circular drive near Pen's front door. Amber pulled her Prius in behind Gracie's minivan and walked up; Sandy opened the door before she had a chance to reach for the bell.

"Saw you coming," Sandy said. "Come in. There are some wonderful smells coming from the kitchen."

"The frittata is a recipe I picked up from an author friend," Pen said, pulling a fragrant pan from the oven. "I'm testing it on you before I make it for Benton next week. The muffins came from Mimi's."

Gracie gave a swooning expression at that news. They followed Pen's invitation and took seats in the dining room.

"We can talk while we eat. I know most of you have commitments." Pen sliced the frittata and carried the hot pan to a trivet she'd set in the middle of the table. "Amber, perhaps you should lead off with the question you wanted to pose to all of us."

Taking a swig of her cranberry juice, Amber looked around the table at her friends. "Sandy and I have discussed this a little. I am all set to move the money away from Cody's accounts. The problem now is that he'll see pending transactions if he checks them, and it's possible he could notify the various banks that he didn't make those transfers and could get them stopped before they go through. Sandy says it can take two or three days for it to happen."

"And we need a way to keep him from checking during that time," Mary said.

"Exactly. You get the picture. Cody is a guy who *lives* on his phone, and checking his bank balances with apps is super easy for him."

"We need to get his phone away from him," Pen suggested.

"How?" Gracie asked. "If he's anything like my kids, he knows where that thing is all the time."

"It'll be a challenge."

"One of us could go to his house, wait until he's in the shower, and grab it off the dresser or something," Mary said.

"We don't know where he lives," Sandy said. "I did a little searching and can't find an address for him here in the metro area. His address of record, both at his employer and on his driver's license, is still the one in New Jersey, which we believe is his father's residence."

"So we go there?" Gracie looked eager as she said it.

"You just want an excuse to travel somewhere," Sandy said with a laugh. "Sorry, but he obviously can't be living there while working here. He's got to have somewhere local to stay."

"Maybe I can find out who he hangs out with at work, see if he has mentioned where he lives," Amber suggested. "I know a lot of the after-work hangouts downtown."

"Yeah, but won't you be taking a chance on him knowing you're asking questions?" Mary asked.

"Well … he's been hinting that we see each other. I could meet with him and come right out and ask."

"Or meet with him and just steal the phone right then. It doesn't matter whether we get into his house, if that happens."

"So, trailing Cody and getting his phone away from him is the first priority," Pen said. "Then we must address the issue of his simply walking into the nearest phone store and buying another."

"You're right. We can't let that happen," Amber said. "These new phones store everything in the cloud, so if he can get a new phone and log in with his user credentials he'll be back online with all of his apps, in less than an hour. We need several days."

Gracie peeled the wrapper off a blueberry muffin, giving it an appraising look. "Back to square one—how do we get anywhere close to him?"

"I guess that's up to me," Amber said. "I have his phone number and he wouldn't be surprised to get a call or text from me. Shall I give it a try?"

"Give his number to the rest of us, as a start," Sandy suggested. "That way, we can implement plans, and he won't recognize any of our other numbers."

In less time than it took anyone to pull out her own phone, Amber had gone into her contacts and shared the number with all of them.

"Looks like you're up, girl," Mary said.

Amber took a deep breath and called Cody's number, expecting to leave a voice mail. He came on right away.

"Hey, I've been thinking about you," he said, his voice seeming wistful.

"Yeah, me too. Cody, I know you're here in Phoenix."

An uneasy pause.

"It's okay. Actually, I'm happy about it. And I was thinking ... want to get together after work this afternoon?"

"I can do better than that. My boss gave me the day off and I'm downtown anyway. How about lunch? Thirty minutes?"

Amber looked at her empty plate and her full stomach groaned, but there was no time like the present. "Sure. Name the place."

The call ended and she looked around at the rest of the Ladies. "Well, a girl's gotta do what a girl's gotta do."

Chapter 64

She ordered the smallest salad on the menu and still could barely look at it, her stomach was so full. But one thing about salad, you can push it around the plate a lot and somewhat make it look like it's disappearing.

Cody was already at the table when she walked into the place, and he ordered a burrito that looked like it could choke a horse. He dug into it and didn't seem to notice Amber was barely eating.

"So that's cool, that your boss gave you the day off." She watched his expression for any sign that he knew she had been working all these months in the same building, not two blocks from here.

"Yeah, we're pretty much caught up right now, so it was no problem." Expression as bland as they come.

She wanted to kick him under the table, but refrained.

"So, big plans for your afternoon?"

"What did you have in mind? Maybe I come to your place?" He sent the gorgeous smile toward her.

Uh, that would be a big *no*. But she smiled back. "Afraid I can't. Some of us have to work."

"Oh, I thought you said you were taking some time—" He nearly stuttered. "—but I guess that was last week."

She glanced down at his phone, sitting next to his water glass. He had set it down the moment she joined him, and hadn't touched it since. But there was no way she could reach across the table and pick it up. What could she use as a distraction? She signaled the waitress for more water, but realized as long as Cody sat in that chair he would know the moment his phone moved a centimeter.

"My dad's coming for a visit," he told her. "So I'm thinking I might take the rest of the week, spend a little time with him. He's only been out here once and we didn't really get time to explore the city at all."

"Oh? What does he want to do? There are all the museums and the zoo is really cool."

A flicker across Cody's face told her those were not his father's cup of tea.

"A hike in the Superstitions is great this time of year." No reaction.

"He's really more into ... Well, he loves to gamble."

"Oh, one of the Indian casinos then. Sure, those can be fun." Personally, Amber would rather stab her eyeball out than spend hours in a smoky, noisy place like that, but the full parking lots at the casinos attested that plenty of others felt differently.

"He likes the ponies. Dog races, too, but I guess those are getting less popular. I don't know if they even have them here now." He set his napkin down. "I gotta run to the—" a nod toward the restrooms at the back "—don't let them take my plate. I might finish my burrito."

Finally, a chance. But he automatically picked up his phone and stuck it into his pocket when he stood up.

Rats!

He was back in three minutes. "Got a text from Pop. His flight just landed, so I need to get going."

"Oh sure, not a problem. I guess you'll be driving him to his hotel, or is he staying at your place?"

"Hotel. And a rental car. That's another thing I gotta help him with." Cody put enough cash on the table to cover both their meals. "Sorry to skip out like this. I didn't realize how late it was getting."

"Well, I hope I get to meet your dad. What's his name?"

"Woody. He'd get a kick out of you." His eyes darted to the right. "But we'll have to see. It's looking like we'll be pretty busy."

He still had a grip on his phone, and Amber felt discouraged that her mission had failed. However, even though she didn't have the phone in hand and had no idea how she could keep Cody from noticing the money movement, she'd gained some valuable intel. The moment he was out of the restaurant, she followed.

A half-block away she saw him get on a city bus. The lit banner above the back window said AIRPORT.

It seemed *possible* he'd been truthful about one thing.

She rushed to where she'd parked her car, sat inside, and called Pen.

"We have to figure out where the horse races take place," she said. "Also, the car rental agencies at the airport—is there any way we can learn what make and model car is being rented by Cody Brennan, Cody Baker, or Woody Baker. I'm assuming that last—he just told me his dad's first name."

"It sounds like a nickname," Pen said, "but I have an idea about that. Are you planning to follow him?"

"I'll try. You know how the traffic is around the airport."

It wasn't hard to follow the bus. Amber trailed the lumbering vehicle, fairly confident Cody had no idea she was behind him. The problem came once she reached the airport where she didn't get a clear view of the passengers who disembarked, and the busy curbside was carefully monitored by security for anyone who didn't seem like they were there to pick up someone. There was no way they were going to let her leave her vehicle to pop inside and get an idea where Cody went. And driving out to the parking lots was out of the question—she would lose him for sure.

The constantly moving stream of traffic gave her no chance to make a decision. She spotted the sign for the cellphone waiting area and made a dangerous move across two lanes to get there. It was as close as she could come to waiting around anywhere near the terminal.

Ten painfully slow minutes dragged by. Fifteen.

Amber practically jumped out of her seat when her phone rang.

"The rental car is coming from Alamo," Pen said. "Apparently he has just now completed the paperwork. Cody rented it in his name, using his New Jersey driver's license. A shuttle will take them to the lot to pick up the car. It's a Ford Taurus, but the woman didn't say what color."

Amber had no clue where on the vast airport complex the rental car lots were located.

"Of more use to you," Pen was saying, "is that they gave the Skyliner Motel in Deer Valley as their address while in the city."

"I'll find it. I can probably beat them there if I leave right now," Amber said. "Thanks, Pen, you're the best."

She ended the call and flipped over to the maps app, finding the address and directions to the motel without any problem. It looked like a slightly fancier version of a Super 8. Why wouldn't a guy who'd just come into a half million dollars pick a more upscale place?

When she zoomed the map out to a wider view she figured it out. The Skyliner was only a mile or so from the racetrack.

Chapter 65

"What time do the races start?" Woody asked, before they'd even cleared the airport property.

"I don't know, Pop. Let me get my bearings here, okay?" Cody frantically scanned the dozens of signs all around them as he steered the unfamiliar car off the lot.

Damn. He should have gotten a car while he lived here, should have driven around more in the city instead of using the convenience of Uber and the city buses. The tangle of overpasses and freeway entrances was mind boggling. All he knew was that he needed to get to I-17 northbound, and the stupid rental didn't have a GPS.

He finally found a spot where he could pull over, so he picked up his phone and studied the map. Clearly he was going about this all wrong. *Who the hell puts a major airport smack in the middle of a huge city and surrounds it with a bazillion freeways?* He activated the voice directions and let the phone tell him the turns to make.

An hour later, in a foul mood, he spotted the motel ahead. *Finally!* He whipped into the lot. The tires chirped a little when he stopped in front of the small office.

"I'll be right back," he told his dad.

Inside, the girl behind the desk asked how many keys he wanted. Until this moment, he'd thought he would let Pop have the motel and he would go back to his own room whenever they weren't together. But this city traffic was crap, and he wasn't about to drive back and forth in it, just to shuttle his father around.

"Two keys. Thanks."

She was cute and looked a little like Amber, with dark skin and curly hair. But he could already tell she didn't have Amber's smarts or that sparkle in her eye. And what would be the point? There was no money potential in this one. Pop always said you choose your marks for one reason— profit—not for their looks.

The girl handed over the keys and explained where the breakfast room was. She flashed him a smile as she handed back Pop's credit card. "I see you'll be with us for five days? I'm off tomorrow but I'll be back the day after. In case you need anything."

Cody merely smiled.

He drove past a fenced swimming pool and pulled the Taurus to a stop in front of room 16. Right now, mid-afternoon there were only three other cars in the lot. The place felt like one-night stays. Just off the interstate, it was the kind of place tired travelers would pull off at dark and leave in the early morning. The landscaping had a dry, untended feel, and the pool didn't seem very inviting. But those weren't the amenities his father wanted anyway.

They got out and he pulled Pop's large suitcase and his own backpack from the trunk.

Five days. It was easy to see what Pop would do to stay busy, but Cody wondered how he would spend his time. No job to report to, no travel on the calendar, no plans with Amber. And he'd just now realized he had left his laptop in his room at TV-lady's house. Well, he could drop Pop off at the racetrack later and then he'd drive out to Mesa to get it.

Or not. The thought of getting back out in the traffic held no appeal at all. Maybe tomorrow. He had a clean shirt with him and his basic shaving gear. He could delay having to make the drive.

"So, you think there's any action at the track right now?" Pop asked, the moment he'd dropped his suitcase on the bed.

Seriously? Cody sighed. "I suppose we'd better check it out."

Chapter 66

Amber zoomed her phone camera toward the Taurus and snapped several quick shots of Cody and his father. The older man was a skinnier, slighter version of his son with thick gray hair. The thought flashed through her mind that Cody seemed safe from inheriting male pattern baldness. Forget it. Not important, she told herself.

She slid farther down in her seat to look at the photos. She'd only caught Cody in profile, but there was a good face image of his dad while he stood at the door to their room, waiting for Cody to insert the keycard into the lock. She noted other details. A suitcase for the father, only his normal backpack for Cody. Was he planning to stay, or would he leave his father there and go to his own place?

Quickly, she selected the best three pictures and forwarded them to all the Ladies, along with the name and address of the motel. Now, any of them could take over the mission. She debated going back to her condo, but she still needed to know that Cody couldn't check his bank accounts before she initiated the money movement.

Patience, she coached herself.

Five minutes after they walked into the motel room, Cody and his father emerged. Amber slid even farther down, completely out of sight, until she heard their car start. A peek told her they were backing out, and she quickly started the quiet Prius. When they made a right turn onto Bell Road, she followed.

Bell, one of the busier main arteries through this part of the city, was an easy place for her to remain off their radar. They passed some car dealerships and a Walmart, and then turned right. She saw a sign for Turf Paradise with a running horse on the logo; she knew exactly where they were going. She followed them into the parking lot, staying well behind until Cody pulled the Taurus into a spot near the entrance.

She cruised down a parallel row of parking spaces and watched the two men walk up to the entrance and enter the tan stucco building with its long row of tall windows. There was a lot of open space surrounding the grounds and track, with nice views of the mountains in the distance. It seemed like the type of place that probably once sat out in the middle of nowhere for a long time before the city grew up around it. She pulled into a parking slot at the east end of the lot.

What now? She pulled up the racetrack's website. The peak times of day were from noon to about six p.m. so they were nearing the end of the racing day now. Amber had no idea how these things worked, but it might be fair to assume the men were here to check out the facility, maybe take a look at tomorrow's lineup. A diehard race fan, as Cody described his dad, wouldn't be content to travel all this way just to watch for an hour or so.

She phoned Mary to run her theory by.

"That's what I would think," Mary told her. "I'd bet they'll be back tomorrow. And hey, since we need someone neither man has ever seen, I could do it. I'm not a gambler, but it's fun to watch the horses and see how wound up people get over their bets."

"The mission is still for us to get Cody's phone away from him," Amber said, admitting she'd failed to do that at lunch.

"Got it. I'll figure out something."

"Thanks, Mary."

Amber ended the call and sat there, staring toward the racetrack entrance, when she remembered the other task she needed to accomplish. Mary would figure out a way to get Cody's cell phone, but his laptop was still out there somewhere. She thought back to their lunch together and tried to remember whether he'd handled the backpack as if it was heavy enough to contain his computer. She couldn't say for sure. Laptops were pretty lightweight these days.

She drummed her fingers on the steering wheel and thought about it. No time like the present, she decided. Surely the men would stay put for at least an hour. She started her car and sped out of the lot. Despite the fairly heavy late afternoon traffic, she was back at the Skyliner Motel within fifteen minutes. She parked out of sight of the office and walked back to it.

"Hi," she said to the girl behind the desk, putting on her brightest smile. "My brother and our dad checked in here awhile ago, and Cody was supposed to get me a key to the room. I thought they'd still be here but I guess they went out. I hope to bring us all back some dinner. Anyway, it's room 16. Can you make me another card real quick?"

"Um, I'm not sure ... I may need to check with the manager."

Another guest had walked in behind Amber, a large man who made an impatient sound. "Hey, would you at least get me and my wife checked in first?"

"Excuse me, but I was here first," Amber said. "It's a simple enough request."

The girl seemed torn between not following protocol or having the rude man cause a scene. Her hands dithered over her keyboard.

"*Now*," the man said. "We've had a long day and just want to get to our room."

Amber sent a pleading look toward the girl and mouthed, *Sorry*.

One minute later she held a plastic key card in her hand. One minute after that she was at the door of room 16, slipping inside.

Obviously, the men had done nothing in the way of settling in. The big suitcase she'd seen earlier sat in the middle of one bed. Cody's backpack was on the other. She unzipped it and rummaged. No laptop.

Rats!

He'd obviously planned on spending the night, however, since there was a change of clothing and a shaving kit in the pack. That was good to know. She looked for anything else that could be of use. No papers of any kind. What had she expected, a rent receipt with his home address all written out? No cell phone, which made perfect sense. He carried it everywhere, and what would a guy like Cody want with a spare?

A glance at the clock told her the races were ending

about now. She could only hope the men had stayed to the end.

The suitcase … would Cody have entrusted his father with anything of value to her mission?

She took a moment to open the bag and look through it. There was a checkbook for the First State Bank of New Jersey—she already knew about that account, but she carefully peeled out one of the deposit slips and tucked it into her jeans pocket.

Otherwise, the suitcase only seemed to contain the things an older man would bring on a trip. Enough clothes to last a week, a shaving kit with a couple of prescription pill bottles inside, two magazines—*Playboy* and *Racing Weekly*— not subscriptions, so they'd probably been purchased at the airport.

Amber tried to leave the bag as undisturbed as possible. Something told her Woody would be the kind of man who would know if his stuff had been tampered with. On the other hand, the TSA could always take the blame. She had to get out of here.

She scanned the parking lot through a slice of space at the edge of the drapes. No Taurus yet. She slipped out the door, pocketing the spare keycard. No telling when it might come in handy.

She'd made it halfway to her car when the Taurus pulled into the motel driveway. Amber spun toward the closet labeled Ice Machine.

Chapter 67

Cody couldn't help thinking about his laptop. Why hadn't he thought to bring it when he left the house this morning? He knew he'd be stuck with his dad's choice of television for the evening. Sure, he could bring up a movie or some YouTube videos on his phone, but watching the tiny screen would get old.

"Hey, get over here and eat while this is hot," Woody said. He'd carried their take-out Popeye's Chicken dinner to the small table in the room.

Oh well, that's what the visit was all about—spending some quality father/son time together, right? Plus, he loved Pop's choice in food. He'd just polished off his third piece of chicken when an incoming text sounded. He wiped his greasy fingers and pulled the phone from his pocket.

Pop made a *pah* sound and created a lot of noise with

the food wrappers, but Cody read the text anyway.

Amber: Did your dad get here okay?

Cody: Yeah he's got me held captive in some motel out near Deer Valley.

Amber: At least you're having fun. Nice that you got so much time off work.

Cody: Yeah, well....

Amber: What?

Cody: Didn't want to tell you, I quit that gig. May move on to something else.

Amber: Really?

There was a pause of three or four minutes, during which he tried to imagine what was going through her head. How much of this whole scam had she figured out?

Amber: Sounds like big news. Eager to hear your plans.

Cody released his pent-up breath. Sure. Later.

Amber: Gotta go. Hi to your dad.

He sent her a heart, then wondered if that was the right thing to do. Pop would say no. In fact, Pop would be furious if he knew how Cody was feeling about Amber. He'd already gotten that lecture, so he told Woody this was a girl he'd met in a bar. And he didn't share anything about the messages.

He didn't have to say much of anything. The TV began blaring an old western, punctuated with wild bursts of drumbeats at the dangerous plot moments. Cody propped pillows against the headboard of his bed and stretched his legs out before he noticed he was taking up exactly the same position as his father. He shook his head. Ma had probably been right—the two Baker men were too much alike.

He thought ahead to the day tomorrow. If they got out of the motel a little after the rush hour traffic, they could make good time out to Mesa and he could pick up his laptop from the landlady's house. Another couple of clean shirts and jeans wouldn't hurt either. Then it would be an afternoon at the races with Pop. Sometimes the betting was kind of fun, and he wouldn't mind a warm day outdoors with nothing to do but put away a few beers.

They ended up sleeping until nine. Cody wasn't complaining. He'd hated the months of getting up practically at dawn to catch the bus downtown. Maybe he would follow his father's example and start to enjoy some of the new money. Pop took the first turn at the shower and by the time Cody finished and dressed, the old man was antsy to get going.

"The racetrack doesn't open until noon. We got plenty of time," Cody told him. "We'll grab some breakfast and do this one errand I've got. We'll get you there."

Or so he thought, until they walked out the door and saw that two of the tires on the rented Taurus were flat. *Well, crap.*

"Grab the jack," Woody said. "We'll just put the spare on."

"And which tire do you propose we leave flat?" Cody already had his phone out. "I'll just call the rental agency and they'll send someone out."

It took another twenty minutes to get the right person on the line, explain the problem, and feel halfway confident that assistance was actually on the way.

"There's a pancake place a few blocks east of here," Cody said. "We can get breakfast there."

"You gotta be here when the repair truck comes, don't you?"

"The lady said it would be forty-five minutes or so. I'll give the cute girl at the desk my number and ask her to call if it shows up."

The cute girl had been replaced this morning by a fat guy with an attitude who didn't seem too inclined to keep an eye out the window.

Cody turned to his dad. "Come on. We gotta eat and they've already cleared away the stuff they had here. So let's go up the road."

Woody shrugged and the two set off walking.

They each wolfed down a plate of pancakes and bacon, then hurried back to the motel. The car still sat there, listing to the starboard side. Woody went into the room and turned on the TV. Cody checked the time, chafing at the waste of a whole hour of their time. They could have driven to Mesa and been halfway back by now.

The truck didn't show for another sixty-seven minutes, and the guy clearly was being paid by the hour as he dawdled along with the exchange of the tires.

"I don't see no damage to these," he told Cody. "Seems like a loose valve stem or something, but the boss says change 'em out. Guess he don't want me having to come back out if they go flat again."

No kidding, Sherlock. At this rate I'll be my dad's age before we start our day.

He signed the work order and watched the truck make a complicated four-point turn and pull away. In the room he found Woody studying the racing form.

"Okay, Pop, all set. We'll go pick up my stuff and then it's off to the track."

"Can't do that."

"What?"

"Didn't you tell me it'd take an hour, maybe two to make that round trip? Well, the track opens in twenty minutes and the first race is the one I gotta get in on."

"You're kidding."

Woody stood straighter and stuffed the racing form into his shirt pocket. "I am not. What's this bug you got, this obsession, with getting some spare clothes and stuff from your room? There's that big Walmart right by the track. Run in there and get you a couple shirts, maybe a pair of jeans ... you're all set."

Cody opened his mouth to protest but the look on his father's face told him this was one battle not worth winning. The man could make your life miserable when he didn't get his way. He let out a sigh and drove to the track.

Chapter 68

Mary sat in her car at Turf Paradise, enjoying the cool breeze that flowed through her open windows, smiling at the satisfying memory of that sound, the hiss of air leaving Cody Baker's tires. Heh-heh. Definitely worth getting up a little early so she could perform her little task in the dark.

She'd hung nearby long enough to see that the men didn't find some alternate transportation to get across town. They'd walked to a restaurant, then back to the motel, and from across the road she'd seen Cody talking to the driver of the repair truck. Another few minutes passed, and she had followed them here. The long brown wig was beginning to itch, but she couldn't take the risk that the men would later remember her short, spiky blonde style.

The parking lot wasn't terribly crowded this early in

the racing day. Spotting Cody's red t-shirt and baggy denim shorts shouldn't be that hard. She locked her car, pocketed her keys and sauntered toward the same entrance where the men had gone, five minutes ago.

Not surprisingly, she immediately spotted Woody at the betting window. He seemed to know exactly what he wanted and the transaction took only a minute. Cody was at a concession stand, apparently deciding noon was the perfect time of day to start with a beer or two.

When the men joined up, Mary noted their direction and followed, picking up a racing form along the way. Woody seemed right at home, and he led the way down the sloping bleachers to the front. The front-row seats right at the finish line were all taken—a fact that the father seemed to be pointing out to his son—but they were able to get on the third row in the same area. Mary slipped on her sunglasses while she made sure they settled down, then she edged her way along the fourth row, which wasn't crowded at all.

The timing was perfect. Horses were lining up at the gate and the smallish crowd seemed excited. She peered over Cody's shoulder and saw his father's racing form, marked up with his choices. He'd circled number 21 in this first race. The horse started slow out of the gate but made its way quickly to the middle of the pack. Rounding the second turn he edged forward into third place, then second.

The crowd was screaming and cheering, everyone on their feet, seemingly yelling for a different horse, but Woody maintained a calm shell. The only sign that he'd put money on this longshot was the tension in his knuckles as he gripped his racing form.

Mary let out a yell, "Come on, twenty-one!"

When the horse edged ahead in the final turn and gathered speed to finish by half a length, the crowd went wild. Mary used the excitement of her supposed win to grip both Cody's and Woody's shoulders. "Woo-hoo! Oh—sorry."

"Nice!" Woody shouted as he gave her a high-five.

She played the next two races the same way, cheering madly for one of the horses, watching the two men, noting their little routine moves. Cody got more in the spirit with each beer he finished. When she decided he was sufficiently relaxed, she made her move and unzipped the front pouch on her waist pack.

Just as the horses were rounding the bend in the fourth race and the crowd was on their feet, she leaned forward and pinched the edge of the cell phone that stuck enticingly out of Cody's pocket. Into the waist pack it went, and Mary was on her way out of the stands by the time the final results were announced. No one noticed as she quickly stepped through the crowd and past the payout windows.

Out in the car, she stuffed the brown wig and sunglasses under the seat, sent a one-word text, and started her engine. Even if Cody realized his phone was missing, there was only a slim chance he would figure out who the woman behind them really was.

Chapter 69

Amber's heart pounded when she read Mary's text. It was time. All she could do was hit the button to start the money transfers she had set up—and then hope and pray all their tactics for keeping Cody offline would work.

She hit the button.

Then she called Sandy. "Did you get all the account information and routing numbers I sent?"

"Yep, exactly what I needed. Don't get your hopes completely set on this, Amber. Internally, I can monitor the cash movement, but I can't promise that I can speed things up for you. But I'll try."

"Anything you can do. Oh—what about that deposit slip I gave you?"

"Woodrow Baker. You said the account belongs to Cody's father?"

"The checkbook was in his suitcase. Cody told me his dad's name was Woody."

"Right. I made an interbank request this morning, for more information on the account holder. Pretended that we're considering Mr. Baker for a loan."

"Is he the one behind their dummy corporation?"

"Probably. Technically, the corporation has the name Woodrow Wilson Baker. Cody's father is Woodrow Harrison Baker. A small difference, but it could be the thing they'll use if they really get in deep trouble. He could pull the old 'that's not me' argument."

"I'll get online and see if I can find more," Amber said. "Maybe there is a Baker, middle name Wilson, somewhere in the picture too."

She opened a new browser window and typed a search, mainly so she wouldn't forget to do it later.

"I'll start some quiet inquiries," Sandy said, "and I'll let you know if I'm able to green-light any of your transfers to make them go faster. But don't count on it."

"I know. We need to plan on this taking a few days. What else can we come up with to stall for time? What if their car exploded?"

"With or without them in it?"

"Either."

"Careful, sweetie, you've already got the police watching you pretty closely."

"I know," she said as Sandy hung up.

But that just made it more of a challenge. Keep Cody away from his phone, while not letting him suspect her involvement, and make every roadblock she could throw in his way look and feel like just a bad twist of fate. Sure—no problem.

All this was running through Amber's head when a

string of search results came up for the name Woodrow
Wilson Baker. A lot of them were about the former
president, with the surname Baker deleted, but she did find
one—at a genealogy site. She went there, created a profile
for a free trial subscription, and began prowling around.

She had just hit upon a promising list of Woodrow
Bakers with different middle initials when Mary called.

"How's it going? Operation Money Move is underway?"

Amber laughed at the not-so-subtle code name. "Yeah.
So far, so good. Sandy is monitoring some of it through
the bank, although she has to be careful since her bank
technically isn't at all connected to it. What about at your
end? Are you still at the track?"

"No, I left. But I got to thinking it might be smart if
we keep watching the two of them. We don't *think* Cody
can get to his laptop quickly, but what if he can? We have
no idea where it is right now."

"True. That's been worrying me."

"So I propose to go back there and spy some more.
Those couple hours at the races were actually kind of fun."

"He'll be suspicious, won't he? What if he puts it
together that the moment his phone disappeared was right
when a certain blonde was sitting behind him?"

"For one thing, she wasn't blonde when she pulled the
dirty deed. And for another, I'm staring in the window of
a wig shop in the mall right down the road. I'm thinking
with different hair, glasses, and clothing styles I could keep
him from spotting me."

"I don't know … con men are pretty good with faces."

"I'll accessorize. Plus, when I go back, I don't need to
sit close at all. I can be twelve rows above them or twenty
seats over. As long as we know they're at the track he can't
be heading off somewhere to get that computer."

"Actually, I like it."

"I'm looking at a gray, feathery style that's very cool. I'm thinking it goes with something from the country-club-chic department at Macy's. And tomorrow I can have long blonde dreadlocks."

"Just don't stand out *too* much. Better to blend in as a housewife from the neighborhood than to let them notice you."

"You take all the fun out of it." But Mary laughed as she hung up.

Chapter 70

Woody went to cash in his winnings on the first six races, happy with his take, although he'd misjudged a couple of them. Well, you can't win them all, he'd said to his son. Cody decided while Pop wasn't looking over his shoulder it would be a good time to check and see if he had any new messages from Amber. He reached for his back pocket and froze.

No phone. He searched his seat, Woody's empty seat, even asked the man on the other side of him to look around his seat. Down on his knees he looked under, around, and at the rows above and below them. The phone was simply gone.

"What are you doing? That concrete is grungy." Woody was standing over him.

"You got my phone? I can't find it anywhere."

"I don't have your phone. Did you check all your pockets? Those shorts got a million of them."

Cody knew without looking—the phone was heavy enough to be noticeable—but he checked anyway.

"Maybe you left it in the car."

Had he? He couldn't specifically remember looking at it since they'd arrived at the track. But when he returned from the parking lot ten minutes later he was empty handed. Woody was already intent on the lineup for the next race and he barely noticed Cody's rising panic.

"Well, it's back at the motel then, son. You'll find it when we get back. Meanwhile, if you gotta call someone there's pay phones in the hallway by the restrooms."

Calling someone was the least important thing the phone did for Cody. His whole life was on that phone. Without his list of contacts he wouldn't even have the faintest idea of anyone's number that he *could* call. It was a disaster.

"Cody, sit down. You're driving everyone crazy."

"I should go back to the room."

Woody's impatience nearly boiled over. "Don't be stupid. You can live one afternoon without a damn phone in your hand. Your neck is getting all bent over from staring at the thing. Here, let me buy you another beer. Or maybe something stronger?"

Cody shook his head. "Beer's fine." He sank down in his seat, legs sprawled, a pout on his face, and drank the beer while Woody jumped up and cheered his favorite horses.

"Ha!" Woody plopped down in his seat at the end of the race. "Trifecta! I got 'em all on that one."

His face was flushed with excitement, his smile wide. Until he noticed Cody's expression.

"You gonna keep this up all frickin day?"

"Maybe."

Woody gripped a wad of Cody's shirt and pulled his son close. "Listen, you little puke. We came out here for a good time, a father-son visit. We were having fun until the damn phone thing came up. Straighten up your act, buster."

Cody recognized the tone from his childhood. Woody meant business. When Cody was a kid the next step would be a smack across the mouth.

Pop's tone softened. "It's gotta be back at the motel. So just drop the attitude and enjoy the rest of the afternoon. I'm gonna treat us to a nice dinner at that steak place we passed earlier."

With a sigh, Cody downed the rest of the beer. "Okay. Steak sounds good."

Cody ended up having a couple of scotches with his porterhouse, Pop's treat. The old man was in an ebullient mood after the trifecta win. He couldn't stop going on about the fact that they were in shirtsleeves in late October. Everything about the racetrack was to his liking.

Unfortunately, not everything about Cody was the same. Every time he subconsciously reached for his phone, Pop sent him a withering stare.

It was a little after eight when they reached the motel and Cody's worst fear came true. The phone was nowhere in the room. He went back out to the car, but his prior search had been thorough and it wasn't there either.

Walking over to the motel office, he insisted the manager call the maid who had cleaned their room. The girl denied having seen a cell phone in the room. Even when Cody himself got on the line and described its navy blue case, she swore she had never seen it. When her denials turned to sobs he felt bad about practically accusing her.

He debated about what to do as he headed back to the room. He could call the carrier and have his account suspended, but that would involve getting a new number and a whole bunch of other hassles. He could notify Apple and have them remotely lock the phone, but it already had password protection and facial recognition. It was useless to anyone who found it.

What bothered him the most was the simple fact that he'd lost it. Cody Baker did not lose things.

"No luck, huh?" Woody said when he walked back into the room. "Well, tomorrow we'll go to the lost and found place at the track. Somebody probably found it on the ground and turned it in."

Cody should have thought of that. He mentally chided himself while he brushed his teeth. If worse came to worst, he could locate an Apple store and go buy a new one. It was a thousand dollar phone he'd lost, and he hadn't bought the protection plan—because he never lost things—but he would just have to bite the bullet and do it. At least money wasn't a problem.

Chapter 71

Amber felt the clock ticking as the evening slipped by. In between making queries on the genealogy website she switched over to the banking transactions she'd initiated earlier in the day. None of the transfers were showing as completed yet. She knew they wouldn't, not this soon, but some kind of magical thinking made her keep checking anyway.

She'd constructed a very limited family tree for the Bakers. One problem was that it was a very common name, but she'd located a Woodrow Wilson Baker. Obviously, he was not the man who'd set up the paperwork for Blandishment Inc.—the man had been dead more than twenty years. Woodrow Harrison Baker was about the right age to be Cody's father, so that little fact tied nicely to what she knew. The checkbook she'd found in the suitcase belonged to Cody's dad, Woody.

Putting the few clues together, it appeared Cody himself had set up the corporation using his grandfather's name. It wasn't possible to question the family patriarch about the company, and his name left a trail to no one in the modern day. The corporate address of record was the company in Delaware that had facilitated the filing. All perfectly legal, even though it did seem a bit iffy.

She was about to switch back over for one last look at the banking transactions before bedtime when her phone chimed. Gracie.

"Hey, just wanted to report in. I picked up Co-Wood's tail right when they left the track."

"Co-Wood?"

"Yeah, I thought we needed a code name for the Cody and Woody team."

"Um, catchy."

"So, they ate dinner at a steakhouse. I grabbed tacos and ate in my car, but don't feel sorry for me. They were good."

"Okay, I'm not feeling sorry for you."

"They're at the motel now. Mary told me their room number and I'm in the one next to it. I can hear their TV through the wall. When it shuts off, I'll watch their car to be sure no one sneaks out. Planning to give them an hour or so to fall asleep and then try to grab some sleep myself. But I'll set my alarm and be awake in plenty of time to follow, in case they get an early start. Mary said this morning they came rolling out around ten."

"From what I saw, Cody is not an early riser. Must have been a challenge for him to work at B-G, where the report-to-your-desk norm is seven a.m."

"What's the latest on the transfers?"

"Just what Sandy had told me. Nothing will move for at least twenty-four to forty-eight hours. Maybe longer. I'm making myself go to bed so I'll quit checking it every ten minutes."

"I'll be right behind Co-Wood tomorrow. My guess is, with Woody's love of gambling, they'll spend the day at the track again."

"If Cody breaks away from his dad or makes any moves other than the track, be sure you're on his tail. These next two days, we can*not* let him get his hands on his computer."

"Or let him buy a new phone. Got it."

They ended the call, but Amber wasn't tired any more. The thought that Cody could easily buy a new phone and have all his apps and data transferred to it wouldn't leave her alone. She paced through the condo for a minute and debated going down to the garage to clean up her car. She tended to toss food wrappers and used tissues into the back seat, and she had left a box of miscellaneous office supplies in there, things she'd purchased the day she set up her home office.

Oh, forget it—the car can wait. She returned to her computer and clicked over to the bank transfers, promising herself this was the final time she would check them tonight.

Chapter 72

Gracie stretched her stiff limbs. The mattress was a board, the pillows horrid lumps that refused to be pounded into any decent shape. She should warn Mary to bring her own pillow from home, since the room would be hers tonight.

At least she was accustomed to waking before dawn. Scott's work normally took him out on the road by six, and the kids needed much time and nudging before school. She left the bed and stood with her ear against the connecting wall to room 16. Not a sound.

She peered out through a crack in the drapes. The Taurus was right where it had sat last night when she'd checked at midnight. She'd parked her own minivan on the opposite side of the double row of rooms, near the office and somewhat behind a giant agave plant.

There was a tiny, one-cup coffee maker on the vanity and she set it up to brew. The Skyliner offered a breakfast bar, but Gracie had picked up her own from a nearby convenience store: two protein bars and a bottle of cranberry juice. She didn't want to be seen, in case the men did choose the motel's fare. If she made any face-to-face contact at all, it needed to happen later, probably at the track.

While her coffee sputtered and dripped into the itty-bitty carafe, Gracie washed her face and brushed her teeth. Her sundress and light jacket from yesterday would have to do. She hadn't exactly come out to this job equipped for a multi-day stint.

She poured her coffee into the paper cup provided, took a sip and added the contents of all the little sugar and creamer packets. It wasn't quite as vile, but it wasn't like her medium roast Ruta Maya at home. The room next door still seemed quiet. She peeked out the window once again.

The Taurus was gone.

Oh no, oh no, oh *no*! She set the coffee down a little too hard on the dresser, grabbed her purse and room key, and dashed outside. If she could make it to her minivan ... surely the men couldn't be more than five minutes ahead of her.

Okay, ten. She had spent at least that long getting dressed and making the coffee. She dashed for her van anyway. She started it and wheeled about to face the street. But which direction? Interstate 17 was right there—one minute to the on-ramp, and they could be miles away. If they'd gotten on Bell Road, it stretched for miles both east and west. Her mind worked frantically, looking for the next logical move.

Just as she made the decision to go east on Bell, away

from the interstate—it was, after all, the section of the neighborhood the men were most familiar with—a white Taurus pulled into the Skyliner parking lot. A gray-haired man was at the wheel.

Gracie backed into an empty space beside the motel office and picked up the tiny binoculars Mary had left with her. It was Woody Baker, all right. He parked directly in front of room 16 and stepped out of the car, a small shopping bag in hand. It was imprinted with the logo of a CVS Pharmacy. She watched as he locked the car and let himself into the room.

Great binoculars, she thought. And a way too close call. If both men had been together, she would have lost them. She moved her van closer, parking it three doors away from her own room, hoping like crazy that neither man had paid much attention to the vehicles in the lot.

"I suck at this," she muttered as she locked her vehicle and went back into her room.

Once again, everything was quiet in the next room. She stood with her ear pressed to the wall for a good five minutes, but the TV didn't come on, no voices in conversation. Nonetheless, she'd learned her lesson about being prepared. She gathered everything she had brought with her, decided to forego the now-cool cup of bad coffee, and went out to her van.

Even a casual glance out the window of room 16 and the van would be seen. She pulled back to her previous spot and dashed into the motel office for a fresh cup of coffee from the breakfast bar. Even primo detectives needed their coffee in the morning.

The curtains were still closed on 16 and the Taurus was still in place. Crisis averted.

It stayed that way for three more hours, and Gracie

was stiff and desperately needing to pee by the time the curtains parted. Note to primo detective self—don't have two cups of coffee when you'll be stuck in the car. She supposed men had easy answers—such as an empty soda bottle—for these situations. But that option wasn't open to her. Until she knew Cody wasn't on the move, she would have to hold it.

From what Mary had told her when they switched places, it seemed Cody and Woody followed the same routine as yesterday. Left the room late morning, had breakfast at a pancake place (where she wandered in and used the bathroom), and then it was straight to the track. She followed them inside.

Cody stared around the open lobby for a minute, then headed toward a door marked Lost & Found.

Heh-heh-heh, still looking for the phone. That was good.

She edged a little closer as Cody joined his father in the line at the betting window.

"No, we're not leaving now. We just got here," Woody said. "Relax, you can get yourself a new phone on the way home tonight. Those stores probably stay open pretty late."

Cody grumbled a little, but Woody held up a keyring with an Alamo tag on it. Clearly he'd remained in charge of the car.

"I'm gonna place my bets. Why don't you grab us a couple beers? It's warm out there today."

Interestingly, Cody did as he was told. Gracie turned her back as he passed within four feet of her. She watched the two men join up again and head for the stands. They sat in the first row, midway down, exactly even with the finish line. She took the seat on the aisle, two spaces away from Woody. No way were they getting out of here without her knowing it.

She pretended to study the racing form she'd picked up as she walked in. A minute later she felt eyes upon her and noticed Woody looking in her direction. Could she use this to her advantage?

"Who do you like in the first race?" he asked.

"Gosh, I don't know. I actually don't know a whole lot about horses, but my sister wanted to come here. And now she's called to say she's running late."

He scooted over to the empty seat between them. "Maybe I can help?"

"Really? Would you? I'm afraid I'm going to be really bored if I'm not doing anything half the afternoon."

"I follow the ponies a lot. Let me see your form."

She glanced beyond his shoulder, toward Cody. He gave his father an eye-roll sort of glance then proceeded to drink the second of the beers.

"Do you win a lot at places like this?" she asked, batting her eyelashes, just a little.

He beamed. "I've been very successful in my betting career."

"Oh my, you've made a career of this? You certainly must make a lot."

He did a little aw-shucks shuffle with his feet and edged closer, pointing at a line on the form. "Now here's the horse you want in the first race. Odds aren't real long, but this is just the warm-up for the day. Yesterday I picked a trifecta—that means choosing the first, second, and third place horses in the right order. Carried home a pretty decent amount on that one. Course, the more you bet the more you win."

"Oh, I wouldn't feel confident about betting very much. Can I just do a few dollars?"

"Sure. Let me show you how." He stood, ready to lead

her to the betting window.

What could it hurt? She knew Woody had the car keys, so Cody wasn't going to get away.

"If you didn't bring cash, there's an ATM," he pointed out.

She noticed the window also accepted credit cards, but didn't point that out. He was up to something and it could be interesting to see how it played out.

Chapter 73

Woody noticed how the woman kept touching his arm when she spoke to him. Little brushes with a hand, a flick of the fingertips. It had been some time since a woman flirted so outrageously with him. He pinned her age as being somewhere between his and his son's. Late thirties, maybe forty. Yes, he was nearly old enough to be her father, but there was something extremely flattering about the attention of a younger woman.

Cody wasn't immune, it seemed. For the first time since they'd arrived at the track he was laughing. Not a polite little ha-ha now and then, but genuinely enjoying the woman's company. She'd told them her name was Grace. It suited her perfectly.

He'd set her up for the simple 'sure thing' bets on horses after learning she didn't know anything about betting. She'd started with two-dollar bets, upped them to five, then ten. She was beginning to feel confident enough to start pulling out twenty-dollar bills any time now. All he had to do was convince her to let him carry the money to the window while she simply sat back and enjoyed the view.

"Hey, let's get a table in the turf club upstairs," he suggested. "They got better drinks and food up there. Somebody will come around and wait on us."

Cody spoke up. "I want to duck out for a couple hours and find an Apple store so I can replace my phone."

Woody took his son's arm and steered him toward the stairs that led upward. "You don't want to be rude to our guest, son. We can go phone shopping on the way to the motel or after dinner."

The woman put on a look of concern. "Plus, you've already had a few drinks, Cody. You'd have to drive quite a way to the Apple store, and I'll tell you, the cops are not at all lenient when it comes to DUI around here. Have you heard of tent city?"

Woody knew by Cody's reaction that he had. "It's a place where they make you sleep in tents, no matter how hot or cold it is outside, and they say it involves doing hard labor."

Grace nodded. "That's right. And, the prisoners have to wear pink, like pink boxers. Pretty humiliating, as well as being uncomfortable."

Woody chuckled at the image of his know-it-all son out in a tent in pink boxers.

Apparently that was enough to make Cody change his mind. He grudgingly walked up the stairs with them. Woody pointed out a table right at the windows where they could watch the races and hear the announcements easily.

"Here we go. Let's get some snacks." He summoned

over a waitress, a past-the-prime woman in black jeans and a Turf Paradise logo shirt. After ordering margaritas, nachos, and three kinds of wings, he turned back to Grace.

"Now, let's have some fun with our bets," he said. "Here's one I play all the time. It's not described on your form, but the idea is to pick ..."

He scooted his chair over closer to hers and sketched a diagram on a napkin. It involved a complicated way of choosing four horses that would finish the race in a certain sequence and each needed to beat its own best record time. The whole setup was total bull, of course.

"The beauty of it is, hardly anyone knows about this system of mine," he told her, "so nobody is picking your same horses. The jackpot comes in and it's all yours. I've made big bucks with this, over the years."

"Really? It sounds super difficult," Grace said.

"It is. That's why it pays off so good."

"Well, how do you ...?"

"Place the bets? Don't worry about that part. I'll take your money and mine—Cody, you in?"

Cody reached into his shorts pocket and pulled out two twenties.

"Aw, that ain't much," Woody said.

Cody pulled out three more.

"Okay, so here's what I'll do—"

The waitress was back with a tray loaded with plastic baskets full of food and a big pitcher of margaritas. "I didn't have space for your glasses," she said. "Be right back."

Woody continued where he left off. "I'll go down to the betting window and get all our bets placed. I studied the form last night, and the best race for this move is not the next one up but the one after that. I'll get it all set up," he said to Grace. "You don't have to worry about anything."

She handed him forty dollars, and he couldn't manage to get any more out of her.

"If this pays as great as you say, I'll definitely bet more next time," she said.

"You watch, baby. It's amazing." He stood. "You two get started on the food and drinks. I'll be right back."

On the concourse level he glanced around. Of course there was no bet to be made. He picked up three discarded tickets from the floor, scuffed them up enough that the race number was no longer readable, and stuck them in his pocket. A quick visit to the men's room and he was ready for food and the second half of the con. He would hand Cody's hundred and Grace's own forty back to her. Maybe sweeten the pot a little with some of his own winnings, so she would bet it all on the last race of the day. Then he'd claim that one didn't win, and he'd pocket everything.

When he got back to the table the woman was gone. He glanced around, a little frantically.

"Where'd she go?" he asked Cody.

A shrug. "Said she was going to the bathroom."

"Downstairs?"

"How should I know? I think she just went to the one over there." Cody indicated the back of the turf club.

Just then Grace came walking out, right where Cody had said she would be. Woody breathed a sigh of relief. Everything was going to work out just fine.

Chapter 74

Amber picked up the phone the instant she saw it was Gracie.

"I can't talk long," came Gracie's voice in a whisper. "I'm in the restroom. Cody says he's going to buy a new phone this afternoon. I tried to scare him out of driving too far, you know, stories about tent city and all that. But he's genuinely in a panic over not having his phone. He's going to take the risk of driving, find the closest Apple store, and get a new one."

"Hang on, I'm looking them up now," Amber said. "Rats—there are at least a dozen stores. I don't know how well he knows the city. I suppose he could keep driving around a lot."

"Or not. He'll just ask someone where the nearest one

is. Is there any way the transfers will be done by, say, seven o'clock tonight?"

"No way. I've been checking them all day, and Sandy has access from the bank. I think one of the smaller ones is all that's gone through."

"Okay, so now what?"

"I guess we have to figure out a way to get all the Apple stores in the valley to close early."

"Amber ... how are you going to do that?"

"Not sure. But you just keep them busy. I'll figure out something. Have you seen Mary out there?"

"Huh-uh. We talked early this morning and decided I'd take today's shift and she'll hang around them tomorrow. Look, I'd better go. I've set my phone on silent mode but I'll sneak a peek at it now and then if you want to send me a text."

Amber hung up, wondering exactly how she was supposed to convince a dozen different stores that they needed to close early. Or convince them not to sell a new phone to one Cody Baker. It just wasn't going to happen.

Then her gaze fell on Cody's phone, sitting there benignly on her desk. What if ...

She picked it up.

It came as no surprise to discover the phone was locked and password protected. When her own face didn't pass the facial recognition test, and swiping upward on the screen only brought up a demand for a passcode, she noticed something she previously had never paid much attention to. A phone will allow an emergency 911 call without the delay of waiting to be unlocked.

She wrote down what she intended to say. When she had the words right she picked up the phone again and hit the Emergency Call button.

"911—What's your emergency?"

The message needed to be delivered monotone, as robotic as she could make her voice sound. That meant no stammering around for words. She read the message she had written out. "I have it on good authority that one of the Apple computer and phone stores in the state of Arizona will be the victim of a bombing sometime in the next fifty-one hours. I cannot say which store or an exact time when this will happen. I suggest the police contact the store managers and have them evacuate every store and close it."

"Please stay on the line while I notify the police."

But Amber had hung up. Her heart was pounding and she felt a little faint. She'd probably just committed a felony worthy of federal, state, and local attention. The cops were likely to track the phone and come pounding on her door at any second. She dropped it on her desk and tried to think logically.

"Okay, first thing, I have to get my prints off this thing. Second thing, I gotta get it out of this building."

The plant only bloomed encouragingly.

Amber grabbed her messenger bag and a container of Clorox wipes. Then she dashed for the door. Riding the elevator to the garage level, she wiped every centimeter of the phone until it gleamed. She glanced around the parking garage. No cops. This was good.

She eyed the dumpster. No, no, no. Couldn't have the phone anywhere near her residence.

She got in her Prius, thinking frantically. Where could she dump it? The Ladies had originally planned to only hold onto Cody's phone until the bank transfers were completed, then figure out a way to return it to him so he would only think he'd misplaced it.

But maybe there was a way to do that *and* achieve justice. A smile crossed her face as she pulled onto Goldwater Boulevard and headed toward downtown Phoenix.

Chapter 75

Gracie put on a smile, but she was growing a little weary of being Woody and Cody's babysitter. The younger Baker was bored and grumpy, chafing to get the car keys from his dad so he could get out and replace his missing phone. Apparently the fear of a DUI on his record only went so far. He'd cut way back on his drinks and consumed a big share of the snack food, so he might pass a test anyway.

On this side of the table, the old man was blatantly out to scam her. Plus, he kept finding little ways of brushing up against her thigh and she was ready to smack him.

"Here's the payout from that play we made," Woody said after returning from downstairs again.

He fanned out a stack of twenties and gave Gracie and Cody each a share. Some kind of a look passed between the two men. Obviously, both were in on it. But Gracie had to pretend to be super impressed.

"Oh, wow, Woody. This is amazing!"

"I tell ya, this system works at least ninety-five percent of the time." He pocketed his 'share' and reached for the last of the hot wings. "I'm doing it again in the last race of the day. Who's in it with me?"

Cody shoved his winnings across to his father and pulled out his wallet. "Me, for sure. Bet it all. Gotta love these kinds of results."

Woody turned to Gracie. "You too?"

"Hmm ... I'm not sure." She'd slid two twenties from her stack—all of her original bet—and slipped them into her pocket while he was devouring his wing. "Well, okay," she said. "Bet it all. This is fun!"

They whiled away the next hour, until it was nearly time for the final race of the day. Woody went downstairs to place their bets. Gracie brought out her phone, saying she was checking with her babysitter. There was one text from Amber: Watch the news.

Gracie flipped over to her news app and spotted the headline right away. **Terrorist attack on major computer maker?** She clicked the video and a newscaster began talking.

"Uh-oh," she said.

Cody perked up. "What's going on?"

"Looks like they've shut down all the Apple stores in the state. Sounds like someone phoned in a bomb threat."

"What!" He reached out and she let him take her phone and listen to the newscast.

Details were sketchy, but the journalists were happy to provide a lot of speculation as to what this might mean, how deep the terror threat might go, was the gigantic company the only one being targeted, and why only in Arizona?

Oh my god, Amber, what have you done?

Cody looked like he wanted to throw something, so Gracie gently took back her phone. He stomped over to the bar and ordered a Scotch—double.

Woody came back to the table and suggested they watch the final race from the trackside rail. "It's so much more exciting down there. You can feel the ground vibrating, hear the horses breathing." He slipped an arm around her shoulder when she stood up.

"Ooh, Woody, that does sound like fun," Gracie said. *Gag me.*

The two of them walked down multiple sets of concrete steps until they were on the level with the dirt track. Cody had stayed behind, but Gracie was pretty sure Woody still held the car keys. Conveniently, he never did mention which horses they wanted to cheer for, but he did a credible acting job when he delivered the news that theirs didn't win.

"Well, I need to get going," Gracie said after a show of disappointment. "Say goodbye to your son for me. It's been a very informative day."

Before he could come up with a reason for her to stick with them—heaven forbid it should involve dinner—she scurried out the exit and checked back to be sure he hadn't followed. She attached herself to a large group that was headed toward a tour bus, dodging when they rounded out of sight and tucking herself into the back of her minivan.

An informative day. No kidding. She got out her phone and texted Amber. WTH? Do we need to talk?

Chapter 76

FedEx drivers were such nice people. Amber smiled as she headed her Prius back toward home. Imagine anyone else who would let you put an unidentified package into his hands, plead being in a huge hurry, and then they run an errand for you where you didn't want your face to be seen.

It was the first thing that came into her mind as she approached the entrance to Blackwell-Gorse. Her original plan was to pretend to discover a phone lying on the ground near the door, take it to the security desk, and turn it in as lost. But one of the security guards might remember her.

And, Cody might *know* he hadn't lost the phone right here, at his old workplace. Then again, by the time this whole thing was over, the Heist Ladies would have messed with his head so much he might not actually be certain.

But when she spotted the FedEx driver parked at the curb, his arms full of packages as he headed toward the building, she acted on a plan even more brilliant. Good thing she hadn't cleaned out the car last night, after all. An unused bubble-lined mailer bag provided the perfect solution. Using one of the sterile wipes she picked up the phone and slipped it inside, leaving the bag top unsealed.

A dash to the front door, holding it open for the driver. "This was lying on the ground right here," she said. "I think maybe you dropped it."

By the time he discovered it was unsealed and unaddressed, she was long gone. Most likely the bag ended up at the security desk.

Now, all she had to do was make sure the bank transfers continued to move along as they should. She went immediately to her computer when she reached home. Three more of the transactions were showing as completed. She was about to call Sandy to see if there was anything further she could learn, when her phone rang. It was Gracie.

"Hey, lady, how was your day?"

"I can't wait to get home and have a shower," Gracie said. "Woody's middle name should be grabby-hands. I'm weary of dodging him. I followed them to a Mexican restaurant where they seem pretty well settled in. As soon as Mary gets here, I'm heading home."

"At least I think we foiled Cody's idea of heading out to buy a new phone right away. I even heard other stores are pulling those products until this whole bomb scare goes away."

"Speaking of which, what did you do?"

"Do? I have no idea what you mean." She adopted an innocent Southern accent, teasing.

Amber had turned her personal computer on to a news channel and was watching the headlines scroll across the screen. It seemed the police were involved and the investigation was moving quickly.

"Oh, here's Mary. I'm turning over surveillance and intercept duties to her."

"Good. Well, enjoy your shower and an evening at home with the family."

"I wish. There's a football game at Dylan's school and I just remembered I'm the mom picking him up afterward, along with a bunch of his fourteen-year-old buddies."

Amber wished her luck, but her attention was now fully on the newscast.

"Police are on the scene at the computer store on North Street, thought to be the central target of the threat. An unnamed suspect is being sought for questioning after authorities tracked the phone number from which the threatening call was made. Channel 3 News has it on good authority that the suspect is a twenty-nine year old male who may have only moved to the city recently, and it is believed he may work in this downtown office building where the phone has been tracked."

Amber recognized the Blackwell-Gorse Tech building, surrounded now by yellow tape and guys in black SWAT gear stomping around. Wow. These guys took bomb threats pretty seriously.

Chapter 77

Cody was tired and bored. Pop's idea of a great time wasn't at all where he wanted to be right now. They'd chosen Mexican food for dinner, but Pop complained that the chili was too hot and he barely ate anything. But instead of simply going back to their room, now he'd insisted they check out this bar he'd noticed on their way to the Mexican place.

It was one of those where country music blared from the sound system, which made Cody's headache all that much worse. The two of them had taken seats at the bar. While Pop ordered a whiskey, all Cody could stomach was a soda. He nursed it to keep pace, hoping they could leave after one drink.

A TV set above the bar was tuned to football, so he entertained himself by watching the people. Two couples were keeping lively time with the music, over on the small dance floor. Most of those at the bar itself looked like working class guys who'd been home for dinner and then made an excuse to get out with the guys. Their wives were probably happy they chose to watch the game away from home.

A few small tables lined the room and that's where the business types were, including one woman on her own. With her gray hair in some kind of feathery style and her tailored dress and jacket it seemed more likely she'd be at one of those high-end watering holes or something, but how would he know? Maybe she had a husband who'd invited his buddies to their house and she just needed to get out. He was surprised Woody hadn't latched onto her as a potential mark. But maybe Pop had already got his fill of betting for today.

He hoped so. He didn't want this evening to stretch on any longer. In fact, he was about ready for the whole visit to be done. His normal evening was spent locked away in his bedroom where his current project was to devise a new fantasy role-playing game. He'd recently connected with a guy who knew a guy, and Cody was hoping to get the beta version of the software ready to show. If what his new buddy said was true, some of the big players in online gaming were looking for exactly what he was developing—right genre at the right time.

Now he just needed to get Pop on a plane back home.

And then what? Cody knew he could go back to Jersey too, could write programming code just as easily from his bedroom there. Too bad he couldn't dip into the money yet. He'd be on a plane to Jamaica or somewhere, get himself a room near the beach, and skip the upcoming Jersey winter. Then again, he could do that here, and he might still have a chance with Amber.

He tamped down thoughts of all things tropical. The money needed to sit right where it was for at least six months, and then he'd need to pull out small increments so as not to arouse suspicion. And that was another reason he was antsy to get to his phone or computer. He needed to be sure all those foreign transactions had gone through at the correct exchange rates.

Did this new distrust of bankers mean Cody was more like his father than he wanted to admit? Ugh.

Woody's drink was getting low. Cody chugged his Coke and tapped his dad's shoulder, giving a nod toward the door. "Hey, you can watch the end of the game back at the room. We got TV there."

Chapter 78

Something was wrong. Mary felt the change between the two men, as strongly as if a jolt of lightning had rocked the turf club.

The morning of the third day had started in what was becoming a predictable pattern. Breakfast, racetrack, bets, turf club around noon, and an order for snack food. She'd donned an over-styled blonde wig that a housewife in her seventies would choose. That, and a muumuu that added twenty pounds and covered her athletic build, provided the perfect cover. She'd placed a tiny pebble in her shoe to create a realistic limp. She was certain Cody had noticed her in the bar last night where her chic outfit had been out of place. She'd made sure she looked nothing like that woman now.

Mary had whiled away the past two hours by tracking

the news via an app on her phone. Cody was still being referred to as 'an unnamed suspect' but the details fit. He was from New Jersey and had been in the Phoenix area a short time, although they weren't quite admitting the police didn't have an address for him here. He had worked in the building where the phone had been located, abandoned, at the lost and found. He had recently quit the job with no notice.

Much was being made of the fact that the threat had stated the bomb would detonate within the next 51 hours. Endless pundits speculated on why that number had been chosen. There was even a countdown timer at the bottom of the screen showing 29:32:04 left against that deadline.

If Cody was monitoring the news, he would know in a moment that he was the suspect, and since he was not exactly making any attempt to hide, Mary could only assume he wasn't following the story.

Now, just as she was limping toward the bar to order a soda, the older man raised his voice.

"I just don't understand why you need your computer. You got no job to go back to. Why can't we just have a nice day out together?"

"Pop, it's three days now. Sorry if my new project interests me more than watching horses run around a track. I'm happy you're winning, but it's driving me nuts, just sitting here."

"Fine then, go! I'm sick of hearing about that damn computer. You can't spend a couple days with your old Pop and just relax? Go get the damn thing."

Standing at the bar with her back to them, Mary did her best to conceal her reaction. At all costs, she had to keep him away from his laptop. She asked the bartender to put her Coke in a paper cup.

Cody was on his feet when she turned around, and Woody was fishing in his pocket. The keys. Gracie told her it seemed the old man controlled the car keys, but now he was about ready to hand them over. Mary limped her way toward the exit where she could keep an eye on the outcome.

When Cody came down the stairs from the turf club, dangling the key ring from his finger, she walked outside. He strode out the door, not even giving her a glance. There was no way she could keep up the convincing limp and keep up with him. She kicked off her shoe and dumped the pebble out, then dashed to her little red sedan and got inside.

By the time he steered the rented Taurus to the exit, she was twenty yards behind him, tapping her phone to raise someone. Pen was the first to answer.

"Cody's leaving the track and he's headed for his computer," she said, a little breathlessly as she ran the yellow light.

He was heading for the interstate and she couldn't lose him.

"Do you know where?" Pen asked.

"Wherever he lives. I have no clue."

"Describe to me where you are now."

"I-17 southbound."

"How can I help?"

Mary thought fast. "I should be able to tail him, but I don't know how it'll go once he gets to his place and gets the computer."

"Shall I put Amber and Gracie on alert?"

"Yes, please. I'll let you know what happens." Ahead, Cody appeared to be taking the ramp toward I-10, right through central Phoenix. She left her phone on the console, ready to hit redial if she needed to.

This is where it could get tricky. If he exited downtown, there were a number of one-way and crowded, narrow streets where she could easily lose him. She thought of the news scenes shown outside Blackwell-Gorse. Surely he wasn't planning to go back there. What, exactly, had he said to his father? She tried to remember.

But Cody stayed to the middle lanes, passing through the tunnel. Mary was three cars behind him when they emerged. At the junction where I-10 headed south toward Tucson, Cody merged onto the 202. From here, the exits were spaced farther and were well marked as the freeway took them toward the East Valley cities.

He bypassed chances to go north to Scottsdale or south to Chandler or Gilbert. It looked as though he was heading toward Mesa. Mary reported it to Pen.

"I've spoken with Gracie. She's on the move and can meet you."

"Let me find out where that is."

"It might not be a bad idea to let him actually get his hands on the computer," Pen suggested. "It probably contains evidence the police can use." There was a pause. "However, at that point you *must* stop him. Once he sees his bank accounts, our cause is lost. Amber says only half the money transfers have been completed."

"I'm on it." Mary closed the gap to two cars between them. This time of day, with rush hour not due to begin for another hour or more, there was enough space to keep an eye on him from a distance.

She tapped Gracie's number and reported. "We're passing Gilbert Road."

"Good. I'm not far behind you. Let me know what turns he makes. I have an idea."

While Gracie outlined the basics of her plan, Mary didn't take her eyes off the white Taurus.

Five minutes later, Cody edged into an exit lane.

"He's getting off at Power Road. I'm closing in so there's only one car between us."

"I see you ahead," Gracie said. "I'll be two minutes behind you."

Cody roared through the major intersection at McDowell, but slowed at the next one as traffic exiting a Home Depot joined the flow. Mary had tossed her wig aside and was now right behind their quarry. She hardly dared check the rearview for Gracie. Right now she had to keep her eyes on Cody's plain white vehicle, which could easily blend with the hundreds of others at the busy commercial intersection.

If she'd blinked, she could have almost missed his last-minute signal before he turned right, onto a side street. He drove two blocks and made a right turn again. Smallish, middle class houses filled the area.

Wary of being spotted, Mary pulled to the curb and watched as Cody came to a stop in front of one of the houses on the left. He got out, leaving his car on the wrong side of the street, and went inside. He planned this as a quick stop, she realized. Gracie had suggested they create a diversion, cause an accident if necessary.

In less than two minutes Cody walked back out of the house, a briefcase-sized bag in hand.

Mary's heart rate picked up as she realized this was it—this was the time.

Chapter 79

Amber stared at her computer screen. Lines of numbers scrolled past, account numbers and dollar amounts. As the word Confirmed showed up at the end of a line, the list scrolled upward. Next line, Confirmed. Two more to go.

Her phone rang. It was Sandy. "How are the transfers going?"

"Nearly there. Just one more ..." She swallowed hard. "And they're done."

Sandy let out a sigh of relief.

"I'm switching over to the other server now," Amber said. "Just need to check and be sure ... Yes! the B-G account has the new deposits. I'm going to make a couple of entries within their own system."

"I probably don't want to know this."

"So true. Okay, I'll let you go. Sandy—thank you."

Amber raised her eyes to the ceiling as the call ended. *Thank you, Sandy, thank you, banking system, thank you, whatever gods of money are out there watching over me.*

She turned back to the internal B-G server once again, and entered dates beside each of the new deposits, effectively postdating them so it appeared the money had never actually left their account. It would give the auditors and accountants a headache, but eventually she hoped they would just assume an error had been made on their part and accept that everything really was back to normal.

Picking up her phone she tapped Gracie's number. "It's all done. Do you have the evidence?"

"It's all coming down right now. Call the police and send them to this street," she said, reading a name off a street sign. "I gotta go!"

Amber made the call, talking directly to Detective Howard. "Be sure to confiscate Cody Baker's computer. The answers are in his bank accounts."

Howard sputtered a little but agreed to at least have the Mesa Police Department detain Mr. Baker.

"And send someone out to Turf Paradise to get his father, Woody Baker. He may have been the mastermind behind the whole thing."

Howard started to protest that Amber was not the one in charge here, but she hung up. She still had a few loose ends to tie up, starting with completely wiping the hard drive on the borrowed computer.

Chapter 80

W e've got to stop him!" Gracie said, leaving her van at the curb, rushing up to Mary, and assessing the situation.

Mary seemed to be undressing, right there beside her car. From her gym bag on the passenger seat, she'd pulled stretch pants and a workout top. "I can't let him know I'm the same person from the track. The street's a cul-de-sac," she told Gracie. "He's got to turn around to get out of there."

She'd already pulled the pants on and ripped the baggy muumuu off over her head. She yanked the stretchy top over her sports bra and got back behind the wheel. Without even closing her door, she pulled forward and blocked the narrow street. Cody had returned to his car, set a computer bag on the back seat, and now from half a block north, was turning the Taurus around to leave.

Mary got out of her vehicle and walked around front to raise the hood. "Stay out of sight, Gracie. Once he's out of his car, you grab that computer bag."

"Will do." Gracie tucked herself behind an enormous bougainvillea, two seconds before Cody's car swung around, facing south again.

Mary stood in front of her vehicle, hands on hips, staring under the hood. For a moment she was afraid Cody would try to edge around, but she was blocking the road well enough that he would have to hop the sidewalk and take out a fire hydrant to do it.

He edged the Taurus closer, clearly impatient.

Mary threw up her hands and stared at him. "What do you want me to do? It just quit."

He got out of his car and walked toward her.

"Could you take a look here and see if you can tell what's the matter?" Mary tried for a helpless-female attitude, but it was a little hard to pull off. With her spiked blonde hair and toned body in workout gear, she seemed far more capable than the computer geek standing beside her.

Still, males will be males, and Cody walked over and made a show of peering under the hood. Mary glanced up in time to see Gracie dash from the cover of the big flowering shrub, circle to the far side of the Taurus, and pull the bag from the passenger seat.

"Maybe it's this thingy right here," Mary said, pointing to the fuel injector. "Does this hose look loose to you?"

Cody had no choice but to take a closer look.

Gracie sprinted back to her van and disappeared through the passenger side door.

Mary heard sirens out on Power Road. They seemed to

be getting closer.

By the time the sound registered with Cody, two City of Mesa police cars had roared to a stop on either side of Mary's vehicle.

"Seems like overkill for a stalled car," Cody commented.

Four cops emerged, one strode forward.

"I was just about to suggest we push the lady's car out of the way," Cody said. "We won't be blocking the road much longer."

"Cody Baker?" said the cop.

Realization dawned. Cody's eyes went wide and he stepped back, but a second cop was right behind him. Cody chose to take the innocent approach.

"What's this about? I swear I don't have any tickets."

"We have orders from downtown Phoenix PD to bring you in. They've got questions."

"I can't just leave my car—" Cody was looking around, a little frantically. "My computer—"

Gracie stepped forward, holding the computer bag. "I believe the police will want to see this."

"You! From the track yesterday?" Cody stared. "Wait, officers, this woman … she's got something to do with this. My dad can identify—at the racetrack. My dad's at the racetrack. He can tell you—"

Two of the officers led Cody to a patrol car; another one took the computer bag from Gracie.

"Tell Detective Howard he'll find the evidence he needs, right here."

Chapter 81

Three nail-biting days went by while the Ladies waited for news. When the call came from Detective Howard, Amber had to sit down before she could take it all in. He said she would need to come downtown to finalize some paperwork. She called her attorney and her four best friends.

"Cody Baker and his father are both in custody," Howard told them, when they met him in the downtown squad room.

He nodded toward the other man in the room, who spoke up. "Our forensic computer team are still putting together the fine details of the case against them, but we do know this. Using Cody Baker's personal computer, money was routed out of Blackwell-Gorse Tech, sent through a complex series of transactions all over Europe and the

US, through at least one dummy corporation, and into the personal accounts of these men."

"So you can now put your hands on that money and return it to the victim, the corporation Blackwell-Gorse?" Mariah Kowzlowski asked.

"Well, that's a little way down the road," Howard said. "There've been more transactions, even as the two men were seemingly spending leisure time at the racetrack."

Amber held her breath.

"Bottom line, for our purposes here today, is that Blackwell-Gorse has dropped the charges against Amber Zeckis. You're free to go."

There was a collective sigh of relief and smiles all around.

"What will happen to Cody?" Amber asked.

Gracie gave her a look, but the detective didn't seem to notice.

"The charges are serious. Both men will likely do prison time."

"But you said the money is no longer in his account?"

Howard looked a little impatient at being questioned. "We're still working on the money trail. All we've discovered so far is that the last set of transactions were apparently done from a different computer than the laptop we confiscated."

The forensic tech spoke up. "The ID on that computer isn't registered to anyone, as far as we can tell. But we're staying on this until we prove the connection."

Mariah Kowzlowski stood and gathered the forms she and Amber had signed, and the group moved out of the room. The lawyer said goodbye, apologizing for her abruptness by saying she had another case in court in ten minutes.

The Heist Ladies made their way out of the big judicial complex and stood in the parking lot near their cars. "What about that other computer?" Mary asked.

"Shall we say, what you don't know won't hurt you," Amber told them. No one asked for further details.

"Be sure you call your parents," Gracie said. "They've been worried."

Amber promised she would. She gave each of her friends a long hug. "Thank you, all of you, for helping me get through this. It was a scary time."

One by one, they got into their cars to get back to their routines. Sandy was the last to leave. "Thanks for not saying more about the extra computer."

"It's all good now? I don't want any trouble for you, in case—"

Amber had delivered the borrowed computer back to Sandy, later the same night Cody and Woody were arrested.

"You might want to put this one at the back of the shelf, make sure it's one of the last to be given out to any of your employees," she'd said. "Just in case a serial number can somehow be pulled from the data the police have. I was careful, really careful, but I'd hate to take the chance."

"Oh, this one's going into a bin of old machines that are headed for recycling. It won't ever be registered to anyone." Sandy had taken the machine there herself.

Now, Amber pictured an Indiana Jones-type warehouse filled with old equipment that was stacked to the ceiling. By the time the police could figure out which machine they were looking for—if they ever did—there was virtually no way they could pinpoint its location. Besides, once computers were recycled, the old hard drives were normally bashed beyond usability.

At least she hoped so.

* * *

She got the call from Blackwell-Gorse the next day.

"Ms. Zeckis, it seems there's been a terrible mistake," the woman from HR said. It was the same voice she'd talked to before, but Amber couldn't remember her name. "In checking further, we've located the money our auditors had thought was missing. Every cent of it is back in our accounts."

"How lucky," Amber said.

"I'm calling to say that your job is still here for you. And the C-suite folks have authorized me to offer you a twenty-percent salary increase."

Rumor around the office had always been that raises were seldom and low. When a three-percent increase came, it was usually tacked on to a fifty-percent increase in workload.

"That's extremely generous," Amber told the woman. "I've promised my parents an extended visit before I decide what to do next. So I'll think about it over the next couple of weeks."

"Take your time. We look forward to having you back."

Amber wasn't sure, but she got the feeling it was corporate-speak for *please don't sue us for wrongful termination.*

* * *

She heard from Cody while she was in Santa Fe. She'd been skimming the news, just to be sure no permanent harm had come from her fake bomb scare. When nothing actually exploded, the media moved on to a bloodier story. The stores reopened with little fanfare, as no one wanted to bring up such an unpleasant situation. She was beginning to feel relaxed again, when she saw the unknown number appear on her phone.

"Hey, Amber," Cody said. He was using that sexy Cody Brennan voice again.

Her b.s. radar went on alert, but this time he seemed sincere.

"I just wanted to let you know that the police convinced me to make a deal. They seem to believe my dad engineered the whole thing."

"And did he?"

"He's always been the idea man. I'm the programmer."

"So you'll testify about that in court?"

"Most likely. We're both going away for some kind of prison term. I'm just hoping mine will be lower than it would have been."

How convenient.

"What I'm really calling for is, besides saying goodbye for now, I want to ask you if you'll wait for me. Stick with me, babe. I've learned a lesson from all this, and I'm not listening to Pop's schemes ever again."

"Cody ... I just ... That wouldn't be a good idea. I'm sorry to say it, but after Paris and what happened on the way home ... I'll never fully trust you again."

She stopped herself short of condemning his ability to create elaborate programs and to move money around. She was still a little bit in awe of that part of him.

There was a long pause at his end, then he said, "I'm glad you and your friends put the money back."

"I don't know what you mean."

But she did know. Exactly. He could read her, read her touch in her programming code. They were, in a way, kindred spirits. And therein lie the danger. It wasn't that she didn't *want* to ever see Cody again, it was that she didn't *dare*.

Chapter 82

Texts began flying among the Heist Ladies, right before Thanksgiving. Change was in the wind, and they each wanted to share their news. Gracie took the role of organizer and sent out invites to each: Thanksgiving dinner at my house. Hubby is away on business, kids will be unsociable teens, I could use the company. I've got all the food, just bring wine.

They gathered early to help with the cooking. The turkey had gone in the oven a couple hours earlier and was already sending that distinctive, heavenly scent through the house. Amber was assembling the dressing, while Sandy peeled potatoes.

"So, what's with Scott being away on a holiday?" Mary asked, from her station at the relish tray. "Nobody in the country works on Thanksgiving weekend, unless they're in retail, and I know he's not."

"But it's business as usual in Thailand," Gracie said with an enigmatic smile.

"Wait—what? He's in *Thailand*?" Amber nearly dropped a bowl of chopped onion.

"His firm got a big engineering contract over there, and ..." Gracie gave it the air of an announcement. "It looks like our family is moving to Bangkok!"

A hundred questions erupted at once.

"The contract is for three years, the kids will attend an American diplomatic school, interspersed with classes at the local school, and I plan to tour every historic site, eat local food every day, and learn the language."

"Whoa, ambitious," Sandy said. "Good for you!"

She had set down the large chef's knife she was using on the potatoes.

"Okay, Sandy, spill. You've got news too. I can see it on your face," Amber said.

"Well, Pen will remember, during our trip to the UK and France last month, how I absolutely couldn't get enough. The history, the buildings, their accents— the whole ambiance of England and Scotland really grabbed me. Not to mention Paris. I applied with one of the major banks, and yes, I'll be taking a cut in salary and position ..."

"You got the job!"

"I did. I'm so excited, I cannot tell you."

"Is this a temporary thing, like our situation?" Gracie asked.

"I hope it can become permanent," Sandy told them. "The bank is arranging my work visa, and it looks like I'll be in London at least six months, but I'm planning to apply for a long-term visa. Unless it turns out I can't stand a much rainier climate than here."

Several chuckles. "*Everywhere* has a rainier climate than here," Gracie said. "Sounds like we both have some adjustments to make."

"What about Heckle and Jeckle?" Mary asked. "I could take them. I love your cats."

"A neighbor said the same thing," Sandy told them. "I haven't quite made the final decision yet. All I know is that it's somewhat tricky to take pets from the US into the UK, so I'll need to decide soon."

"Soon? When do you leave?" Pen asked.

"Um, next week."

"Oh gosh, before Christmas?" Pen seemed a little dismayed. "It's not the ideal time of year to adapt from Arizona to England."

"I know. I figure this will be the big test for me," Sandy said.

The potatoes were boiling now and the casseroles were in Gracie's second oven. The Ladies had poured glasses of wine and seemed in a pensive mood.

"Our lives are taking new turns. That's all it is," Pen said, taking a deep breath and blinking damp eyes. "As for myself, I plan to explore my other creative side, to pursue my painting. Writing has been my life for decades now. Painting challenges a different part of my brain. Plus, there are views of the Superstition Mountains that are crying out for me to put them on canvas."

Nods from Amber and Sandy. "You have genuine talents in both areas. Write and paint—neither has to be exclusive," Amber said.

"We five shall always remain friends."

"Always. No matter where in the world we happen to be," Gracie said, then she caught something about Amber's expression. "What about you? Now that you have your passport back, I get the feeling you're itching to use it?"

"I was going to save this for after dinner," Amber said, "but I do have some news. I think I told you Blackwell-Gorse Tech offered me my old job back."

"But you were a little on the fence about that," Sandy said.

"Right. I had a hard time imagining myself there, thinking how people would treat me, after the cloud of that embezzlement charge."

"And so …"

"And so, I applied for a work abroad program. I'll pack my computer and a few clothes and lease my condo to someone. Remote work is all the thing now. And it's right for me because I don't have a husband, kids, or cats to tie me down."

"Hey—that hasn't stopped the rest of us," Gracie said.

"I know. And I'd figure out a way anyhow. And someday maybe I'll have those things, all of them." She caught their expectant looks. "Okay, so I leave January third, and my first new home will be in Croatia."

"*First* new home?"

"We get to travel about. I'm with a group, mostly young women, mostly my age, and we'll sample several countries. I can do that until I decide where I'd like to settle. You know, it's basically reliving the lifestyle my parents had before I came along."

Everyone offered Amber congratulations and hugs, then all eyes turned toward Mary, who hadn't said much.

"This has been the best time of my life," she said, "ever since I met all of you. I can't tell you what it has meant to me."

Her eyes welled up, and then everyone's did.

"We've each had an experience that required the help of good friends," Pen said.

Nods all around.

"And for the future?" Mary continued, "I'll be right here in the Valley, Pen, and we'll get together anytime you want. I've mentioned my new guy. He's a fitness buff, a little younger than I am, but we've hit it off *so* well. There might be a future together."

"That's great, Mary," Gracie said. "We're all so happy for you."

"And if it doesn't work out, look at all the places I can head off to, places where I'll have at least one very dear friend waiting for me."

Pen raised her glass. "To very dear friends."

Author Notes

The idea for the Heist Ladies came to me quite a few years ago. I'd been writing my Charlie Parker series and my Samantha Sweet mysteries, both of which were traditional murder mysteries. But the idea nagged at me that I'd like to write something a little different, mysteries that didn't involve murders. And so I began with that premise, knowing nothing more than I wanted the central characters to be five women. They would be of different ages and have different talents they could bring to the stories. There would be five stories, one featuring each of the Ladies, who would bring a problem to the group to help her solve it.

The whole thing came together in 2010 when I happened to be on a family car trip. My dad was driving and I was the backseat passenger, with nothing to do for seven hours but think and make notes. With my handy composition book and a pen in hand, I began jotting down every idea that came to me.

During that trip the characters of all five Heist Ladies came to me. The basic plots of each of their stories popped into my head, as though the ladies were sitting there in the car with me and talking about what was going on in their lives. I divided that notebook into sections and wrote furiously until I had character sketches and plot lines for everything on paper. Seven hours in a car is a long time, and I made good use of it!

Then real life intervened. I had deadlines for other books. Charlie and Samantha fans were calling for more. And I needed to do research about con men, as I had decided the thing that would pull the Heist Ladies together was the fact that they, or someone near and dear to them, had been taken in by someone unscrupulous. It wasn't until I began the actual writing of the first of those stories, *Diamonds Aren't Forever*, that I discovered it was really interesting and kind of fun (I'll admit it), to get into the heads of the bad guys as well. To show their cocky attitudes and bulletproof demeanor. They believed themselves to be invincible and uncatchable—that is, until this great team of women moved in to outsmart them and take them down.

It's been great fun writing this series and seeing it come to a conclusion. At this point I have no plans to write more books in this series, but then again … I never say never. So we'll have to see. I hope you have enjoyed the Ladies and their antics. Visit my website at connieshelton.com or drop me a note.

People ask where we writers get our ideas. Sometimes it's on an empty stretch of Arizona highway, snuggled into the back seat of a Lincoln Town Car.

Happy reading!

Connie

Get another Connie Shelton book—FREE!
Visit connieshelton.com to find out how

Thank you for taking the time to read *Show Me the Money*. If you enjoyed it, please consider telling your friends or posting a short review. Word of mouth is an author's best friend and is much appreciated.

Thank you,
Connie Shelton

* * *

Books by Connie Shelton

The Charlie Parker Series

Deadly Gamble
Vacations Can Be Murder
Partnerships Can Be Murder
Small Towns Can Be Murder
Memories Can Be Murder
Honeymoons Can Be Murder
Reunions Can Be Murder
Competition Can Be Murder
Balloons Can Be Murder
Obsessions Can Be Murder
Gossip Can Be Murder
Stardom Can Be Murder
Phantoms Can Be Murder
Buried Secrets Can Be Murder
Legends Can Be Murder
Weddings Can Be Murder
Alibis Can Be Murder
Escapes Can Be Murder
Old Bones Can Be Murder
Sweethearts Can Be Murder
Holidays Can Be Murder - a Christmas novella

The Samantha Sweet Series

Sweet Masterpiece
Sweet's Sweets
Sweet Holidays
Sweet Hearts
Bitter Sweet
Sweets Galore
Sweets Begorra
Sweet Payback
Sweet Somethings
Sweets Forgotten
Spooky Sweet
Sticky Sweet
Sweet Magic
Deadly Sweet Dreams
Spellbound Sweets – a Halloween novella
The Woodcarver's Secret

The Heist Ladies Series

Diamonds Aren't Forever
The Trophy Wife Exchange
Movie Mogul Mama
Homeless in Heaven
Show Me the Money

Children's Books

Daisy and Maisie and the Great Lizard Hunt
Daisy and Maisie and the Lost Kitten

Sign up for Connie Shelton's free mystery newsletter at connieshelton.com
and receive advance information about new books, along with a chance at prizes, discounts and other mystery news!

Contact by email: connie@connieshelton.com
Follow Connie Shelton on Twitter, Pinterest and Facebook

Connie Shelton is the *USA Today* bestselling author of more than 40 novels and three non-fiction books. An avid mystery reader all her life, she says it was inevitable that this would be the genre she would write. She is the creator of the Novel In A Weekend™ writing course and was a contributor to *Chicken Soup for the Writer's Soul.* She and her husband currently reside in northern New Mexico with their two dogs.